D1287565

Dear Reader,

I grew up in the small farming town of Pomeroy, Washington, during the 1970s. When I return, the first place I go is to the little city park along Pataha Creek. In the middle of the park is a green gazebo. Surrounding it are picnic tables and play equipment, and in the far corner sits a tennis court.

I don't think of the park much in everyday life, but when I return to my hometown I'm filled with childhood memories. School outings and church picnics. Fun with my siblings. The triumphant day I finally conquered the monkey bars. Neighborhood water fights. And learning to play tennis with my best friend.

In *A Cup of Grace*, Elaine and Nathan and other characters are reminded of a special place from their childhoods, the World's Largest Snow Globe. It was a nearby roadside attraction that closed years ago—but soon their memories return as if they'd skated on the forested property's frozen pond and then posed in the oversized snow globe just a few years before.

Those past connections—and their current delight in remembering them—draw them into a mystery that unfolds in an unpredictable way. They learn that an open heart, filled with grace, goes a long way in sorting out how the past impacts the present.

As I wrote the story, I prayed that I too would be willing, whenever possible, to be full of grace. Life is full of heartache and the more we can connect and show love to those around us, the more hope will fill all of our souls.

That's my prayer for you too, as you read *A Cup of Grace*.

Leslie Gould

Tearoom Mysteries

TEAROOM
mysteries

A Cup of Grace

LESLIE GOULD

Guideposts
New York

Tearoom Mysteries is a trademark of Guideposts

Published by Guideposts Books & Inspirational Media
110 William Street
New York, New York 10038
Guideposts.org

Acknowledgments

Every attempt has been made to credit the sources of copyrighted material used
in this book. If any such acknowledgment has been inadvertently omitted or
miscredited, receipt of such information would be appreciated.

Scripture references are from the following sources: *The Holy Bible,* King James
Version (KJV). *The Holy Bible, New International Version.* Copyright ©1973, 1978,
1984, 2011 by Biblica, Inc. Used by permission of Zondervan. All rights reserved
worldwide. www.zondervan.com

Cover and interior design by Müllerhaus
Cover illustration by Ross Jones, represented by Deborah Wolfe, Ltd.
Typeset by Aptara, Inc.

Printed and bound in the United States of America
10 9 8 7 6 5 4 3 2 1

A Cup of Grace

CHAPTER ONE

The lazy snow flurries drifted to the ground outside the window of the upstairs sitting room as Elaine Cook searched Pinterest ideas on her laptop for the tearoom's Valentine's Day Gala. Next to her on the comfy sectional sat Nathan, sorting through a stack of mail, attempting to catch up on his office work.

He was in a busy stretch with his auction business, with several upcoming estate sales and a conference he was scheduled to speak at in Boston soon. He used an antique silver-plated letter opener on the envelopes. Most, after he skimmed each document, went into the paper bag he'd brought along for the recycling.

A gust of January wind shook the windows of Tea for Two, and Elaine stood and pulled the drapes tighter, hoping to block the cold from seeping into the old Victorian house. When she sat back down, she scooted closer to Nathan. He dropped another envelope into the bag at his feet and then put his arm around her, pulling her close, his blue eyes lively.

"Even a boring task like this"—he nodded toward the bag of junk mail—"is enjoyable when I'm spending time with you."

Elaine leaned into him, breathing in the scent of his spicy cologne. "I feel the same way," she said, doing her best to be content in the moment. But she couldn't help thinking of her cousin Jan's upcoming wedding just over a month away. And the engagement of her daughter, Sasha. Both reminders that although she'd been dating Nathan Culver for quite some time, he hadn't proposed.

At Christmas, Nathan's odd behavior had made her dread the idea of having to make a snap decision on their future together. But since the misunderstandings had been cleared up, in the past few weeks Elaine had begun to think more and more in terms of Nathan as not just a boyfriend, but a husband.

She felt sure marrying Nathan was in her future, but she longed for him to confirm the idea with a proposal. The sooner the better, as far as she was concerned. Sure, at first she'd had cold feet with Nathan. But it had been a couple of years now. Things had changed. A lot.

Nathan released her and reached for another envelope as she continued scrolling through Valentine's Day ideas. For their tearoom event, they planned to have a high tea with a string quartet playing Victorian music. Elaine wanted everything to be perfect and welcoming and inclusive. She stopped at a photo of tables decorated with old love letters, photos, and Victorian valentines, all under glass. They didn't have glass like this for every table, but it wasn't a bad idea. They wouldn't have to use glass all the time—just having it as an option for special events would be great though. They could avoid worrying about spills and changing the tablecloths in the middle of special occasions such as bridal showers and weddings. She turned toward Nathan and pointed at the old cards. "Do you have any of these?"

He shook his head. "I found some old valentines in an estate sale a few months ago but they all sold."

Perhaps Elaine could find some elsewhere. Love letters too. Maybe people in the community would loan them to Elaine and Jan for the Valentine's Day Gala.

She kept scrolling and then stopped at a photo of heart-shaped scones. She'd have to speak with Jan about that.

They had a few weeks to pull off a fabulous Valentine's Day event. It would be perfect this time—it was their third try to get it right. It wasn't that the two previous times hadn't gone well. It was just that some people, mainly Macy, had after the fact expressed hurt feelings that they'd been excluded. It wasn't entirely true, but Valentine's Day could be difficult for single people, and Elaine truly hoped to do better.

Absentmindedly, she scrolled down to an image of tea sandwiches cut into heart shapes. She'd ask Jan about those too.

She turned her full attention to Nathan. He was right. It was so nice to have an evening together, even though they were both technically working. She hoped their future would be full of such evenings.

She nudged him. "Anything interesting in your mail?"

"No. Mostly junk and a few bills." He tossed another envelope into the recycling bag.

The next piece was a large white envelope with a fancy return address label. He held it up. "I wonder how I missed

3

this." He read the return address. "It's from an attorney in Tampa."

"My," Elaine said. "That sounds important."

Nathan slid his letter opener under the flap and slit open the envelope. "Except I don't know anyone in Tampa." He pulled out a packet of documents and began reading the cover letter.

Elaine turned back to her laptop and Googled *Valentine Tea ideas*.

But she was distracted from clicking on the first entry by Nathan holding his letter in midair. "Wow."

"What is it?"

"I'm mentioned in Berl Newton's will."

"Berl Newton?" The name was familiar but Elaine couldn't place the man.

"He owned the roadside attraction, you know, the World's Largest Snow Globe."

"Oh, of course," Elaine said. It had been years since she'd thought of the place. Back in its heyday, everyone shortened the name to simply the Snow Globe.

"He and my dad were friends, way back when," Nathan said.

Elaine and Nathan's fathers were friends too, but she didn't think her own father was particularly close to Mr. Newton. She certainly didn't remember him and his family ever coming for dinner or anything, but she did remember her family visiting the World's Largest Snow Globe. "That skating rink was the best," Elaine said.

Nathan nodded. "I remember my dad saying that Berl put a lot of work into that rink. It started as a shallow pond, but he redesigned it into a rink that opened in late October and didn't close until March."

"Wow, that really is a blast from the past," Elaine said. "I have such fond memories of the place."

"Me too." Nathan smiled at her. "I wonder if we ever skated there at the same time."

Elaine laughed. "I'm sure we did on some wild Friday night during junior high."

Nathan nodded and a sweet expression passed over his face. "I wish I could remember it."

"Me too," Elaine responded. She'd known Nathan much of her life. They were friends growing up and then, as they both married other people and lived their lives, didn't have any contact from the time they graduated from high school, except at her father's funeral, until she returned to Lancaster three years ago.

She loved that Nathan and she had shared experiences from the past—even ones in which they couldn't recall all of the details.

She pointed to the document still in his hand. "So why are you mentioned in Mr. Newton's will?"

"You're not going to believe this."

"Try me," she said.

"He left me the old roadside attraction property. And his snow globe collection."

Elaine's eyes grew wide and she pressed her hand against her chest, her fingers splayed. "You're kidding."

"That's what this attorney, a man by the name of"—he read from the bottom of the page—"Andrew Marner, wrote. Apparently he's handling all of Berl Newton's business. He said that Mr. Newton had taken care of nearly every detail of his will, businesses, and finances. Everything was in order. The attorney doesn't expect it will take long to settle the estate."

Elaine caught her breath. "When did Mr. Newton die?"

"Three months ago." He glanced at the date at the top of the letter. "This was sent just before Christmas." He sighed. "Wow, I totally overlooked it."

It wasn't like Nathan to miss an important letter, but she could see how it could happen. He'd been really busy the last few weeks.

"I hope this doesn't sound odd, but why would he leave it to you?" she asked.

"It doesn't sound odd at all." Nathan ran his free hand through his light-brown hair that was touched with hints of gray. "I have no idea." He put the letter beside him and glanced at the next page of the document. "Like I said, he and my dad were good friends. And several years ago, Mr. Newton contacted me about selling his snow globe collection at auction."

"Did you take it on?"

Nathan shook his head. "He found a collector here in Maine to sell it to, so he didn't need me, but then he changed his mind. He said it had too much sentimental value to sell it after all. I didn't actually see the collection, just photos of it, but it appeared to be quite extensive. Probably one of the best collections around, maybe *the* best."

Elaine had always loved snow globes. "What about that huge snow globe he used to have? The outdoor one."

Nathan turned his attention to Elaine. "You wouldn't be referring to the world's largest one, would you?"

Elaine grinned. At one time, the snow globe put Lancaster on the map, even though the roadside attraction was nearly ten miles out of town. "That's exactly which one I mean."

"Well," Nathan answered, "after the new highway bypassed the place, business gradually died down and Mr. Newton finally dismantled it. My dad had told me that he was afraid it could be hazardous to someone who might trespass on the property."

The globe sat on a pedestal with steps leading to the opening. Inside was a bench with pine boughs suspended over the top of it. The floor was painted white, and white confetti floated down from the ceiling.

She remembered going skating at the rink with her parents and brother several times and then sitting in the snow globe. Mr. Newton occasionally hired a photographer and once her dad paid to have a family photo taken. She'd have to ask her mom about what had happened to the picture.

On Monday mornings at school, the kids would talk about skating there over the weekend. It was the place to be, for a time, for the children and the teens of Lancaster. Skating at the Snow Globe, tucked away in the forest, was much better than skating on Chickadee Lake. There wasn't any wind and lights hung over the top of the rink, allowing night skating. It had been a magical place.

She took Nathan's free hand. "Did you go skating there a lot?"

"All the time," Nathan answered. "I didn't have to pay because of Mr. Newton's friendship with my dad. I was quite the skating pro." He grinned. "Nearly as good as Scott Hamilton."

"So you could do jumps? Axels? Doubles? And triples?"

He laughed. "Maybe not quite that good. But I definitely killed it under the disco ball. You should have seen my funky chicken moves."

Now it was Elaine's turn to laugh. "I'd forgotten all about that." The ball had been hung high over the middle of the outdoor rink. It really had been a magical location.

Sadly, by the time she was in junior high, the place had started to fall off the map. By high school, it was closed.

And now Nathan was going to inherit it. It seemed unbelievable. Of course, it wouldn't be the same place now that it had been. It was probably just a collection of run-down buildings. "Do you know the history behind it all?" she asked.

"Vaguely. Mr. Newton's dad owned the property and opened it as an auto camp back in the 1920s when cars were first becoming popular, but those Model Ts couldn't travel very far at once. He had a gas station and a garage and fixed a lot of flats, I imagine."

Elaine remembered her mother talking about family trips as a child when they'd get multiple flat tires in a day because of the thin tires and rough roads.

"According to my dad, Berl's father had little cabins for travelers to rent, and he stocked the pond with fish in the spring," Nathan said. "He had fire pits and hiking trails, a destination along the way for travelers. He added a store and a little gift shop too so he was making a profit from taking care of both the cars and the customer."

Elaine slipped her laptop to the side, and turned toward Nathan, tucking one leg up on the sectional. "When were the skating rink and globe added?"

"Oh, Berl added those after his father passed away. The rink first, in the fifties. And then the globe later, probably in the '60s."

It had been the 1970s when Elaine had skated there. "Did you ever hear why he added them?"

"Yeah, he wanted to draw in year-round business." Nathan had a faraway look in his eyes as he remembered the details. "Travelers took their trips in the summer, which brought in plenty of business, but he wanted an attraction in the winter to draw the locals out. That's why he came up with the rink and the snow globe. He sold little snow globes in the gift shop too, which were a big hit. Of course, they were cheap, nothing like the ones he collected. He also turned the cabins into rustic European-style cottages."

Elaine remembered those. They had pitched roofs and shake siding. They looked as if they were lifted right out of the Bavarian countryside. There was also a little chapel on the grounds with a double steeple and miniature stained-glass windows. As far as she knew, services were never held in the building, and she guessed that Mr. Newton had built it as a place where his guests could reflect and pray.

Nathan explained, "He was a sort of Renaissance man. He had a degree in engineering, which he definitely put to use around the property. But he made his living, at least most of it, from selling real estate in the area. I think the whole World's Largest Snow Globe project fed his creativity. His goal was to make the place a winter wonderland, with a snow globe theme."

"Well, he certainly succeeded. I can still vividly remember how magical all of it was. It was like a fairy tale come to life."

She smiled at the memory. "So did Mr. Newton move to Florida because the business declined?"

"I'm not sure," Nathan replied. "Perhaps he would have anyway. But I do remember his wife died and he felt restless. He was a good businessman and a big dreamer, and I'm guessing he figured he'd have more opportunities in an urban area."

Elaine could see that.

Nathan slipped the document into the envelope. "The will is dated a few months after the last time I spoke with Mr. Newton, so six years ago." He pressed the flap of the envelope down. "I'll call the attorney in the morning and see if there are any more details."

"This is wild," Elaine said and Nathan nodded, clearly stunned and a little confused. "I guess I just wonder why he wouldn't leave the property to a relative."

"I don't know," Nathan said. "He did have a daughter. She was several years older than we are."

Elaine smiled, recalling the girl, although she couldn't remember her name.

"I can't imagine why he didn't leave it to her," Nathan said. "But even more so, I can't fathom why he'd leave it to me."

CHAPTER TWO

The next morning, after she'd spent some time petting Earl Grey and listening to his grateful purrs, Elaine fed him on the back porch. Then she brewed a pot of English breakfast tea and told her cousin about Nathan's inheritance.

"You're kidding!" Jan Blake stood with her pastry cutter poised over a bowl of bacon maple scone dough. "That's absolutely wild."

"I know, right?" Elaine retrieved two cups from the rack. "He's flabbergasted why Berl Newton would leave him the property. He's fine with me telling you, but he doesn't want the news to hit the community grapevine yet."

Jan shook her head in dismay. "Yeah, I can understand that. What a surprise." She lowered the beaters but didn't start them. "Mr. Newton has a daughter, right?"

Elaine nodded.

"I remember going out there with you and your family when we were kids," Jan said.

Elaine hadn't thought of that, but now the memory took shape in her mind. "That's right. We had our photo taken in the globe and had to brush confetti out of our hair afterward." Hopefully her mother had that photo too.

Jan laughed. "It was the cool place to be, as a fifth grader. Even as an eighth grader."

Elaine agreed. "Nathan said he used to go out to the rink all the time back in the old days." Elaine glanced out the window, over the snow-covered lawn and toward the frozen lake. "I wish I could remember him then."

The pond by the Snow Globe had been just the right size for a rink. Large enough to spread out but not so much that everyone was far apart, like on the lake. Even though she knew it was unrealistic, she imagined Nathan opening up a rink there again. They could skate together with their kids and grandchildren, sharing a slice of their own childhoods with those they loved.

As Jan started the mixer, Elaine poured the tea and then grabbed her notebook. When Jan was done, the two sat at the table to talk over the day. Elaine and Rose, their employee since the tearoom's first month or two, would be serving. It probably wouldn't be too busy, but they could still hope. The specials were bacon maple scones along with sour cream lemon tartlets, a last-minute recipe Jan was considering for her wedding tea, which would be held the day before the ceremony. Elaine had witnessed Jan become absolutely obsessed with choosing the menu items for the tea and for her reception, but that had all evened out over the last couple of weeks, and Elaine was grateful.

Jan had decided on a big wedding because her first one had been small and intimate. Elaine, along with Rose and Jan's daughter Tara and her daughter-in-law, Paula, were going to be bridesmaids. Jan's other daughter, Amy, had decided she would be too far along in her pregnancy—and maybe even have given birth by then—to stand up in the wedding. Jan had told Elaine that she'd totally understood Amy's decision and ultimately agreed. Amy's support wasn't limited to standing beside Jan that day. Elaine had witnessed Amy being an incredibly supportive daughter the whole way through Jan's relationship, and she knew that support would continue.

Elaine thought about how the bridesmaids' mauve-colored dresses were all purchased, pressed, and hanging in her closet upstairs, and their matching shoes would be arriving soon. Elaine was thrilled her cousin was going to have the day of her dreams—and that everyone who loved her most would be celebrating with her.

As Jan reached for her teacup, her engagement diamond sparkled under the overhead light.

Elaine smiled as she glanced back down at her notes. She was truly happy for her cousin. "We should talk more about the Valentine's Day Gala." Elaine shared her idea about ordering glass to cover the tables, adding that she would get estimates and place the order, and explained the idea of collecting old-fashioned valentines and love letters. "But let's make it more inclusive, so people like Macy, who aren't in a relationship, feel included too."

"Oh, I love it!" Jan cradled her teacup. "Rose could make a poster today, requesting that people loan us what they have, including photos."

Elaine wrote *Rose—poster* under the Valentine's Day category even though she knew she'd remember to ask her about it. But this way she could cross it off her list. "I have ribbons and lace she could use, and some paper doilies. And paper and a board. I'll pull the easel out to put it on."

"Perfect. She'll just have to communicate that we'll take good care of each item."

Elaine nodded. "I'll set up a recording and file system to make sure we keep track of everything. Then we won't put the items under the glass until the night before—and we'll return them as soon as possible afterward."

"Sounds good. We'll all trust your organizational skills to make it work."

Elaine couldn't help but smile as she glanced back down at her list. Her administrative work, combined with Jan's baking gift, had created a viable business. "We should also start asking people to buy their tickets for Valentine's Day."

"Definitely. In fact, wouldn't it be great to make invitations we could pass out to customers?" Jan took a sip of tea.

"Great idea," Elaine said. "Who could design something like that?"

"Maybe Tara—I'll ask her."

Elaine wrote down Tara's name and *invitation*. Jan's youngest daughter made jewelry and had a knack for design.

"I've already booked the quartet from Augusta," Elaine said. She had done that in November, knowing she needed to take care of that detail early.

They chatted some about the menu for the tea, and Jan said she needed to put more thought into it.

"I've been thinking. Besides the music, it would be great to have the Bookworm Book Club read some poems from the Victorian era."

"Oh, that sounds lovely." Jan clasped her hands together. Then she said, "Did you know Pastor Mike and Sarah's twentieth anniversary is right after Valentine's Day? The sixteenth, I think. Wouldn't it be great to do something to honor them?"

"Yeah," Elaine said. "For any particular reason, besides how much they do for all of us?"

"Oh, I've just picked up from Sarah that things are stressful right now. Nothing specific."

Jan probably had more information than what she wanted to share. That was fine. Elaine didn't need to know the details. "What do you have in mind as far as honoring them?"

"Maybe a gift certificate to a B and B for a weekend. Something like that."

"That would be lovely," Elaine answered.

"I'll see to it," Jan said. "Well, actually I'll ask Bristol to help with it. And I can ask her about the poetry reading too."

"Perfect!" Elaine jotted that down in her notebook too.

Jan finished the last sip of her tea as Elaine drank her first, and then stood. Elaine stayed at the table, her thoughts drifting back to the Snow Globe. As Jan took her cup to the sink, she said, "I'm just going to slip across the street and see how my new kitchen is coming along. I'll be right back."

Elaine smiled at her cousin. Jan and Bob had bought the old Victorian across the street and were nearly done renovating the kitchen, along with having other repairs done. At least once a day, and probably more, Jan slipped across the street to check on the progress.

When Elaine heard the click of the front door as Jan closed it behind her, her thoughts fell back to Nathan. She hoped he could get more information from the attorney soon. As much as she thought it would be fun if he reopened the World's Largest Snow Globe, she knew it wasn't realistic, not with his auction business.

She took another sip of tea. Besides knowing every detail of Jan's upcoming wedding, Elaine had been helping her daughter, Sasha, plan her wedding for next summer.

Elaine wanted what was best for Nathan and for herself. They had been taking their time because, after losing Ben, she'd felt cautious. Could she have a second marriage as good as her first?

Even though Nathan had never been hesitant about their relationship, he was currently overwhelmed with other things. She hoped the Snow Globe property wouldn't add even more stress to his already busy life. He needed less stress—not more.

When Rose got her poster assignment later that morning, she was thrilled. First she spent some time in Elaine's office at the computer, doing some research and printing off a few things. Next she gathered all of the supplies during slow times during the day and worked on the project in the dining room, her blue eyes serious with the task. Elaine retrieved the easel from the attic and set it up in the spacious entry, ready for the poster once Rose finished it.

Business was steady all day, but slow enough that Elaine had a chance to interact with the customers and answer any questions they had about the tea. She loved giving little lessons about the different types they carried. They'd just gotten a new tea in, one from a company in Portland, called Acadia Vanilla. It was a black infused tea and was full-bodied and very satisfying, especially on an icy day. Everyone who tried it liked it, and one woman bought a whole bag.

Of course, Jan's scones, tartlets, and other treats were a big hit too. Elaine delighted in the comfort that the tradition of tea brought to customers. Taking time out of the day for a freshly brewed, hot cup of tea and something sweet or savory was a time-honored tradition that brought a little joy to the day of everyone who partook.

By midafternoon, however, business had slowed to a trickle and Elaine was able to handle it, allowing Rose to finish her project. Soon, Rose sashayed out of Elaine's office with the poster in her hand. A few strands of her wheat-colored hair had fallen out of her high bun and she looked the part of a Victorian valentine herself with her rosy cheeks and bright eyes.

Elaine clapped her hands together in delight at the sight of the poster. Rose had played up the theme. She'd printed photos of cupids out on Elaine's printer and cut the paper doilies into hearts. The ribbon and lace were used as accents. She'd also printed off the information, using a vintage font, and also requested the loan of old photos of "sweethearts, friends, and family" and valentines from "everyone," all to be "well cared for, to be used as decorations on Valentine's Day, and to be returned in the same condition they were received."

"It's perfect," Elaine said, motioning toward the easel by the counter. "We might as well put it on display now. The sooner the better." She was pleased that it truly did sound all-inclusive.

A half hour before closing, Elaine's cell buzzed in the pocket of her apron while she was in the kitchen plating an order of the bacon scones. *Nathan.* She answered it quickly.

"Are you busy?" he asked.

"Not particularly."

"Can you finish early?"

"Maybe..."

Jan took a tray of tart shells from the oven.

"Can you come out to the Snow Globe property with me?" Nathan asked. "I want to look around."

Jan put the cookie sheet on top of the stove and turned toward Elaine.

"Just a sec." Elaine put the phone on mute and told Jan what was going on.

"Of course you should go," Jan said. "Rose and I can easily close and clean up."

After Elaine told Nathan yes, she slipped her phone back into her pocket. They'd need to be on their way as soon as possible before it grew dark.

After she took off her apron and hung it up, she grabbed a flashlight just in case looking around took longer than Nathan anticipated.

She also put on her warmest coat and pulled on her boots. The snow was bound to be deep and it would be hard to get around. They had at least a foot in town and there was apt to be more out in the forest.

As soon as Nathan pulled up in front of Tea for Two, she started out the door, clutching the flashlight in one hand and her purse in the other.

Nathan jumped out of his Cadillac and hurried around the car. He greeted her with a kiss, causing her heart to race, and then opened the car door for her. Always the gentleman. He'd make a great husband someday, she was sure.

She slipped into the car, settled into the comfy seat, and fastened her seat belt as Nathan did the same. The interior of the car was spotless and cozy. She took a deep breath, feeling—as always—safe and secure in his presence.

He pulled away from the curb. The snow around the tearoom was piled up in two-foot banks on both sides of the street from the last time the city plowed, but the trees were all bare from the strong winds the night before. Elaine hoped they'd be flocked again soon. She loved that look. It reminded her of a snow globe.

As they drove past the shops, Elaine could make out a couple of boys playing along the shore of Chickadee Lake. The temperatures hadn't been higher than twenty-five for weeks and the lake was as frozen as could be.

More snow was predicted overnight, perhaps even within the next hour. Of course, Nathan had a winter emergency kit in the back, plus he had studded tires and all-wheel drive too.

As they drove past the shuttered ice cream stand on the way out of town, Nathan said he'd talked with the attorney.

"I figured you had," she said.

"Mr. Marner said he wasn't sure why Berl Newton left the property to me, but he did fill me in more on the man's life after he left Maine." Nathan turned onto the highway toward Waterville. "He invested in real estate development in Florida, and also invented a super strong concrete that was used in buildings he financed."

"Wow."

"Yeah, it made me think of that snow globe he built. I think he was probably ahead of his time with a lot of his ideas."

Elaine agreed.

Nathan smiled at her. "Anyway, he made a fortune in Florida. The attorney only sent me the part of the will that applied to me, but he said that Mr. Newton left the rest of his assets to charities."

"You're kidding. Nothing to family?"

"No. He left money to homeless shelters, churches, colleges, and a builders' association, among other good causes."

"Any idea if his daughter is still alive?"

"No," Nathan said. "Berl's attorney recently died and Mr. Marner is new to the firm and just took over. He's guessing the daughter is deceased but doesn't know for sure. I'll ask around here and see if anyone has heard anything."

"How odd." Elaine exhaled. "What did he say about the snow globe collection?"

Nathan glanced at her, his eyes wide, and then back at the road. "That's especially interesting. The attorney doesn't know where the collection is."

"How could he not know?"

Nathan slowed for a curve. "He said it was really strange. Berl was meticulous about every detail of his will except for the location of the snow globe collection. It wasn't found in his home or office. The attorney has no idea where it is."

"How odd," Elaine said. "Do you think he left the collection somewhere here in Maine?"

"It's hard to fathom that he would. I doubt any of the buildings at the old property are secure."

"How about in a safety deposit box or something?"

Nathan chuckled. "It would have to be an awfully big box."

Elaine laughed with him. She had no idea how big the collection was, but it sounded as if it was large.

They passed the speed limit sign, and Nathan accelerated. "I have that auction this weekend, starting tomorrow."

Elaine remembered.

"The attorney was interested in the Snow Globe property and what it was like. I enjoyed telling him about it from what I remember, but it's been years since I've been by it. I have no idea what it's like now. So I told him I'd call him back and let him know what the property looks like after I checked it out."

They rode along in silence for a couple of minutes. The afternoon was growing dark. As they entered the forest, Elaine was happy to see that the evergreens were still flocked with snow. The wind wasn't nearly as strong here as back in town.

Nathan turned onto the old highway and the narrower roadway, with trees on either side, appeared like a tunnel in the waning light. Elaine remembered that from childhood. It was part of the fairy-tale feeling she'd sensed as a child traveling to the Snow Globe. Ahead on the left was a clearing, but Elaine didn't realize it was the property until Nathan turned into it. The old parking lot was partially cleared of snow. It appeared the state highway plows had turned into the lot recently, maybe to turn around or for the drivers to take a break. The result was a place where they could park without getting stuck.

A group of cottages, eight in all, sat to their left. Considering they'd been vacant for over thirty years, they appeared to be in good shape with metal roofs and shake siding. When they lived in Germany, Elaine and her family had visited the Bavarian countryside. As a child, she hadn't known the cabins were renovated to look like rustic Bavarian cottages with the peaks of the roofs covered with snow, but now it was obvious to her. To their right was the gift store, which also had a metal roof. Set back from it, between the first cottage and the store, was the little church. More like a chapel really, that also had a Bavarian design to it, with its double steeple and narrow windows.

"I don't remember the metal roofs from when we were little," Elaine said, "but maybe I just didn't notice."

"I think they're fairly new," Nathan said. "At least in the last couple of decades."

"That's interesting that Mr. Newton would have invested the money for that."

Nathan shrugged. "He probably didn't want the cottages to weather so badly that they collapsed."

That made sense to Elaine. Straight ahead was the garage. The gas pumps were long gone, but the garage door was still there, although several panes of glass were broken.

Elaine glanced back at the chapel and cottages. She couldn't see any other broken windows.

Far to the right was the warming shed, which was much, much bigger than the term sounded. It was narrow and long, probably sixty feet in length, and all made of wood. The pond, although it was hard to tell exactly where it started and stopped, was covered by a few feet of snow since it was no longer cleared for skating. No lights were strung over it, but the poles that once supported them were still in place. There was no sight of the World's Largest Snow Globe, of course.

Nathan left his car idling. "Boy, it brings back memories, doesn't it?"

Elaine nodded. She felt like a girl again.

"Want to get out?" Nathan asked.

"Of course."

He turned off the engine and they both climbed down. Elaine left her purse but took the flashlight with her. Nathan headed toward what had once been the gift shop, but the door was locked.

"Did the attorney say anything about keys?"

"There aren't any in his possession," Nathan answered. "He's looking into whether there might have been a local caretaker of some kind who has them. If there wasn't one, I'll have to hire a locksmith. Andrew Marner said I could take possession immediately—there are clearly enough assets to pay off any debts Berl had, although he's pretty sure all of the last bills have already come in and been paid."

Nathan looked around. "Look at the exteriors of these buildings though. It's hard to believe that someone around here doesn't have a key. It's not like the buildings are in pristine condition, but they're not falling down either."

Elaine agreed. They'd even been painted in the last few years—if they hadn't, the harsh elements would have stripped the wood bare. "Why do you think Berl Newton held on to the property all these years? Why didn't he sell it?"

"I'm guessing it must have had sentimental value to him, because it definitely wasn't making him any money." Nathan trudged through the snow to the little church and tried the door. It was locked too. And so was the first cottage. "I'm guessing they're all locked!" Nathan called out.

He rejoined Elaine and then they walked together to the gas station and attached garage.

That door wasn't locked. Nathan swung it open and tried the switch, but no lights came on. That wasn't surprising. Elaine would have been shocked if Mr. Newton had been paying to keep the electricity on all of these years.

There was a counter at the front of the room and a tool bench at the back. Elaine shone the flashlight that way. There were a couple of old gas cans under the bench and a few wrenches on top of it.

Nathan turned toward the attached garage and Elaine swung the flashlight that way to light his path. The cement floor was swept clear, except where the snow had drifted in through the broken panes.

Elaine swung the flashlight at the two bays. "I wonder who kept the place maintained—except for the broken glass."

Nathan frowned. "I'm thinking he must have hired someone, but I wonder who."

"Or perhaps," Elaine said, "someone who had fond memories of the place kept an eye on things." It was off the beaten path now, but that didn't mean it was forgotten. Not entirely. Although she had all but put the place out of her mind until Nathan uttered the words last night.

Nathan shrugged as if he didn't agree. He was right. There was no way anyone would paint the buildings from a place of sentimentality.

She shone the flashlight in the corners of the garage, and the beam cast eerie shadows around the shop.

There were a couple of lifts on the floor and another tool bench, but this one was cleared. However, there was a half-filled burlap bag underneath. Elaine stepped forward, just as a mouse scurried across the floor.

She gasped and Nathan laughed. Elaine stepped backward as Nathan said, "I can't imagine what he's eating. He must be tunneling under the snow to find anything at all."

"Maybe there's some sort of seed in the bag," Elaine said. She remembered driving by the place in the summer as a child and seeing lush lawns around the cottages.

Another mouse scurried after the first. Elaine took another step backward. "Let's go look at the warming shed."

"Sounds like a good idea." Nathan led the way, as Elaine shone the light on the concrete floor until they stepped back outside. The sun was just riding the top of the trees as they started toward the pond.

"Look." Elaine pointed as she spoke. "Don't those look like footprints?"

She turned the flashlight back on as Nathan stopped.

"They do." He crouched down.

It had snowed a couple of days before so the footprints had to be fairly fresh. "The attorney didn't send someone out to the property to check things out, did he?" Elaine asked. "Without telling you?"

Nathan shook his head and then stood. "No. He hoped I'd come out." He started toward the pond again. "Perhaps someone was curious about the buildings and stopped to take a look."

Elaine walked alongside him. "Probably so." But she wasn't so sure. There weren't any tire tracks, but there weren't enough footprints to tell where the person went. It seemed the snow had drifted enough to cover most of them.

Elaine clicked the flashlight off. Maybe whoever had been maintaining the property had been there but hadn't had a chance to fix the broken glass.

"I'll definitely follow up with the lawyer about the care-taker. I'll ask him when I call tomorrow."

As they neared the warming hut, Elaine glanced up at the roof. It was steeply pitched, enough so that the snow had fallen off the top and landed in drifts around the perimeter. Back in the day, Mr. Newton had a snack bar where hot chocolate, cof-fee, sodas, hot dogs, popcorn, and candy were sold. The skaters would gather around inside it for a snack and then go back out on the rink.

The warming hut had a counter at the far end where the snack bar was, and had only two full walls, which was why it was called a hut. The wall facing the pond was half size with several gates opening into the shed, as was the one facing where the World's Largest Snow Globe used to be.

Nathan marched through the snow that had drifted up against the shed to the back door. Elaine followed as the sun dipped behind the trees. She shivered, whishing she'd put on another layer underneath her coat. At least her boots were warm and high.

Nathan reached the hut and turned the handle. It wasn't locked. He pushed hard and it opened.

There were no longer chairs and tables in it and the wooden floor had several rotten boards in the middle. "Be careful."

Elaine followed along behind, turning on her flashlight. A starling flew out of the rafters, and Elaine screamed again.

This time Nathan turned toward her and took her arm. He seemed to be startled too.

Embarrassed, Elaine said, "I'm fine."

"Me too," he said and then smiled. She clasped his gloved hand with hers.

The half wall, on the pond side, blocked some of the light, but not all of it. Dusk had fallen, but the last light bouncing off the snow mostly illuminated the interior of the shed, although the flashlight helped.

They walked across the plank floor to the end, and looked out over where the snow globe used to be. Perhaps the old pedestal was under the snow, but nothing was visible. Just the snow.

Nathan let go of Elaine and leaned against the half wall. "I remember sitting here and watching people in the snow globe getting their photos taken."

"Me too," Elaine said. "In fact, I remember getting my photo taken with my family, and then another time with Jan. She reminded me of it this morning."

Nathan turned toward her. "Any chance you still have the photos?"

Elaine shook her head. "But maybe Mom does. I'll ask her."

They turned toward the pond, and Nathan put his arm around Elaine and drew her close. In the dim light, both of them could see that there were tracks in the snow covering the pond too.

"Doesn't it look like the snow in the middle of the pond has been shoveled?" Elaine leaned closer to the half wall.

"Yeah." Nathan stepped away from her toward the gate. She followed and they stepped out onto the pond.

The breeze had picked up as the sun set, sending chills through Elaine, but she pushed forward, following Nathan's footsteps. She shone the light off the snow, which helped illuminate their way.

Soon they reached a circular area that had a wall of shoveled snow around it. Skate marks covered the area.

"Interesting." Nathan crossed his arms.

"Someone's been trespassing," Elaine said, shining the light around the space.

"Well, way out here, no one would consider it trespassing. It's a frozen pond. They're pretty much fair game."

"True," Elaine said.

They were now far enough from the warming hut that they had a view of the gift store, garage, and cottages. Both turned that way, the evening breeze now blowing against their faces.

Elaine whispered, "What will you do with this place?"

Nathan paused for a long moment and then responded, his voice low too, "I have no idea. But I'd like to do good with it, as Berl Newton did all those years ago. I've been praying about it, and I'm trusting God to show me what He wants."

Even as she shivered from the cold, Elaine's heart warmed at Nathan's wise words. He'd been given a gift—but what he wanted most was to use it in a way to glorify God and bring happiness to other people.

In the distance the last rays of color faded from the sky and night fell completely.

"We'd better get back." Nathan reached for her hand. "You're shivering."

They stepped across the ice, off the shoveled area, through the wall of snow, and back toward the edge of the pond, shooting for the bank past the warming hut.

Just as they reached the edge, Nathan's cell phone rang.

"It's Andrew Marner," he said. "It's odd he'd call so late." He pulled off his glove and put it on speaker and then slipped his glove back on. "Hello," he said. "I didn't expect to hear from you again so soon."

They chatted for a moment and then the attorney said, "I don't think this is anything to be alarmed about, but I wanted you to know the will is being contested. It's most likely just a formality. Very rarely, in only one percent of the cases, is such a thing successful."

"Wow." Nathan held the phone closer to his mouth. "Any idea who contested it?"

"Not yet, but it's most likely a relative. I'll find out and let you know. I just wanted to alert you that things will take a little longer than expected. What I said earlier, about you going ahead and taking possession of the place no longer holds."

"Uh-oh," Nathan said. "We're out here right now."

"Oh, that's all right," the attorney said. "Just don't try to sell it. Or raze any buildings. But there's no problem with you being there. Like I said, there's very little chance anything is going to come of this." The attorney added that he'd update Nathan as soon as possible.

After Nathan thanked him, he said, "I have a question for you. Any chance you found out who was maintaining this property for Berl? From the outside most of the buildings appear to be in good shape."

"Yes," the attorney said. "That was the next thing I was going to mention. I found the name and number of a handyman that did odd jobs around the place. His name is Otis Schmidt, and he lives in Waterville. Most likely he has a key. I'll text you the number."

Nathan thanked him and then asked if he'd found anything about the snow globe collection.

"Not yet," Mr. Marner said, "but I'll let you know as soon as I find that information. And I'll keep you updated about the will being contested." Then he said goodbye and disconnected the call.

"How odd," Elaine said.

Nathan slipped his phone back into his pocket. "Who do you think would contest the will?"

"I have no idea." This time Elaine reached out for his hand as they crossed the rest of the pond together and then trudged over the bank, heading back to Nathan's car as fluffy flakes began to fall. The wind picked up and splattered the snow against their faces.

Grateful they were nearly back to the car, Elaine quickened her pace as much as she could and Nathan matched his stride with hers.

But just as they were about fifty feet from the Cadillac, an explosion, followed by a loud boom, rocked the garage.

Nathan grabbed Elaine and turned her away as debris, glass, and wood, flew toward them. Then he lowered his head over hers as Elaine knelt, pulling him down beside her.

CHAPTER THREE

J an put the last teacup in the dishwasher, added the soap, and then hit the start button as she talked with Tara on the phone. "Yes," Jan said. "That's what we were hoping for. Invitations with a Victorian design that we can pass out to our customers, and to other people who might be interested too."

Jan rattled off the details: *Valentine's Day Gala. 5 p.m. High Tea at Tea for Two. Open to all.*

As Jan continued talking with Tara, Rose untied her apron and dropped it in the laundry hamper next to the door to Elaine's office. It had been an extra-long day. They'd had a rush fifteen minutes before four, soon after Elaine left, and the last of the customers hadn't left until a few minutes after five.

Tara said she'd play around with a few ideas and get back to Jan.

"Thank you so much, sweetheart. Both Elaine and I really appreciate it."

"Oh, how's your and Bob's house coming along?"

"Great. I was just over there this morning." Jan had hoped to get back over that afternoon, but with Elaine leaving, that wasn't possible. And she'd just checked a few minutes ago and the contractor's truck was gone. "The quartz counters and refinished cupboards are all done, and the new appliances are in the garage, ready to be installed." They were brushed steel and gorgeous. "After the flooring goes down, the crew will install them." The two chatted for a few more minutes about the project and then Tara said goodbye, and Jan slipped her phone back into her apron pocket. It was a toss-up what she was more excited about—the wedding or the house. She'd had a tiny, intimate wedding the first time. For her second marriage, she and Bob had decided to have a large wedding with four attendants each, a beautiful candlelit ceremony, and a lavish reception. She couldn't wait.

Something began to buzz, but Jan was thinking about her wedding—and her new house—again...

Rose patted her back pocket but then said, "I think that's your phone."

"Oh, you're right." Jan retrieved it from her apron pocket again, expecting that Tara had called back with a question. But it was Elaine. Maybe she and Nathan had decided to go out for the evening.

"Hey," Jan said.

Elaine's teeth were chattering. "We're all right, but—"

Jan's heart began to race.

"Nathan's car was damaged in an—"

Jan expected the word *accident*, but Elaine said, "Explosion."

"What?" Jan gasped. "Where are you?"

Rose shot her a concerned look.

"Out at the Snow Globe property." Elaine's teeth continued to chatter. "We were by the pond when an explosion went off in the old garage."

"Oh no."

"The glass and window frames blew, and one of the boards slammed up under Nathan's car and punctured the radiator."

Jan put her hand to her face. "What?"

"Yeah, and that meant that we couldn't start the engine to warm up until Dan got here, and I've gotten chilled." The chattering grew louder.

At least Trooper Dan Benson was there. "When did Dan arrive?"

"Just a minute ago. Nathan called the state police because they have an explosives unit, and Dan was available. That's why Nathan told me to call you. Could you come get me while he and Dan look around and wait for the tow?"

"Yes, of course!"

More chattering and then Elaine managed to say, "Thank you."

Jan untied her apron as she headed to the hamper. "Where are you right now?"

"In Dan's vehicle. With the heat on, but I'm just not warming up."

"Sit tight," Jan said. "I'll be there as soon as possible."

Once she hung up the phone, she told Rose what happened and then called Bob and explained the situation to him.

"Want me to go with you?" he asked.

"Yes, please," Jan said.

"I'll pick you up in just a few," he said and then hung up.

"I'll start some tea," Rose said. "For you to take along. You go get bundled up. The wind's been picking up and the snow just started again."

Jan had heard the wind wailing. It wouldn't be as bad in the forest, most likely, but it wasn't the kind of weather for anyone to be out in. She put on her heaviest coat, fur-lined boots, scarf, and gloves. Just as Bob gave a quick honk, Rose came with a fuzzy blanket as well as a large thermos of tea in a basket with extra cups and some pastries. "Don't worry about anything here. I'll lock up."

After Jan gave the girl a quick thank-you and hug, she stepped out into the cold. Jan had been a Mainer her entire life but still gasped at the icy wind and the pelting flakes of snow. It was a wickedly cold night.

It was so cold and she was so worried about Elaine that she almost forgot to look at her future house across the street. But a light had been left on in the living room, which caught her attention. It was painted a light shade of taupe, with ivory and chocolate trim. It looked so cozy and welcoming in the snow. And it was nearly done. Bob would move in permanently a couple of weeks before the wedding, and then once they were married, she would join him. She was flooded with warmth, even in the cold, at the thought of sharing the home with her beloved.

She climbed into Bob's Acura and put the blanket and basket on the floor at her feet. "Thank you." She fastened her seat belt.

"Where are they?" Bob asked as he pulled away from the curb.

"Out at the old Snow Globe property. That's where the explosion occurred."

"I thought that's what you said over the phone, but why in the world are they out there?"

Jan quickly explained that Nathan had inherited it from Berl Newton.

"Wow." Bob accelerated as they reached the outskirts of town. "Did they figure out what the explosion was from?"

"Elaine didn't say."

"Probably a propane tank or something."

Jan smiled in her relief. "You're probably right." Here she'd been thinking that some sort of sabotage was going on. She'd most likely been looking for a mystery where there wasn't one.

The wind tore through the tops of the trees, bending the boughs and sending showers of snow toward the highway.

"Help me look for the turn," Bob said to Jan.

It had been so long since either one of them had been out to the Snow Globe that Jan feared they'd miss it.

"I think this is it," Bob said, turning left.

"Yes." Jan recognized that it was where the old highway intersected the new one.

The old road was narrower with barely any shoulder on either side. The snow zipped toward the windshield, mesmerizing Jan, and she turned her head and peered into the trees. The Snow Globe property was surrounded on three sides by forest—she remembered that much, and she guessed it still was.

Bob slowed. "How soon?"

"It's up here on the left," Jan said. "But I can't remember how far."

They continued on until Jan spotted taillights. "Maybe right here."

Bob slowed even more and then turned. Sure enough, it was a trooper's SUV with Nathan's Cadillac parked to the side of it. A puddle of antifreeze had flowed out from underneath it and the green glistened against the white snow.

Jan grabbed the basket, opened the door, and climbed down. She continued around the passenger side of the state trooper's vehicle as Bob followed behind her. Elaine had her eyes closed and her head against the back of the seat.

Jan knocked on the glass and Elaine startled, her eyes flying open.

"Sorry." Jan waved.

Elaine opened the door. "I didn't hear you."

"Are you okay?" Jan asked. Elaine was shivering and pale.

"I think so. My head hurts, but I didn't get hit or anything."

"Hit?"

"By the window casings and glass and boards that came flying toward us."

Jan turned toward the garage. Sure enough, the windows were blown out. "Where's Nathan?"

"He and Dan are checking around to see if they can find anyone." As Elaine spoke, the two men came around the side of the gift shop. Nathan called out a hello, and Dan waved. He wore his heavy trooper coat, a hat with earflaps, and thick gloves, while Nathan wore his wool overcoat.

The two men started toward the SUV. As Elaine climbed out, Jan said, "I should get you home."

Nathan reached them, with Dan right behind him, and said to Jan, "Could you take her by the clinic? I'm afraid she might have a concussion."

"No, I'm sure I don't," Elaine answered Nathan. "If anyone has one, it would be you." She turned to Jan. "He protected me."

Dan nodded a hello to both Jan and Bob and then, meeting Elaine's eyes, said, "Concussions are hard to predict. They don't always affect the person closest to the explosion. It has to do with the way the force radiates."

"Really?" Elaine responded but then shook her head. "I'm fine. Just shaken and cold."

"Go anyway," Nathan said, taking out his phone. "I'm calling the clinic to tell them you're on your way."

Elaine wrinkled her nose but didn't protest any more.

"Why don't you take her?" Bob said to Jan, pulling his key from his pocket. "I'll stay here and ride with Nathan in the tow truck."

Jan guessed he wanted to help Nathan and Dan snoop around more, but she didn't say anything. Instead she put out her hand for the key. He gave it to her as Nathan ended his phone call.

"They're expecting you." He put his hand on Elaine's shoulder.

"What about you?"

"I don't have a headache. And I'm not chilled to the bone. I'll find you after we're done here—either at the clinic or back at the tearoom."

Nathan gave Elaine a hug and then walked with her, while Dan told Bob they hadn't found anything suspicious. "Some tracks in the snow, but they're blurry. We took photos but they aren't clear enough for evidence. Nathan and Elaine saw some before the explosion but there's no way to know if they're relevant or not." He looked up at the sky and the flakes twirling toward the ground. "They'll all soon be covered anyway."

"Did you go in the garage?" Bob asked.

Dan shook his head. "I'm waiting for the explosives unit."

"Good idea," Bob said.

Jan retrieved the basket of tea and goodies, which Nathan and Dan were happy to see, and handed it over. Then she told Bob goodbye.

Once she and Elaine were back on the road, Elaine's teeth continued to chatter even though Jan had wrapped her up in the blanket and turned the heat on full blast.

Jan hated to ask her any questions when she could hardly talk. But finally, as she concentrated on the road through the falling snow, she was so curious she couldn't help herself. "Did you find any sign about who might have set off the explosion?" Jan asked, keeping her eyes on the road.

"No," Elaine stuttered. "Just the footprints and then the middle of the pond was shoveled and someone had been skating."

Jan kept her voice as calm as she could. "So someone's been trespassing? You think the explosion was on purpose?"

"It seems to be a possibility." Elaine closed her eyes.

"Bob thought it was probably a propane tank or something."

"We wondered that too. Nathan and I didn't see any inside the garage when we looked though, before the explosion, but maybe we just missed them." She paused for a moment and then added, "There were some gas cans inside the garage, but we didn't check to see if they were full or not."

Jan asked, "Does Dan think someone purposefully caused the explosion?"

Elaine shrugged. "Hopefully it was just a defective tank or something like that. However, there's been a new development as far as Nathan's inheritance." She went on to tell Jan about the will being contested, most likely by a relative of Mr. Newton's.

"How odd," Jan tightened her grip on the steering wheel as a gust of wind rocked the vehicle. "Do you think it's someone local?"

"I have no idea," Elaine answered. "But hopefully we'll soon find out."

As JAN ESCORTED Elaine up the walkway to the clinic, Sarah Ryder, the pastor's wife and local nurse, swung the door wide open. Her long hair was braided, and she wore a long-sleeve navy T-shirt under her baby-blue scrubs.

"Thank you so much for waiting for us," Jan said as she escorted Elaine into the building.

"Of course," Sarah said. "We're worried about Elaine."

"I'm fine—just humoring Nathan is all," Elaine responded, but she blinked under the harsh light of the fluorescent bulbs above their heads. "I'm sorry it means staying late for you, and Dr. McInnis too."

"Don't worry about it." Sarah patted Elaine's shoulder and led the way into an examination room. Sarah looked tired, with dark circles under her eyes.

Elaine added, "And here it is a Friday night. You and Pastor Mike could be out on a date."

She smiled a little. "He's in Augusta tonight. Making a hospital visit."

"Oh."

Jan wanted to ask more but figured Sarah wouldn't be able to tell her anyway. If whoever was ill wanted the congregation to know, it would be put on the prayer chain or announced at church. "Who is with your kids?" Jan asked.

"There's a home basketball game tonight. Leanne and Caleb rode with a neighbor, and I'll meet them there." Jan knew Asher, the oldest Ryder child, was a senior and played on the team. "I should get there in time to watch the varsity players," Sarah added.

As Elaine climbed up onto the examination table, without taking off her coat, Jan said, "I hope Pastor Mike will get home in time for the varsity game too."

Sarah nodded. "That's the plan." When she didn't say anymore, Jan guessed this sort of thing happened a lot because the week before, when Pastor Mike had stopped by the tearoom for a box of maple croissants, he shared that he'd been away from home a lot. He'd said, with a laugh, that he hoped Sarah would be consoled by the goodies. Of course, they both knew there was no substitute in a relationship for time spent together.

Jan shot Elaine a look, and noted her cousin's empathetic expression. She understood what was going on too. Jan guessed her cousin could identify with Sarah. She'd commented before that there were many times that Ben had missed Sasha and Jared's school events because of army obligations.

Sarah took Elaine's temperature, which was normal. "You'll have to take off your coat, at least one sleeve, for me to take your blood pressure."

Elaine wiggled her right arm out of the sleeve. Once Sarah had the bulb pumped high and read the dial, she said, "One-sixty over ninety. That's high, especially for you."

Jan knew it was—as women in their late fifties, they'd discussed blood pressure many times.

"I think it's just the stress of the explosion," Elaine responded. "And I got really chilled."

As soon as Sarah removed the cuff, Elaine slipped her arm back into the sleeve of her coat and zipped it back up, shivering as she did.

Next Sarah took Elaine's pulse. "One hundred and five," she said. "That's high too."

Elaine nodded, obviously feeling embarrassed that she'd reacted so strongly to the explosion. It wasn't like her to be so shaken.

Sarah patted her shoulder again and said, "I'll let the doctor know you're here."

As soon as Sarah closed the door behind her, Jan stood, wiggled out of her coat, and spread it over Elaine's legs.

"Thank you, but aren't you cold?"

Jan shook her head. "Not at all. You, my dear, are chilled."

"I see what you mean about the Ryders. Sarah does seem stressed," Elaine said. "I'm glad you've come up with the idea to honor them."

Jan nodded. She was glad that Pastor Mike had spoken up the week before. Now she just needed to put her plan into action.

About ten minutes later, Dr. McInnis knocked on the door and then stepped in. After they all greeted one another, and Elaine apologized again, the doctor said, "Believe me, you're not detaining me. I usually catch up on charting on Friday evenings. It's no problem at all to see you."

Jan couldn't help but think of all the people in the community who served others on Friday evenings and during the middle of the night and on weekends too. She admired pastors and doctors and first responders who gave so much of themselves to care for the needs of other people.

The doctor pulled out her penlight and said to Elaine, "Sounds like you experienced an explosion. Can you tell me about it?"

Elaine described what had happened and that glass and boards flew through the air. "None hit me and, in fact, Nathan pulled my head down so I doubt any of the explosion affected me. He's the one who should be in here."

The doctor clarified, "But Nathan doesn't have a headache?"

Elaine shook her head.

"Did you lose consciousness?"

"No," Elaine said.

"Do you feel nauseated?"

Elaine tilted her head. "Just a little."

"Irritated? Confused? Grouchy?"

Elaine chuckled. "None of those, as far as I can tell."

Dr. McInnis stepped closer and held up the light. "Look straight at me." She directed the light into Elaine's right eye, and then asked her to look at the corners of the room ahead of her. Then she looked at the left eye.

"Where does your head hurt?" the doctor asked.

Elaine put her hand on her forehead. "It's the worst here. And my eyes hurt too."

"Are they sensitive to light?"

"A little," Elaine answered.

"Do things look blurry?"

Elaine shook her head.

"You may have a mild concussion. And with your high heart rate, it appears you're in mild shock too. Don't compare yourself to Nathan—two people can experience the same incident and their bodies can react in very different ways, depending on how much of the impact each absorbed. Rest today and tomorrow. No working. No screen time—no TV, cell phone, computer, etc."

"How about reading?"

The doctor shook her head. "You can listen to podcasts or audio books."

Elaine nodded. Jan couldn't imagine how bored her cousin was going to be. Or how understaffed the tearoom would be.

"May I go to church on Sunday?"

The doctor nodded. "If your headache is gone. Otherwise stay home. Either way, come in Monday morning and we'll see if you're better," Dr. McInnis said to Elaine. "If not, we'll do an MRI."

"All right." Elaine slid off the examination table to her feet and handed Jan her coat.

The doctor turned to Jan. "I'm counting on you to keep her in line." She smiled. "I know how hard it is for someone who works as hard as both of you do to take it easy. But this will pay off in the long run, believe me."

Jan nodded as she slipped her coat back on. She'd make sure Elaine obeyed the doctor's orders, and she said so as they stepped into the hall.

On their way to the door, Jan noticed a couple of people in the waiting room across the hall but she didn't recognize them. She looked for Sarah but it appeared she'd already left the clinic. Hopefully she was at the game already.

"You and Rose will need help tomorrow," Elaine said as they reached Bob's car, dashing as quickly as they could through the falling snow, which was coming down hard.

Jan nodded. "I'll call Archie." He was their second employee.

"He's not available. He and Gloria have a fiftieth anniversary to go to. Friends from Waterville. He said he'd plow us out in the morning but then they need to leave by ten."

Jan wasn't sure what they'd do. At least Archie could take care of their driveway with his plow that was attached to the front of his pickup before he left for the party. The way the snow was coming down, they could have a couple of feet by morning.

Elaine took her cell phone from her purse. "I'll call Sasha."

"I don't think you're supposed to use that thing."

"If I can listen to a podcast, I can make a phone call."

Jan wasn't sure, but kept her mouth shut. Keeping Elaine on track might be harder than she thought.

It was obvious the call went to voice mail. "Hey, give me a call," Elaine said. "I need to chat with you about something."

When she hung up, she yawned. "I think I'll go to bed when I get home."

The doctor hadn't said anything about that. Jan had heard of keeping someone with a concussion awake—but she thought that was just until they could be examined. Extra sleep would probably help.

"I'll keep your phone with me while you sleep," Jan said. "That way when Sasha calls, I can tell her what happened."

"Good idea," Elaine said, yawning again.

CHAPTER FOUR

Elaine awoke to voices outside her room.

"Should we let her sleep straight through the night?" It was Sasha.

"I don't think so. She hasn't had any supper," Jan said.

Elaine glanced toward the clock on her nightstand: 9:13. She wasn't hungry, but she wondered how Nathan was doing and how long he, Bob, and Dan had stayed at the Snow Globe. But she felt so warm and cozy under her down comforter that she hated to move.

"Nathan will be here in a few minutes," Jan added. "Let's wait and see what he thinks."

Without missing a beat, Elaine called out, "I'm awake! I'll get up in a minute."

The door opened an inch. "Mom?"

Elaine could see Sasha's face by the strip of light.

"May I come in?"

"Of course," Elaine said.

As Sasha opened the door, Elaine could see her daughter and then Jan behind her. Both had worried expressions on their faces.

Elaine sat up on the edge of the bed. "I'm fine, you two. Don't worry. Please."

"Jan told me what happened." Sasha stepped into the room. She wore workout clothes with a down vest over the top of a long-sleeve T-shirt. Her brown hair was pulled back in a ponytail and her mascara was smudged a little under her big blue eyes. "And of course I can help out tomorrow. Jan called Tara, and she can too."

Elaine smiled. That would be fun for the girls to work together. She, as always, was so thankful her youngest and Jan's youngest had turned out to be such good friends.

As Elaine stood, she teetered a little. Sasha grabbed her. "I'm fine," Elaine said, aware of how often she kept saying *fine*. As if she could convince herself, if no one else.

"I have stew and sandwiches ready," Jan said. "The men will be here any minute."

"Brody's downstairs," Sasha said. "We were on our way to Waterville but turned around after I spoke with Jan."

"Oh, you didn't need to do that." Elaine hated to think of them changing their plans on her account. They were probably headed for a workout at the gym where Sasha was employed. Elaine pointed to her sweater on the end of the bed. "Would you hand that to me, please?"

Sasha, still hanging on to Elaine, managed to grab the sweater and then, letting go, held it up.

Elaine slipped her arms into it and then wiggled her feet into her slippers. "A bowl of stew sounds good, actually."

"Did you warm up?" Jan asked, opening the door all the way.

"Yes," Elaine said. "I really think I'm fine now."

Jan led the way down the curved staircase while Sasha stayed close to Elaine. When they reached the bottom, Brody stepped under the rosette chandelier, his dark eyes full of worry.

"Glad to see you're up and about," he said, putting his arm around her.

"I'm fine." Elaine chuckled, feeling like a broken record. She really needed to stop saying that.

"Brain injuries need to be taken seriously."

"Oh goodness," Elaine said. "I don't have a brain injury." Brody had been in the middle of an explosion in Afghanistan—and had a true brain injury.

"That's what a concussion is." Brody released her. "Don't take it lightly."

She sighed. "Believe me, I won't. I have plenty of people looking after me." She gave him a squeeze, grateful for her future son-in-law.

When they reached the kitchen, Jan said, "Nathan and Bob are minutes away. By the time we have the food on the table they'll be here."

Brody started helping Jan, while Sasha insisted Elaine sit down. Elaine obliged her daughter, simply because she didn't have the energy to protest.

Sasha sat beside her. "I was so worried when Jan called. She said you were fine and all of that, but, Mom, do you think someone targeted you and Nathan on purpose? Do you think they'll come after you again?"

"No. It was nothing liked that. Nathan and Bob both figured it was a propane tank or something."

Sasha shot Jan a look.

"What?" Elaine asked. "What's going on?"

Jan wrinkled her nose and then said, "It wasn't a tank. It was a crude bomb."

Elaine turned her head slowly. "Are you sure?"

"That's what the explosives unit determined. Dan said he secured the area and then they'll return in the morning and do a more thorough investigation."

"Wow," was all Elaine could manage to say.

A few minutes later, Nathan and Bob arrived and they confirmed what Jan had said.

Nathan sat down on the other side of Elaine and said, "I'll go back in the morning too."

"But you're busy tomorrow, right?" Elaine turned toward him. "With the auction."

He nodded. "I'll stop by on my way to Waterville. I really hope we can get to the bottom of this—it's not every day that I'm on someone's hit list."

"Do you see why I'm so worried?" Sasha patted her mother's hand. "You both could have been killed."

"But there's no evidence it was directed at us. Right?" Elaine squinted a little. "It was just a coincidence that we happened along."

"Apparently not," Bob said. "The device had a remote control on it. You two were just lucky it detonated when it did. If you'd gone back into that building or even been a little closer, it could have been deadly."

Elaine didn't respond. *Deadly.* Tears flooded her eyes.

Nathan put his arm around her and his voice broke as he asked, "Are you all right?"

She nodded. "What about you? Did your head hurt?"

"No." He smiled. "Well, maybe a little, but from hunger, not the explosion." He kept his arm around her. "Something hot and hearty sounds mighty good right now."

Jan put the pot of stew on the trivet in the middle of the table, and they all gathered around. After Bob said a blessing, thanking the Lord for protecting Elaine and Nathan, Jan served the stew, filling the bowls one by one.

"What was the bomb made out of?" Brody asked.

"They found both diesel fuel and fertilizer on the site," Nathan answered.

Elaine thought of the fuel cans. At least they didn't explode too. That would have been horrible. "But they haven't confirmed that's what exploded?"

Brody shook his head and Elaine feared he was thinking about all of the bombs in Afghanistan his unit dealt with. He took a roll from the basket, passed it on to Sasha, and then stated, "Whoever detonated it must have been fairly close."

Nathan nodded. "We tried to follow the tracks but lost them in the woods. Tomorrow—"

Elaine gasped. "I don't think you should go back."

"The whole explosives unit will be there..."

Elaine shook her head.

"I'll be fine," Nathan said. "And Otis Schmidt is going to meet us there in the morning with the master key so that we don't have to break into the cottages."

They were all quiet for a long moment and then Elaine asked, "Do you think this has anything to do with the will being contested?"

Sasha's eyes grew large. "What are you talking about?"

Elaine realized she hadn't told her anything about Nathan's inheritance, or the phone call from the attorney.

Nathan jumped in and quickly summarized what was going on, much to Elaine's appreciation.

Once he was done, Elaine asked, "So is the entire will being contested? Or just you inheriting the Snow Globe?"

"I don't know for sure," Nathan said. "I assumed it was just the Snow Globe when the attorney called, but I didn't clarify that."

"It must be the whole thing—why would anyone want just the run-down Snow Globe property?" Jan turned toward Nathan. "No offense."

Nathan shrugged.

"Of course, it varies from state to state," Bob said. "But it's possible to contest only part of a will rather than the whole thing."

"We need to find that out," Elaine said. "And why someone would target Nathan." She could practically feel her blood pressure rising again. She took a deep breath. She couldn't help but take the entire incident personally.

Why would anyone want to harm the nicest guy in the whole wide world?

THE NEXT MORNING, Elaine stayed snuggled under her comforter as long as she could, which was 7:45. She could hear Archie plowing the driveway, and thought about going down to thank him. But she quickly set the idea aside and lounged around for another hour until the scent of cinnamon rolls baking was more than she could stand. She rolled out of bed, showered, and dressed. When she padded down the stairs, she could hear Sasha and Tara chatting in the east parlor. Elaine stopped in the doorway and waved.

Sasha, who wore a skirt, tights, and a sweater, with an apron over the top, asked, "Why are you up so soon?"

"The day's half over," Elaine answered. "I stayed in bed as long as I could."

"How are you feeling?" Tara asked.

"Pretty good," Elaine answered.

Sasha put a hand on her hip. "But your head still hurts, right?" She came across as gruff.

Elaine almost laughed. She wasn't used to Sasha assuming the parental role in their relationship. "It's not bad. I think I'm on the mend."

Tara stepped forward, her bracelets clinking on her wrist as she walked. She gave Elaine a hug and said, "We're just all so relieved you're all right." She glanced back at Sasha. "And still a little worried."

Sasha didn't say anything more and turned back toward the big fieldstone fireplace.

"We were just going to start a fire," Tara said. "It's so cold again today. A fire will cheer things up in here."

"Sounds like a great idea," Elaine replied, looking out the window. At least another six inches of snow had fallen. "I'll get a cup of tea and some breakfast and come in here and sit."

Tara pulled her phone from her apron. "Could I show you my idea for the Valentine's Day invitation first?"

"Of course," Elaine said.

Sasha spun around. "Mom, you're not supposed to look at any screens, remember?"

Tara turned red. "I'm so sorry."

Elaine said, "I'll just take a quick look. It will be my only screen time today."

Sasha shook her head.

Elaine sighed. "Can you describe it to me?"

"Sure." Tara looked at her phone as she spoke. "I used Victorian lace and ribbons, and placed the information inside of a doily with cupids on either side."

"That sounds perfect," Elaine said. "Show your mom. Then can you have them printed? I'll reimburse you for the cost."

Tara agreed to, and Elaine continued on to the kitchen, mulling over Sasha's behavior, both last night and this morning. Elaine knew she was concerned, but she had a gruff way of showing it. It wasn't like her daughter, not at all.

Ten minutes later, Elaine sat in front of the fire as Rose checked in with her and got a quick update about what happened the evening before, straight from Elaine as opposed to the story Jan and Sasha had pieced together in the kitchen as they prepped for the day.

Rose patted Elaine's shoulder when she'd finished. "Don't worry about today. Sasha and Tara are a great pair to take your place."

Elaine nodded. All three of the young women would have fun working together.

Rose left the parlor to flip the sign on the front door to open, and in no time, several patrons had entered the tearoom and were seated around Elaine. All were from out of the area, and perhaps in town for the snowmobile races across the lake over the weekend.

Elaine could hear the buzz of the machines in the background and, honestly, the racket wasn't helping her headache. She'd decided to retreat upstairs when Macy stepped into the parlor.

She glanced around at the full tables and then approached Elaine. "Mind if I join you?" Obviously she hadn't taken the time to wait for Sasha or Tara to seat her.

"Please do," Elaine said. She'd stick around a little longer.

Macy wore jeans and a bulky sweater. A black headband held her short gray hair back from her forehead.

As the woman sat down, Elaine asked if she saw the poster in the entryway.

Macy harrumphed.

"We hope all of our customers will come to the Valentine's Day Gala," Elaine said. "And share photos of people they love."

"We'll see," was all Macy said.

Elaine was grateful that at that moment Sasha approached with a menu for Macy. "Good morning! How are you today?"

Macy harrumphed again. "I'd be better if those snowmobiles would all break down. Who needs that sort of a roar on a Saturday morning?"

Sasha glanced toward the window. "I hadn't even noticed." She shrugged and surrendered the menu.

As Sasha left, Elaine leaned toward Macy and whispered, "I noticed."

Macy smiled a little. "I shouldn't complain. My cabins are full of the snowmobilers so they're bringing in money. It's just so noisy."

Elaine nodded. No doubt the racket was putting Macy on edge.

Macy leaned forward and lowered her voice. "But it's probably affecting you much more than me. I heard about what happened last night."

Elaine was surprised at Macy's empathy—and that she'd heard about the explosion. "Who told you?"

"Well, I first heard about it on the scanner." Macy had told them recently that she'd taken up the hobby of following police activity in the area with a police scanner. The woman wrinkled her nose. "And then someone was talking about it at Murphy's store, saying you had a concussion from the explosion."

Elaine couldn't imagine exactly who would have been talking about her—she knew it wasn't Sarah, the doctor, or Jan—but that's how things worked in a small town.

Macy sighed. "I've been missing the good old days lately, and then hearing about the Snow Globe made me miss it all the more."

"You would have been so little when it closed," Elaine pointed out. Macy was a few years younger than she was, and although the woman's family didn't live in Lancaster during her entire childhood, they lived in town during her elementary years and then in nearby neighboring communities.

"I was in the fourth grade. I was so sad—it was my favorite place."

"Really?"

Macy nodded. "I loved ice-skating. Here on Chickadee Lake. Out at the Snow Globe. Anywhere I could."

Elaine picked up her teacup, imagining a young Macy speeding across the ice. "I had no idea."

Macy smiled. "Well, I wasn't exactly Dorothy Hamill, but I really did love it."

"Do you still?"

"Oh, it's been years. Since my kids were little. I don't even know if I could still do it."

"I heard it's like riding a bike, but I haven't tried in years either," Elaine said. "Wouldn't it be fun to do it again?"

Macy glanced down at her feet. "I'd have to buy new skates. My feet have—grown."

"Mine too," Elaine responded. "Well, they've grown wider anyway."

The two women laughed and Elaine imagined a skating party out at the property on the pond. Perhaps there were others, besides Macy, who would enjoy such an event.

Sasha returned with more tea for Elaine—English Breakfast—and then took Macy's order: a pot of orange dulce tea and a scone with clotted cream.

Once Sasha left, Macy asked Elaine why she and Nathan were out at the Snow Globe.

Elaine wrapped her hands around her teacup. At least that information hadn't been spread all around town. "Nathan was there on business. Checking out the property."

"Oh? Doesn't Berl Newton still own it?"

Elaine chose her words carefully, not wanting to get into the details of Nathan's inheritance—and now the uncertainty around it. "Mr. Newton died a few months ago."

"Oh." A frown settled on Macy's face. "Did Berl's daughter contact Nathan then?"

Elaine shook her head.

Macy didn't seem to notice Elaine's reaction. "What was her name? She was several years older than I was. Older than you too, I'm sure."

Elaine nodded in agreement. She had vague memories of the girl but that was all.

"I was so enchanted by that Snow Globe," Macy said. "It was so big and that confetti that came down was so beautiful."

Smiling, Elaine agreed, thinking it was an experience that many who grew up in the area shared.

Sasha returned with Macy's tea and scone. As she placed them on the table, she turned toward Elaine and asked, a little too loudly, "Are you doing all right?"

Elaine nodded, not wanting to draw any more attention to herself than she already had. Sasha looked as if she wanted more information, but turned away to put another log on the fire instead. Elaine was grateful.

Macy, as she stared into the flames, said, "I loved snow globes when I was a girl, all because of what Berl Newton gave us." She turned her attention back to Elaine. "In fact I used to collect them years ago."

"Really?"

She nodded. "Just cheap ones. Souvenirs, really. I couldn't afford any of the real ones."

"They really are magical. I've always loved them but never collected any," Elaine said. "Do you still have your collection?"

Macy frowned. "No. And I'm not sure what happened to what I had. I suspect I left them at my parents' house and they sold them at a yard sale or something." The woman took a bite of her scone. "I did some research on snow globes years ago. I can't remember much of what I learned, but I do remember many of the first ones had churches in them. They weren't Christmas scenes, necessarily."

"That's fascinating." Elaine wished she could do some research on snow globes herself, but that would involve a screen.

"Early ones were paperweights, displayed at a big fair in Paris in the late 1800s. Then around the turn of the last century, a man in Vienna started making the globes." She exhaled. "I can't remember all of the details, but I do remember it was a remarkable story."

Elaine thought of Mr. Newton's collection. Obviously it wasn't made up of cheap souvenirs but of real snow globes. She took a sip of tea.

"I saw an article in the *Portland Press Herald* several years ago about someone here in Maine who collects snow globes," Macy said.

"Oh?" Elaine wondered if it was the man Nathan mentioned who wanted to buy Mr. Newton's collection all those years ago, before Mr. Newton changed his mind about selling.

Macy leaned closer. "I heard Berl Newton had an amazing collection, but I never saw it. I wish I'd asked him about it." She nodded her head in a knowing way. "He stayed at Green Glade years ago."

Elaine nearly spit out her tea but managed to swallow it. "What?"

"Yes. He came back to Lancaster every few years, from what I heard, but he only stayed at my place once. He said as much as he liked Florida, he never got over Maine. You know, his wife is buried here. And I think he found the whole roadside attraction thing really fulfilling. He told me that he hadn't found any of the projects he'd done in Florida as satisfying." Macy took another bite of her scone and then said, "He'd be shocked to know about the explosion on his property. Why would anyone do such a thing?"

Elaine thought of Nathan. Was he out at the site right now? Was he in danger? She felt her anxiety growing and knew she needed to change the topic. "What are you reading in your book group?"

Macy leaned back in her chair and began describing the plot of *Middlemarch*. Elaine half listened, trying to remember the story from when she read it years ago but she couldn't. She tried to follow Macy's rambling description of Dorothea Brooke's life. Instead, she found herself hoping Nathan would call soon. Or better yet, stop by.

As much as Elaine wanted to research snow globes after her conversation with Macy, she refrained. After Macy left, Jan's son, Brian, his wife, Paula, and their daughters, Avery and Kelly, stopped by. The girls, aged fourteen and twelve, were going to be in charge of the guest book at Jan and Bob's wedding. Jan had purchased the mauve dresses, a shade darker than the bridesmaids', and they'd come to pick them up—in their ski clothes.

"We're going downhill," Kelly said, her dark eyes shining.

"Oh, where?" Elaine remembered those days with her kids and how much they all enjoyed them.

"Titcomb," Brian answered.

That was up by Farmington. "A little out of your way, isn't it?"

He nodded. "But we weren't sure when else we'd get the dresses. The wedding's really sneaking up on all of us."

Elaine smiled. It was indeed. Just the thought of the upcoming celebration made Elaine forget her headache for a moment. It was going to be such a glorious event for the entire family.

She reached out and took both Kelly's and Avery's hands. "Your grandmother doesn't have any cream puffs." They were Kelly's favorite. "But I know for a fact she has some éclairs. Go grab one."

Paula had already headed for the kitchen, and Brian and the girls followed.

Elaine drained the rest of her tea, then retreated back upstairs to the sitting room, and hoped Nathan would give her a call. Sure enough, just after ten thirty, he did. She could tell he had her on speaker by the faraway sound of his voice.

First he asked how she was doing.

"Great," she answered. "How are you?"

"A little tired but fine. Dan Benson and the explosives unit were back on the scene when I stopped by, but of course the new snow covered all of the tracks. They didn't have any new conclusive information, but I'll stop back by on my way home and see if they're still there."

"Are you late getting to the auction?"

"No," he answered. "Everything's ready. I just need to show up."

They spoke for a few more minutes, and then he said he'd stop by and see her that evening.

When Elaine hung up the phone, she clicked to her podcast app and pulled up one on organization. Four hours later she woke up—without the headache—to Sasha peeking into her room, a tray in her hands.

"Oh good. You're awake. I was about ready to rouse you."

Elaine sat up. "I'm feeling better."

"Ready for some lunch? I have a bowl of stew, leftover from last night."

"How lovely," Elaine said, swinging her feet to the floor.

By the time Nathan arrived, Jan, Sasha, and Tara had the tearoom in tip-top shape and Elaine was back in the east parlor, enjoying the fire again. The headache hadn't returned.

Nathan sat down with her, just as Bob arrived to take Jan out for dinner.

Sasha stood in the middle of the parlor. "Brody will be here soon, but I can make some dinner for the two of you first."

"No need," Nathan said. "I can do it."

"I'm not an invalid," Elaine said as Jan and Bob slipped out the door, followed by Tara. "And actually my headache is gone."

Nathan grinned. "Well, in that case I have an idea. How about if we all go out to the Pine Tree Grill? Do you think

Brody would be on board for that? We can walk over." He turned toward Elaine.

Sasha frowned. "Do you think that would be too much for you, Mom?"

Elaine shook her head. "The light in the restaurant is dim. I think I'll be fine. Frankly, I have a bad case of cabin fever."

"All right." Sasha took out her phone. "I'll call Brody."

Ten minutes later, they were all bundled up and walking past the Bookworm on their way to the Pine Tree Grill. The sidewalk was completely shoveled, and the snow was piled in banks on both sides. Stars twinkled above them and a crescent moon rose over the treetops. To their left, the ice on the lake shimmered. By the light of the stars, Elaine could make out some of the tracks from the snowmobiles.

Tonight, the icy air didn't permeate Elaine's coat. She'd worn several layers and wound her scarf tightly around her neck. Sasha and Brody led the way, setting a quick pace. Elaine and Nathan lagged farther behind.

"Did you stop by the Snow Globe on your way back from Waterville?" Elaine asked.

"I did. But all of the officers were gone."

"Any sight of anyone or anything else?"

He shook his head. "But I didn't stop to snoop around either, not without the officers there."

She slipped her arm through his. "I don't blame you, but I'm guessing whoever was there last night is long gone. Don't you think they would've been scared enough to flee the county?"

"I hope so," Nathan responded.

Brody and Sasha waited for Elaine and Nathan on the porch of the restaurant, and Brody held the door. Bianca Stadler, who owned the restaurant with her brother, Mel, waved as they entered. "Welcome! Elaine, I heard about your little mishap yesterday. How are you?"

Elaine just smiled. She couldn't manage to respond to one more person asking how she was doing. Bianca didn't notice though because she ducked behind the counter to grab the menus.

Snowmobilers, still in their bibs, crowded around a large table in the front. One must have told a joke because the others threw back their heads in laughter.

Nathan stepped forward and said, "We need a quiet table."

Bianca whipped her head around, her long brown ponytail swinging back and forth. "Of course."

She led the way, her cowboy boots clicking across the weathered floorboards and her gold bracelets jangling on her wrist. They passed by memorabilia on the wall—the vintage posters, old wooden skis and snowshoes, lobster pots, and syrup taps. Elaine never tired of the Pine Tree Grill. It was one of her favorite places in Lancaster.

Mel nodded toward Elaine and the others from the kitchen door. Elaine waved and Nathan veered across the room to chat with Mel as Bianca led the other three to the table in the far corner.

As Elaine sat, Bianca asked if they figured out what caused the explosion.

Elaine shook her head, not wanting to divulge anything about the case.

"Boy, I hadn't thought of that place in years," Bianca said, passing out a menu to Elaine and then Sasha and Brody. "The property has been pretty much out of sight, out of mind, hasn't it? For the last forty years or so." She left the fourth menu at Nathan's place. "Come to think of it though, Berl Newton stopped in here every once in a while over the last few decades. Honestly, I didn't know he'd kept the property out there. He never said anything about it."

"Oh?" was all Elaine needed to say to keep the woman talking.

"Sometimes he came in alone, but sometimes his daughter was with him. I heard that she had a son, but I never actually saw him."

"Berl has a grandson?"

"That's what I understood," Bianca said as a customer across the room stood. "At least he did." She took a step away from the table. "At one time the boy disappeared, and I honestly don't know how it all turned out. Hopefully nothing happened to him."

The customer was waving at her now. Bianca rolled her eyes before heading toward him.

Elaine smiled. The clientele at the restaurant was a little more forward than at the tearoom. Then she shivered. If Berl's grandson wasn't mentioned in the will, chances were something had happened to him.

"Mom," Sasha asked, "are you chilled?"

"No," Elaine answered. "I'm fine." But she did leave her coat on, for the time being at least.

A moment later, Mel followed Nathan to the table. After greeting everyone, he said, "Nathan told me Berl Newton passed, and the two of you were wondering about his daughter. Ilene is her name. I knew her fairly well, even though she was a few years older. She loved that property, and especially skating."

Elaine listened and then said, "Bianca just said Ilene had a son."

Mel nodded. "Ilene married a guy from Toronto. I can't remember his name, but it didn't go well. He wasn't a nice guy from everything I heard."

Elaine shot Nathan a questioning look and then asked Mel, "So did they divorce?"

He shrugged. "To be honest, I don't know for sure, but I'd definitely look into him," Mel said. "As far as the explosion. I only met him once and that was probably thirty years ago now, but the guy gave me the creeps." Mel rubbed the back of his neck. "Come to think of it, there's someone else you might want to talk to."

Nathan leaned back on his heels. "Who's that?"

"I don't know his name but he's a businessman from Boston and owns the property that borders Berl Newton's land. He was in here a few months ago. I overheard him saying how much he'd like to purchase that property and that he'd been trying for years, unsuccessfully."

Nathan thanked him for the information. After Mel left the table, Nathan sat down beside Elaine. She took her notebook out of her purse. "It's time to start making a list of people to talk to," she said, writing *Ilene Newton's ex* at the top of the page. Followed by *snow globe collector* and *property owner of the land next door to the Snow Globe.*

CHAPTER FIVE

Elaine felt even better the next day, and decided to attend church. Nathan picked her up, but he would have to leave as soon as church was over to go back to Waterville to wrap up the details of the auction.

He'd left a message for Dan Benson but hadn't heard back from him. "He'll call soon enough," Nathan added.

The prelude music had already started as Elaine led the way into a pew toward the back of the church. Jan and Bob sat a few rows ahead, and Sasha and Brody were across the aisle.

As the prelude continued, Elaine bowed her head to pray but soon her thoughts were on Jan's upcoming wedding and then Sasha's. Elaine had no doubt that Nathan would propose to her, in time. But there were times, like today, when it seemed it was taking forever.

As the music faded away, Elaine raised her head and watched Pastor Mike step to the pulpit. Nathan slipped his arm around her and pulled her close. Elaine patted his hand and settled against him.

Pastor Mike welcomed the congregants and then read the opening scripture from Psalm 86. "All the nations you have made, will come and worship before you, Lord; they will bring glory to your name. For you are great and do marvelous deeds; you alone are God." His voice was clear and deep. But his eyes appeared tired and his face pale.

Elaine hoped he wasn't getting ill. As they rose for the first hymn, Nathan took his arm away from Elaine's shoulder and reached for her hand. The service continued with more hymns and then the sermon, which was about God giving His followers a spirit of power and love. Pastor Mike repeated a phrase from the scripture from earlier, "For you are great and do marvelous deeds; you alone are God." Pastor Mike went on to say that God was in charge of all things.

Elaine reflected on the pastor's words. God was in charge of her relationship with Nathan, the explosion out at the Snow Globe, including the mystery surrounding it, and the whereabouts of the snow globe collection. As Pastor Mike continued to preach, Elaine said a prayer that they'd discover the truth, that Nathan would end up with the property if that's what God wanted, and that they would be kind and loving to all involved in unraveling the mystery.

Perhaps Ilene's ex-husband was responsible. Or maybe the collector who had been interested in Mr. Newton's snow globe collection. Or the man who owned the property down the road. At this point, it could be pretty much anyone.

She also said a prayer for Pastor Mike, Sarah, and their children.

After the sermon ended, they sang another hymn, and then before the closing prayer, Pastor Mike said, "We have quite a few prayer requests today." He started with an elderly woman who was in the hospital in Augusta. That was probably who he'd been visiting on Friday. Then he mentioned a man in the congregation who'd been injured in an accident a week ago. Then a family who was in need of financial assistance and had recently been evicted from their home. He didn't give the family's name and Elaine couldn't even guess who they might be, but her heart went out to them.

He scanned the congregation as he said, "I know there are many other unspoken requests too. Let's pray for all of those." As he bowed his head and prayed, Elaine joined him and prayed silently, asking God to help the people mentioned and the unnamed family. She also prayed for the other requests.

"Amen," Pastor Mike said. He seemed tired as he walked down the steps off the stage. Sarah stood and walked with him toward the back door to greet the congregation.

When Elaine and Nathan reached them, Sarah whispered, "How are you?" to Elaine.

"Better," she replied. "My headache's gone."

"Wonderful." Sarah gave her a quick hug.

"How are all of you?" Elaine asked.

Sarah's eyes watered a little. "It's been another busy weekend. Hopefully this afternoon really will be a day of rest."

Elaine hoped so too. "See you in the morning," she said.

Sarah nodded and reached for the hand of the woman behind her. "Pastor," the woman said, ignoring Sarah. "I have another request for you. My neighbor is having heart surgery tomorrow—I'll be driving her over to Augusta first thing in the morning. She's scared and would like to speak with you..."

Elaine followed Nathan down the stairs into the bright sunshine, knowing Pastor Mike would go visit the woman and pray with her. It was the right thing to do, but she felt for Sarah.

Elaine slipped her sunglasses on. Her head no longer hurt, but her eyes were still sensitive to the light—especially as it reflected off the snow. But that didn't matter. She was thankful for all that she had. She and Nathan were safe. Jan was happy, and she and Sasha would soon marry. She'd aim to count her blessings instead of dwelling on what she longed for.

After Nathan dropped her off, Elaine ate slices of cheese and apples and crackers for lunch and then braced herself for another boring afternoon in the sitting room. Jan had texted her that she and Bob were going on a drive. And she guessed that Sasha and Brody were probably on their way to the gym. Elaine yawned. She might as well take another nap.

She really didn't mind being alone. In fact, the quietness was what she needed today. Yes, her headache was gone, but she still felt out of sorts.

Instead of climbing into bed, she decided to curl up in the sitting room and listen to a podcast in there—until she fell asleep. As she pulled an afghan over herself, she heard the door downstairs. Jan and Bob must have returned early. She slipped her ear buds in and leaned back against the pillow, but then she thought she heard someone call out, "Mom!"

Elaine took one ear bud out.

"Are you upstairs?" It was Sasha.

Elaine removed her other ear bud, surprised at how relieved she was to have someone stop by. "In here, sweetie!"

Sasha stepped into the room. "Hey, Brody dropped me off on his way to work out."

Elaine scooted into a sitting position. "Why didn't you go with him?"

As Sasha shrugged, her blue eyes grew a little watery.

"What is it?" Elaine hoped nothing was wrong with Sasha and Brody's relationship. "Is everything all right?"

"Yeah. I'm just still a little shaken."

"Whatever about?"

Sasha sat down beside Elaine. "You."

"Me?"

Sasha's eyes grew downright teary.

"Sweetie." Elaine put her arm around her daughter. "I'm fine."

"I know that, but you scared me." Sasha swiped at her eyes. "What would I do if something happened to you?"

Elaine touched her daughter's chin and lifted her head. "Honestly, I'm fine. But I am really happy you stopped by."

"Are you sure you're okay?" Sasha asked. "Maybe a nap would do you good."

Elaine shook her head. "I was just going to listen to a podcast and rest, but I'd rather spend time with you."

They sat silently for a moment and then Sasha asked, "Do you need me to do anything for you? You know, that you haven't been able to do? Laundry. Cleaning. Cooking."

"You know what I've been dying to do? Research on the Newton family."

"Are you sure that's a good idea?"

Shocked, Elaine leaned back so she could see her daughter's eyes. "Sasha, you're always up to solving a mystery. What's going on?"

"It just seems like maybe it's better to let this one go. Why wade into danger, right? Wait and see what happens with whoever's contesting the will. In the meantime, you and Nathan should stay away from that property."

Elaine exhaled, remembering Sasha's grief after Ben died. She'd lost her daddy. Her security at the time. The possibility that Elaine could have been badly injured—or even killed—by the explosion seemed to have truly shaken Sasha.

"Not knowing the truth isn't going to protect anyone," Elaine said, gently. "While knowing the truth could." She meant Nathan. Hadn't she been as worried about him as Sasha was about her? "Plus it could protect someone else too."

Sasha seemed to consider that for a moment.

Elaine squeezed her daughter's hand. "You've always been game for finding out the truth, sweetie. Don't let fear get the better of you."

Sasha leaned back against the sectional and exhaled. Then she let go of Elaine's hand. "Where's your laptop?" she asked as she stood.

"In my room, on my desk."

"I'll be right back."

"I'll make us some tea," Elaine said, standing too. "Meet you back here in a jiffy."

"I'll come down and carry the tray..." Sasha's voice trailed off as she reached the hall.

71

Fifteen minutes later they were settled on the sectional, the tea tray on the coffee table and the computer on Sasha's lap.

She opened it up. "Where should we start?"

"With Berl Newton. See what you can find."

Sasha typed for a few seconds and then said, "Here's his obituary from a Tampa newspaper."

She read it out loud while Elaine sipped her tea. *"Berl Newton was born in Lancaster, Maine, in 1926 to Horace and Maria Newton."* As Elaine already knew, Berl grew up on the family property that had been developed into an auto camp during the early 1920s. He graduated from Forest High School in 1943 and immediately joined the army. He served in World War II in Europe during the last months of the war and was discharged in 1948. After attending college and graduating with a degree in engineering, he took over the operation of the family business. He met Nanette Young in 1952 and built the skating rink for her. They fell in love and then married the next year. Soon after, he renovated the cabins and then added the World's Largest Snow Globe, which became a favorite roadside attraction. He had one daughter, Ilene, who was born in 1955.

Sasha took a drink of her tea and then continued.

"His wife died in 1973, and in 1980, several years after a new highway was built, Berl Newton relocated to Tampa, where he worked as a real estate agent, a land developer, and a builder." Sasha continued, reading that he'd invented a concrete that didn't crack in that climate. He was intrigued with solar energy and alternative ideas to housing too, including earth-berm houses. The writer included that Berl often spoke fondly of growing up in Maine but lamented there weren't the opportunities for

him in his place of birth that he'd found in Tampa. He also mentioned his snow globe collection on occasion too, saying it allowed him to preserve a little bit of the past.

"Besides his wife, his daughter, Ilene, also predeceased him."

"Oh, how sad." Elaine took the last sip of her tea.

Sasha nodded in agreement and then read, "He has no survivors."

Elaine gasped. "But Bianca said he had a grandson. If he's not deceased, why wouldn't he be mentioned?"

Sasha frowned and shook her head. "That is odd." She looked up from the computer and picked up her cold cup of tea. "Regardless of that, it sounds as if Berl was a great guy."

It certainly did. But there were still a missing part to the story. Why wasn't his grandson mentioned in the obituary?

THE NEXT MORNING, Elaine drove to the clinic and entered the waiting room at 8 a.m., as soon as it opened. Sarah greeted her, asking how she was doing.

"Great," Elaine said. "The headache didn't come back. I'm sure I'm cured."

Sarah smiled. "Oh, that's so good to hear."

Elaine asked how Sarah's weekend had gone without thinking through the question first.

"Busy," Sarah answered, crossing her arms. "Family time was hard to come by."

Elaine shot the woman an understanding look, remembering that Pastor Mike had probably spent some of Sunday afternoon with the woman who was having heart surgery this morning.

"I'm not complaining." Sarah sighed. "It's part of Mike's job. Honestly, I'm used to it."

"But?"

"Well, Asher will be going off to college next fall, and I wonder what he'll remember from his childhood. His dad serving everyone else while missing out on family events?" Sarah shook her head a little. "I'm sorry. I *am* complaining—which I really shouldn't be doing."

Elaine smiled at Sarah and then said, "You're not complaining at all, and believe me, I understand. Being an officer in the army isn't the same as being a pastor, but there were many times when Ben missed out on the kids' activities or family celebrations because of his job. And not just because of scheduled trips and events—but because of emergencies with a soldier or a soldier's family too. It's difficult to balance the responsibilities of a job, being a good leader, and a family."

Sarah nodded. "Thank you for sharing. It helps to know it's not just our family that struggles." She disappeared down the hall.

It wasn't long until Sarah returned to take Elaine back to a room. She took her blood pressure. "It's back to normal, one-twenty over eighty. That's good."

Within ten minutes, Dr. McInnis had examined and then released Elaine, saying it appeared she was fine. "Don't overdo," she said. "And if the headaches do return, go back to no screen time and limited activity."

Elaine assured her she would, grateful she could resume her normal life. Because Elaine knew Rose was coming into work, she called Jan and asked her if she minded if Elaine did some research before returning to the tearoom.

"Are you sure you're up to it?" Jan asked.

"Yes," Elaine said, appreciating her cousin's concern, even if she was weary of everyone doting on her. "Dr. McInnis cleared me."

"Go ahead then," Jan said. "I'm guessing we'll have a quiet Monday morning."

A few minutes later, Elaine parked in front of the tax assessor's office in Lancaster, located in the town hall. She knew the information was public, and she hoped it wouldn't take too long to acquire it.

Nathan had said that he and Dan had driven down to the property at the end of the road to see if the owner had been around the evening of the explosion. The man wasn't, but Nathan commented that the house was huge. Three stories with a three-car garage.

Elaine had a number of questions. What was the owner's name? Did he still want the Snow Globe property? If so, why? Did he want a buffer to his property? Or did he hope to develop it?

She stepped into the town office and then headed upstairs to the assessor's office. The door was unlocked so she let herself in. The assessor was a man who appeared to be in his forties, whom Elaine didn't know. The nameplate on his desk read Tyson Griggs. Elaine introduced herself and explained what information she was looking for. She said the property was behind the Snow Globe land and provided the address for it.

"Wasn't there an explosion out there on Friday?" the man asked.

Elaine nodded.

"Is that why you want the owner's name?"

Elaine paused for a moment. "Partly. But I've been told the owner is interested in the Snow Globe property." She hoped she hadn't said too much.

"Interesting." The man clicked on his computer.

Elaine stood silently until the man said, "Here it is." He reached for a pen and pad of paper, wrote down a name, ripped the paper off the pad, and handed it to Elaine.

Adam Slater. Boston, MA.

"Thank you," Elaine said, tucking the piece of paper into her pocket. "I appreciate it."

Once she reached her car, she took her notebook out of her purse and added *Adam Slater* next to the *property owner of land next door* entry she'd added earlier. Then she Googled the name on her phone. There was a man by the same name who worked for an investment firm in Boston. She called the number that was listed. A receptionist answered, and Elaine requested to speak with the man. The receptionist said she couldn't put the call through, but Elaine could leave a voice message. Elaine did, explaining that she'd like a return call, and then hung up.

In no time, she was back at the tearoom and helping Rose and Jan get everything ready to open for the day. Soon the first customers began trickling in. By eleven the east parlor was full, and they'd started seating people in the west parlor. The special for the day was Jan's mini maple croissants and a savory Brie scone, and in no time both were flying out of the kitchen.

Elaine worked on placing orders when she had a spare moment and educating customers on the different types of tea when she was on the floor. A mother-daughter duo from Augusta couldn't decide between the Darjeeling and the Earl Gray. Elaine brought them samples, slipping in tastes of the Acadia Vanilla too.

"Ooh, I like the vanilla one," the daughter said. "That's lovely."

The mother agreed and Elaine brought out a teapot for each of them.

Just after noon, Nathan appeared in the doorway to the west parlor, carrying his briefcase. He motioned to Elaine. "Do you have a minute? I have a couple of updates."

"Give me just a sec," she said. "Go sit in the dining room. I'll meet you there."

She retreated to the kitchen and let Jan and Rose know she was going to take a break. Then she started a pot of English afternoon tea brewing, loaded a plate with cucumber sandwiches, and put all of it on a tray. She knew Nathan had a busy day, and perhaps this would be his only hope of a lunch.

She grabbed her notebook from her office, tucked it under her arm, and then carried the tray into the dining room and turned on the chandelier as she entered. The crystals sparkled, shining light down on Nathan.

Elaine slid the tray onto the table. "How about a little snack?"

"Thank you." He beamed. "I've had such a busy morning—I ended up having to wait until this morning to pick up my car at the shop—and didn't have a chance to eat breakfast. This is perfect."

Elaine poured a cup of tea, handed it to Nathan, and asked, "What's going on?"

"Two things." Nathan took a drink of tea and a bite of sandwich before he continued speaking. "First, the attorney called again. He said that the person contesting the will is only challenging the Snow Globe property."

Elaine poured herself a cup of tea while she spoke. "You're kidding! Why would they want that dinky property and not his money?"

"Maybe because they don't have a strong case for the money."

Elaine sat down next to Nathan. "Give me an example."

"The attorney said that only a relative could contest a will and usually it's a child or grandchild. But perhaps a distant cousin wants the property because it belonged to Berl's grandparents originally. Something like that. The attorney's assistant was supposed to get a copy of the paperwork that was filed, but he left early for the day. The attorney said he'd get it himself except that he's swamped with a trial for the next few days. He'll let me know who is contesting it once he knows." Nathan reached down and pulled out a packet from his briefcase.

"The attorney faxed me the entire will instead of just the section that concerns me." He placed the document in the center of the table. It was nearly an inch thick.

"Did you read all of it?"

He laughed. "No. Just skimmed it. The beneficiaries are a number of charities, the ones the attorney already mentioned along with a homeless shelter, a ranch for at-risk youth, and a food bank."

Elaine thought of the obituary Sasha came across.

"There's no mention of his daughter," Nathan added.

"She's deceased," Elaine said. "Sasha found Berl's obituary."

Nathan nodded. "The attorney confirmed that she'd passed away."

"What about the grandson?"

Nathan picked up his teacup again. "The attorney said he did have a grandson, but he wasn't included in the will. No one seems to know whether he's still alive."

"What do you mean? There would be a death certificate if he'd passed away."

"Not necessarily. He'd disappear for years at a time, traveling in third-world countries, that sort of thing. It seems he hadn't been on Berl Newton's radar for years."

Elaine took a sip of her own tea and then put it down. "Not even his father's?"

"The attorney didn't know anything about that. But he did say, after talking to other people in the firm, that Berl and his grandson had a falling out years ago. At some point it seems Berl disowned him."

"That would explain why he wasn't mentioned in the obituary."

Nathan frowned and took another bite of the sandwich. "What a tragedy."

Elaine agreed. "Well, if no one's heard from the grandson, he wouldn't know about the will, right? The attorney would have had to send him a copy of it, and obviously he didn't. So there's no reason to add him to the 'talk to' list."

Nathan shook his head. "Not necessarily. Once a will goes to probate, it's public. He could have found it that way."

"Or his father could have."

"That's an idea..." Nathan rubbed his jaw line.

"Maybe the grandson is deceased, and his father's contesting the will."

Nathan exhaled. "But why would he want the Snow Globe property?"

"I have no idea," Elaine said. And she didn't. None of it made sense.

Elaine opened her notebook and added *grandson* to the list.

Nathan peered at the page. "We'll know soon enough who's contesting the will."

Elaine nodded. "But we also need to know who caused the explosion. To stop the person from setting off another one."

Nathan agreed and then sighed. "Back to the property, if it's a relative or something, I believe he or she would have more right to the property than I do."

Elaine nodded. That's what she would expect from Nathan. "But what if it's a scam? To get the snow globe collection?" she asked. "Would you want that stopped?"

Nathan thought for a moment, and then answered, "Yes. Yes, I would. I only want the property if it makes sense for me to have it. But I definitely don't want a scammer to get it."

Elaine agreed. That's how she felt too. "What's your other news?"

"Dan called. The explosion wasn't caused by a bomb made from diesel and fertilizer."

"What?"

"It was a bottle bomb with drain cleaner and bleach in it."

"Wow."

"It was a rather large bottle—a gallon—and activated by remote control."

"But we didn't see anything like that in the garage..."

"We're pretty sure it was placed in there after you and I left."

"And then whoever did it used the remote control to activate it?"

Nathan nodded. "But Dan said the person was most likely in sight of us and if he wanted to hurt us, he would have waited until we were closer to the building."

"So he wanted to scare us?"

"Not necessarily. He could have been anticipating our arrival at some time—although not at that exact time, so most likely he was just messing around. Perhaps a kid. They definitely want to find the perpetrator in case he's planning something else, but they really doubt it had anything to do with me—or us—or the property." Nathan finished his first sandwich.

Elaine wasn't so sure, but she certainly didn't have any evidence to prove otherwise.

"Very few people knew about the will at that point," Nathan said.

Elaine wrinkled her brow. "I'd told Jan."

He grinned. "Well, I think our secret was safe with her. She definitely isn't a suspect. And only she and Rose even knew we were headed out there, right? Even if one of them contacted the perp—which we know neither did—how could someone have collected the supplies and set the bomb in that little bit of time?"

He had a point. Hopefully the bomber didn't have anything to do with the property, besides taking advantage of an abandoned building. She shuddered, thinking what would have happened if the cans of fuel had caught fire too.

CHAPTER SIX

Tuesday, just after noon, Sasha stopped by the tearoom with something in her hand.

Elaine stopped scrubbing the table in the east parlor, which she was hopefully closing up for the day. They were seating all of the guests in the west parlor for the rest of the afternoon.

Sasha raised her hand. It looked as if she carried a stack of envelopes—tied with a red ribbon.

Elaine smiled at her daughter. "What in the world do you have there?"

"Love letters," Sasha answered. "I was over in Augusta this morning, visiting Grandma."

Elaine dropped the cloth on the table and wiped her hands on her apron. "Not between Mom and Dad?"

Sasha nodded.

"How did you talk her into letting us borrow them?"

"She plans to come for the tea and wants to sit at the table where these are displayed."

"Oh, what a great idea!" Elaine put out her hand for the letters.

"She only chose the best," Sasha said and then laughed. "Actually she said she chose the ones that wouldn't embarrass anyone."

Elaine couldn't imagine either of her parents being mushy. They were both such dignified people. She looked at the top envelope. The cancelation date was a year before they married. It was from her father and the return address was in Portland. The salutation read: *My darling Virginia,*

And then the first line was, *Why oh why are you so far from me right now? Why did we ever agree to be separated this year? I ache for you, every single moment. The days I receive no letter from you drag on and on . . .*

Elaine looked up at Sasha. "Are they all like this?"

She smiled. "Pretty much. Isn't it sweet?"

Elaine nodded. Sickly sweet. She couldn't imagine her reserved father being so expressive. At the same time, she truly did find it endearing. She knew she'd benefited from her parents' love for each other.

She wondered if all of the letters they'd receive would be so flowery.

"I had a really good time with Grandma. It made me miss you though."

Elaine smiled. They'd seen each other just two days ago, on Sunday. And they'd talked on the phone the day before.

"I really hope you'll be around when you're Grandma's age—and older. And in good shape."

"I plan to be," Elaine said.

"I realized I've taken your well-being for granted. The explosion woke me up to that."

"Sasha." Elaine reached for her daughter's hand. "Please don't worry."

Sasha smiled a little. "I'm trying not to, honestly. But I was thinking about what Nathan told you, that the explosion had nothing to do with him, or you, or the property..."

Elaine wondered what Sasha was getting at.

"I was going to go skiing today. To train. But then I thought, I don't really need to train today, but I would really like to go skiing with you."

Elaine couldn't remember the last time she'd been cross-country skiing.

"I have an extra pair all ready to go. And we wear the same size boot, so no worries there. All you need to do is grab your coat. And sunglasses. It's bright out today."

"But I'm working." Elaine grabbed the dishcloth with her free hand.

"I already talked to Jan." Sasha grinned. "She said you can take the afternoon off."

"But I already took all of Saturday off."

"She's not worried about it." Sasha nodded toward the kitchen. "Go talk with her."

Puzzled about what to do, Elaine headed toward the kitchen. She didn't know why Sasha would want her to ski with her—there was no way Elaine could keep up.

As she entered the kitchen, Jan slid a pan of apricot scones into the oven. "Did Sasha show up?"

Elaine nodded and then in a quiet voice said, "I don't need to go with her."

Jan stepped to the mixing bowl. "Why don't you, for old times' sake?"

"She probably thinks I can ski better than I can." Elaine wrung out the dishcloth. "I'm pretty out of shape."

"Well, give it a try. If it doesn't work out, just go hang out with her."

"Are you sure?"

Jan nodded. "It's important to Sasha. And it'll be good for you to get outside and get some fresh air."

Elaine didn't doubt that. "All right." She untied her apron. "And thank you."

As SASHA PULLED away from the tearoom, Elaine slipped her sunglasses on and then asked, "Where are we headed?"

"Oh, you'll see."

Elaine guessed they would go to one of Sasha's favorite trails, toward Augusta. But she turned the other way. When they reached the old highway, she turned left.

"I thought we could take a look at the Snow Globe place," Sasha said. "Maybe ski down the road toward the property behind it."

Elaine shuddered. "What if we run into whoever set the explosive?"

"I thought Trooper Benson said he didn't expect the person to still be around."

"Well, yes, that's what he said. But there are no guarantees." Elaine's anxiety level rose. She wasn't sure she was ready to go back there.

"I just thought maybe we both needed to face our fears," Sasha said. "And we're going to have to go there sooner or later if we're going to figure out what's going on."

Elaine nodded. Sasha had obviously had a change of heart. Maybe it was due to learning more about the Newton family.

"What do you think?" Sasha asked.

Face our fears. The words echoed in Elaine's head. Before, she'd been eager to go back and find out the truth, but now it felt harder than what she'd previously anticipated. She'd never shrunk away from a challenge before. And it seemed this was something Sasha needed. "Why not?" she said. "It will do us both good. But how about if you park on the side road? Not in front of the garage."

"Sure," Sasha said. A few minutes later, she pulled onto the road and then over to the side. There was no sight of anyone and no tracks either. Sasha pulled the skis Elaine would use from the rack on top of the car and placed them flat on the ground. Elaine had changed into the boots before they left the tearoom and now took her poles from the back seat. She stepped into the bindings and then clicked down on the holder with her right pole. By the time she managed all of that, Sasha had her skis on too.

"Let's ski straight down the road," Sasha said. "Maybe the owner of that land is around, and we can see who it is."

"Maybe he's the one who set the bomb."

"Mom," Sasha said, starting to ski. "Don't be overly dramatic. He wouldn't be setting bombs. Didn't you say Mel told you he's a businessman from Boston?"

"As we both know, a person's status in life does not prevent them from committing crimes. Right?"

Sasha grinned.

"But I really doubt he'll be here today." Elaine kept up with Sasha as they turned onto the road. It was covered with snow but had been plowed sometime in the not too distant past, with the snow piled up in banks on each side. "Maybe he's on the French Riviera, or somewhere else warm, or more likely in Boston working."

"Well, let's see what we can find."

Elaine was sure Sasha was skiing slower than usual, but it wasn't long until she fell behind her daughter, huffing and puffing as she slid along. At first her motions were jerky, but soon she found her rhythm. And her breathing finally slowed too.

The sky was a brilliant blue and a hawk flew above the tops of the pine trees ahead. Elaine warmed as her legs and arms slid back and forth, back and forth. There was a slight incline to the road but she stayed in Sasha's track and moved along easily, although fairly slowly.

She and Ben had cross-country skied when they were first married whenever they returned to Maine, and then when the kids were small too. Sasha loved it while Jared only tolerated it. Now, Elaine couldn't help but remember Sasha as a girl, eager to ski and going both up and down hills fearlessly.

They took her downhill skiing too. She enjoyed it but preferred cross-country. Soon after that she started target shooting with her father, and then doing biathlons.

Perhaps, with her upcoming marriage, this would be her last year of training. Then again, Brody was so supportive and such a boon to her training, that maybe she'd compete for years.

They reached the top of the hill and then started down the other side. Sasha sped up, bent at her knees, and leaned forward, flying down the rest of the hill, while Elaine did her best to go slowly and not fall down. She just hoped she could make it back up the hill.

Sasha was waiting for her at the bottom. As Elaine reached her, she pointed through the trees. "There's a trail here. I wonder if it goes back around to the Snow Globe."

Now that they were actually skiing, Elaine's courage had grown. "Why don't we try it? After we find the neighbor's house?"

Sasha agreed and the women continued on. As they came around a curve in the road, a large three-story house made of timber and stone with a triple-car garage came into view. It was just as Nathan had described.

Sasha's eyes grew wide. "Wow."

It was definitely an impressive home. But there was no smoke coming out of the chimney and no sign of vehicles. Of course, they could all be parked in the garage. Whoever Adam Slater was, he had good taste in architecture.

"I'll ring the bell," Sasha said, easily stepping out of her bindings.

Elaine skied a little closer. Sasha rang the bell and then knocked. After a couple of minutes she backed away. "Looks like no one is home." She stepped into her bindings once more. "Shall we take the trail?"

Elaine glanced up at the sun. Surely they had enough time before it set, but just in case she asked Sasha if she'd brought a headlamp.

"Yep," she answered. "Two. And emergency supplies also."

That was the last thing they'd need, she hoped. There was no way they'd get stranded—but she appreciated Sasha being prepared just in case.

They headed back up the road and then veered off on the trail. Someone had skied over it recently and Sasha stayed in those tracks with Elaine following behind. Although Elaine's face was cold, the rest of her was plenty warm. The sunshine warmed her body and her soul.

She struggled some going uphill but soon they reached the crest. They continued through the trees. Elaine breathed in deeply, enjoying the scent of pine. She skied on, relishing the activity and freedom of movement.

Sasha put more distance between the two of them and then went around a curve in the trail and disappeared. Elaine began to struggle again, her motions not as smooth as they'd been a few minutes before.

She ducked for a branch hanging over the trail and then struggled to keep her balance. But she managed to keep going without falling. Trees, some flocked with snow and others with bare branches, lined the trail as the afternoon sun wafted through the boughs. Ahead, another trail joined the one they were on. Elaine stopped and peered down at it. There were no ski tracks on it, but there were snowshoe tracks. Apparently, several different people had been recreating in the area. She continued on.

As she climbed another slight hill, slowly, Sasha called out, "Mom!"

"I'm coming!" Elaine yelled back, her heart racing. She hoped Sasha hadn't stumbled upon something—or someone. "Is everything all right?"

"Yes!" Sasha called back. "Just waiting for you."

Elaine struggled on and then reached her daughter, gasping for breath. Sasha pointed ahead. "We're almost there. You can see the cottages."

Sasha proceeded slowly, but Elaine still fell behind. The trail came out alongside the garage. The windows were boarded up. All of the glass and wood splinters were cleaned up too.

"Do you smell smoke?" Sasha asked.

Elaine sniffed. "Yeah..." Had someone set one of the buildings on fire?

Sasha sped up and then called back, "It's coming from the next-to-last cottage!"

As Elaine reached her, Sasha said, "We should call Nathan. Or Dan."

Elaine agreed. "You call while I go investigate."

"Mother!" Sasha called out as Elaine skied forward, surprised at her speed. "You can't just go knock on the door."

As it turned out, Elaine didn't have a chance to knock on the cottage door. Instead she plowed right into a man as she came around the corner of the garage, knocking him off his feet.

Trying to untangle her skis from the man's legs, Elaine blurted out, "Oh, I'm so sorry!"

The man, who appeared to be in his seventies and wore a ratty old coat and torn stocking cap, tried to stand but then tripped over the skis and fell again.

"Stay put," Sasha said. "I'll help!" She stepped out of her skis and rushed to the man's side, offering him her hand.

He took it, and she pulled him up. "Stay put," she said to him again, turning her attention to Elaine, but as she did, the man started a limping jog.

"Go after him!" Elaine yelled, struggling to her feet.

Sasha ran after the man as Elaine released one ski and then the other. She finally managed to step out of them and hurry after her daughter.

She caught up with Sasha, who held the man by his arm.

"Who are you?" Elaine asked, huffing and puffing. "And what are you doing here?"

The man turned toward her. "Nothing illegal, I can assure you. I have permission from the owner to winter in one of the cottages." The man had faded hazel eyes, and his face was gaunt and pale.

"From whom?" Elaine asked.

The man gave her a confused look.

"The owner? What's his name?"

The man muttered something. It didn't sound like Berl Newton.

The man tried again. "He was the one who had the Snow Globe. I can't remember his name."

Elaine stepped closer. "And what did you say your name is?"

"Timmy Calkin," he said. "I used to live in Waterville. I just needed somewhere to stay for a few weeks, until I can get back on my feet."

"But these cottages don't even have the electricity turned on. Aren't you freezing?"

He nodded toward the smoke. "They're insulated really well, surprisingly."

That *was* surprising. Elaine asked, "Do you know anything about the explosion last Friday?"

The man's face reddened. "I heard it."

"But you didn't cause it?"

"No, ma'am. I'd never do anything like that."

"Do you have any idea who did?"

He glanced down at his boots.

As he did, Elaine mouthed "Call" to Sasha. As her daughter stepped away, Elaine said, "Timmy, this is important. You could have been hurt."

He shrugged. "Not much hurts me."

Elaine paused for a moment as she watched Sasha walk toward the gift shop. She turned her attention back toward the man. Perhaps Timmy had been the target of the explosion. Maybe someone was trying to scare him away.

"Please," Elaine pleaded. "Any information you can provide would be helpful."

The man rubbed his chin. "I have seen someone slinking around here with a pack on his back. My eyesight's not so good so I can't describe him. But I've seen him a couple of times."

"Has he seen you?"

"I'm pretty sure he's seen the smoke from the cottage."

"Do you think he's living on the property too?" Perhaps the old Snow Globe had become a haven for the homeless.

The man shrugged again. "I have no idea."

"Have you seen any smoke?"

"I've smelled some, but I think it's coming from the big house down the road."

"Oh? Does the owner spend time there?"

"On the weekends—at least this last weekend."

Elaine thought for a moment, wondering if Adam Slater had been around on Friday.

"The place was crawling with investigators on Friday and Saturday. How did they miss you? Or that the cottage was unlocked?"

"Oh, I scurried out of it on Friday and took all of my things when a car pulled up. I locked the door behind me." The man tugged on his stocking cap, one finger looping through the hole. "I hid in the woods, in a snow cave I dug. That's where I was when the explosion happened. I figured it would take them a few days to clear out."

Elaine could hardly believe he could survive in such cold weather, but she knew it was possible. He was just so old. And fragile looking.

"How did you get back into the cottage if you locked it?"

Timmy's face reddened. "I'm skilled that way." He sighed and in a lower voice he said, "I picked the lock."

"Oh." Elaine hadn't thought of that. Perhaps all of the cottages had been occupied at one time or another. "What food do you have?" she asked.

He shook his head sadly. "I'm pretty much out."

The man needed to be in a shelter, not on his own out in the cold. Elaine nodded toward his leg. "Were you limping before I plowed into you?"

The man nodded. "I've had a bum leg for..." His voice trailed off.

"What happened?" Elaine asked.

"It was a long time ago."

Elaine gave him a sympathetic look.

"I fought in 'Nam," he said. "I took a bullet in my leg that went straight through the muscle. Tore things up pretty bad."

"I'm sorry." Elaine exhaled. The man was a veteran. He shouldn't be hungry, living in a cottage in the woods.

Sasha returned and gave Elaine a quick nod.

"What do you have in your pack?" Elaine asked her. "Any food for our friend?"

Sasha slung it off her back. "I do. Protein bars. A couple of apples. The hot tea Jan sent with us."

Elaine's eyes teared up. She didn't know Jan had done that.

As Sasha dug in her pack, the man said, "I can't take your food."

"Of course, you can," Elaine said. "And you will."

Sasha handed him the apples and the bars and the tea.

"Will you come in with me?" Timmy asked. "I haven't had anyone to talk with for—weeks."

Elaine gave Sasha a questioning glance.

"Look," Timmy said. "I know you called someone. I expected it. And the truth is, I'm relieved. Just come in and have some tea while we wait for whoever is coming to get me to arrive."

Before Elaine could respond, Sasha said, "We'd like that."

Timmy was right—the cottage was quite warm. That was the only positive thing about the space. He had a sleeping bag in the corner, a water bottle, and several empty cans over by the woodstove, which was putting off a fair amount of heat. There was a stack of sticks and small broken limbs in the corner that he'd most likely collected in the forest, along with several bigger pieces of cut wood that he'd probably salvaged from a woodpile somewhere nearby.

Timmy offered the women the sleeping bag to sit on but they said they would stand by the stove. They also declined sharing the apple and protein bars.

"Please," Sasha said. "We want you to eat them."

The man pulled off his gloves, sat on the sleeping bag, and slowly ate the food. As he took the last bite, a car door slammed. He stood and picked up his sleeping bag, folding it up. He placed it by the door and then gathered the empty cans. "Do you think it's all right if I take these? I don't want to leave anything behind."

"Of course," Elaine said.

Sasha took a plastic bag out of her pack and opened it up for him. He dropped the cans inside.

Then Elaine stepped to the door and opened it. Dan greeted her and she introduced Timmy.

He extended his hand and the two men shook.

"I think I should take you to the hospital to be checked over," Dan said. "We'll get a social worker involved and then decide what's next, after we find out what the doctor says."

"All right," Timmy said.

"He's a veteran," Elaine said. "Vietnam era."

Dan's expression of concern intensified. "Roger that. I'll make sure that gets recorded in his chart so the social worker can access those services."

"Thank you."

"Are you two okay?" the trooper asked.

"Yes," Elaine answered. "We were just out... skiing."

"Oh?" He shook his head as he spoke.

"Facing our fears," Elaine explained.

"I can only imagine," he answered.

Elaine and Sasha both told Timmy goodbye. "It's been good to meet you," Elaine said, shaking the man's hand.

"Likewise." He quickly climbed into the back seat of Dan's SUV.

Elaine couldn't help but wonder what the man's story was as they drove away. She hoped, in time, she could find out.

CHAPTER SEVEN

The next morning, before the tearoom opened, Tara spread the invitations across the counter in the entry-way for Jan to examine. They were perfect—old-fashioned but stylized with gold trim and a lacy background. "Everyone is invited!" was printed across the top.

Jan put her arm around her daughter's shoulder. "They're perfect!"

Archie, his hazel eyes shining under his shock of white hair, stepped to the counter. "Goodness, darling," he said to Tara. After all this time, his British accent still warmed Jan's heart. "You've done a marvelous job on these. Excellent work."

Tara beamed in response, and Jan's heart swelled with grat-itude for both of them. The tearoom was clearly a community effort with so many making it a success.

After they'd been open for just over an hour, Jan had a moment of calm in the kitchen and wanted to help Elaine and Archie get the orders out as quickly as possible, so she carried a tray of mini carrot cake muffins and a pot of Rooibos tea, with a Valentine's Day Gala invitation tucked into the side, out to a table in the east parlor.

She was surprised to find Macy at the table, sitting by herself next to the window, watching the snow fall in thick, heavy flakes. The woman had a book in her hands.

Jan greeted her with a hearty "Hello!"

Macy looked up from her book.

"What are you reading?" Jan asked, as she set the teapot, cup, and scones on the table.

She held up the book so Jan could so the cover. "*Middlemarch.* It's for book club."

"That's a good one," Jan said, taking the invitation from the tray and handing it to Macy. "And did you see the poster in the entryway? Asking for love letters or photos—from anyone. Not just sweethearts. Mothers, grandmothers, friends. You know, we all love Valentine's Day."

Macy put the book on the table, read the invitation, and then gave Jan a disparaging look. "I saw the posters and Elaine mentioned the idea too, but I wasn't sure you all were being sincere."

"Oh, we are." Jan smiled, as warmly as she could as she nodded toward the invitation. "We're asking for all sorts of photos—and letters. We're hoping for an all-inclusive Valentine's Day Gala, like when we were kids."

Macy winced. "There was nothing inclusive about Valentine's Day when I was a kid. I got the least number of valentines, that was for sure. And when the girls in my class held parties, I was never invited." She picked up her book before Jan could reply.

"Excuse me. I'm going to keep reading while I enjoy my tea and muffins."

"All right." Jan stepped away from the table. She still felt awkward after her interaction with Macy as she met Archie in the entryway. He gave her a kind, sympathetic nod. Hopefully he could work his charm on Macy and bring her around.

By the time she reached the kitchen, Jan cautioned herself about saying anything to Elaine. She didn't want to talk about Macy behind her back. But she did need to brainstorm with her cousin to see if there was something else they could do to make sure all felt included in the Valentine's Day Gala—most important of all, Macy. Just in case the woman wouldn't warm to Archie about the upcoming event.

As Jan stood next to the island in the kitchen, she couldn't help but become overwhelmed with gratefulness. The tea-room was a dream come true. To be able to bake in such a well-appointed kitchen was more than she ever expected in life. And to serve people in the community, not only tea and goodies, but love and acceptance too. That filled her heart with joy.

But it was her relationships—with her children and grand-children, with Elaine, and with Bob—that truly brought immeasurable blessings to her life. God had been good to her.

And now she had marriage and a new home to look forward to. Her eyes stung with tears of joy.

Which made her ache for Macy all the more. The woman struggled with relationships. If only Macy had one more good friend, preferably a man, that she could interact with. Not necessarily a romantic interest, although that would be wonderful, but even a platonic relationship would do the woman good.

A half hour later, Jan took out a to-go box for Macy of three mini maple croissants that she liked so much. She stopped before the doorway though and listened as Archie, in his British accent said, "Well, all of us sincerely hope you'll join us on the fourteenth. You mean the world to us. You're an irreplaceable part of this community."

Macy's voice was loud and clear. "More likely, Elaine and Jan just want to sell another ticket."

"Oh, you know I won't entertain that sort of talk," he said. "Sure, they have to cover expenses and hopefully make a little bit of a living, but if you think they don't truly care for you, then it's time for you to open your eyes."

Jan froze where she was. A half second later, Archie stepped by her, a frown on his face. When he saw her, he simply shook his head.

She nodded, counted to twenty, planted a smile on her face and traipsed back into the parlor, hoping Macy would somehow, some way, come to accept their love for her.

AROUND NOON, ELAINE said that Pastor Mike and Sarah had a table in the west parlor. After Jan took out a tray of scones from the oven, she stepped away from the kitchen to tell the couple hello.

But as she reached the doorway, she could see they were deep in conversation—until Pastor Mike's cell phone rang. A pained expression passed over his face as he took the phone out of his pocket. He glanced at the screen and then said to Sarah, "I need to take this."

Jan couldn't see Sarah's face. However, she could see Pastor Mike's as he stood, took the call, and started walking toward Jan. She stepped aside. He smiled as he passed her on his way to the foyer and then out onto the porch. Obviously the call needed privacy.

Jan continued on into the parlor and approached Sarah. "Do you need more tea?" Jan asked. "Or another scone?"

Sarah shook her head. "Just my husband."

Jan glanced toward the entryway. "Hopefully he won't be long."

Sarah inhaled sharply and then turned her head toward Jan, a smile on her face. "Forgive me," she said. "I think I'm overtired."

"There's nothing to forgive," Jan replied. "You have every right to be tired. Each of you has a hard job." But Sarah essentially had two jobs, one that she received no pay for. However, Jan was sure she had an eternal reward coming for all that she was sacrificing now.

Sarah put her napkin on the table. "I need to get back to work. But I'll pay on my way out. Who knows how long Mike will be—or if he'll even come back in."

Jan walked with the woman to the cash register. They could both see Pastor Mike through the windows pacing up and down, with the bank of snow in the lawn level with the porch, his cell phone still to his ear.

Once they'd completed the transaction, Jan handed one of the invitations to Sarah.

"Elaine already gave us one." She shook her head. "But I don't want to make a plan only to have to cancel it at the last minute."

Jan put the invitation back on the pile and stepped around the counter and gave Sarah a hug. "Hang in there," she whispered.

Sarah hugged her back and said, "Thank you."

Jan watched out the window as Sarah stopped on the porch and waved at her husband. Mike blew her a kiss and then returned to his call.

As she walked back to the kitchen, Jan sent up a prayer for the couple. A life of service could be a challenge indeed. She glanced down at her to-do list on the counter and added: *raise money for a gift for Pastor Mike and Sarah.*

Later in the afternoon, for a short time, the tearoom was completely quiet. After she caught up with the details at the top of her to-do list for the wedding—working on the seating chart for the reception and then checking with the florist about the corsages and the caterer about the appetizers—Jan took the opportunity to make several phone calls to start raising money for a getaway for Pastor Mike and Sarah. Everyone she talked with thought it was a great idea and promised to spread the word, and Bristol even volunteered to collect the money, saying it would be easier for her at the bookstore than for Jan, back in the kitchen of Tea for Two. Relieved, with her wedding quickly approaching and the wrapping up of the new home renovation, Jan thanked Bristol profusely. She was grateful that the plan had been welcomed with enthusiasm and that she wouldn't have to juggle keeping track of the money along with everything else.

Then Jan finally had a chance to speak with Elaine about Macy just before they closed for the day. Archie had left and Elaine was up to her elbows in soapsuds at the sink as Jan dumped shortbread dough from a bowl into a baking pan for the next day.

"She still seemed defensive," Jan explained. "It seems she was bullied around Valentine's Day as a child."

Elaine's shoulders slumped. "Well, that's not really surprising, is it? The longer we know Macy, the more evident it becomes that her current harsh reactions are based on her past wounds."

Jan nodded in agreement. "Speaking of the wounded, do you think the squatter on the property was lucid? Do you think there really could be another person lurking around there?"

"Weirdly, yes," Elaine said. "I mean at first the easiest thing to suspect was that he was behind the explosion and that part of the mystery was solved—meaning there was no mystery. But the more he talked, the less it seemed plausible that he'd set it at all. He didn't seem to have the energy to. He was definitely in survival mode."

Jan thought about that for a moment. Staying warm in an old cottage with only a woodstove for heat was enough to do anyone in, let alone the time he spent in a snow cave in the forest. Seriously, she didn't know how their ancestors ever survived the freezing Maine winters. "Have you heard anything more from Dan about the man?"

"No," Elaine said. "If I haven't by tomorrow, I'll give him a call."

"Have you learned any more about the Newton family, besides what Mel and Bianca said and what Sasha found?"

Elaine shook her head.

Jan pressed the shortbread dough into the pan. "I'd like to help if you want me to."

"Of course," Elaine said. "I'd love to have you apply your research skills to this! There are three things we need to figure out. Who's responsible for the explosion? Who's contesting the will? And where's the snow globe collection? I don't expect you to solve any of those in a day, although you might surprise me..." Elaine grinned. "But any information you can find on the family that might help would be great."

Pleased, Jan said, "I'll try to get over to the newspaper and see what I can find. I'm guessing there's an article about the daughter's wedding. And something about Mr. Newton when he moved to Florida. And hopefully more information about the extended family."

"That would be great!" Elaine blew a strand of hair that was sticking to her forehead. "Nathan said he had another message from the lawyer about—" The sound of the front door opening interrupted her.

Jan wiped off her hands with a towel. "I'll go see who it is." She hurried to the front of the tearoom, calling out, "Coming!" as she did.

Bristol, from the Bookworm, stood in the foyer with a man who wore a black wool coat and held his cap in his hands. He had silvery hair and a goatee.

"Hello," Bristol said to Jan. "This is Marshall Taylor. He just moved to Lancaster. I know you close soon, but we wanted to squeeze in a cup of tea if possible."

"Of course!" Jan turned toward the man. "Nice to meet you." She introduced herself and extended her hand. The man's handshake was firm and his smile kind.

Jan grabbed two menus. "How about the east parlor? Next to the fire?"

"Perfect," Bristol said.

Jan led the way. "Where are you from?"

"Chicago," he answered. "Although I lived here in Lancaster as a boy."

"Really?" Jan directed the two to a table. "And you missed the cold weather so much that you returned?"

He chuckled as he slipped out of his coat. "I admit, it is a little crazy to move back in the middle of winter. Not that Chicago isn't freezing right now too."

Of course he was right. "Florida doesn't appeal to you?" she kidded as she put another piece of wood on the fire.

He smiled a little. "Well, the sunshine does. But I wanted something familiar. My wife passed away last June."

"I'm sorry." Jan's voice was full of empathy.

"Thank you." His eyes grew moist. Obviously his pain was still raw. "Anyway, even though I don't have any family left here, I wanted to return to a place I remembered well. I have such fond memories of my childhood here. Life was so innocent and simple—and Lancaster still feels that way to me, even now." His faraway look faded, and he met Jan's gaze. "I arrived last week and found my way into Bristol's bookstore right away. Voilà, I'm now in a book group and am having tea with a new friend." He smiled sweetly. "I knew moving back to Lancaster was a good idea."

Jan handed the two their menus and said, "I'm so glad you've found your way back. I grew up here too, moved away, and then returned. There really is no place like home."

Marshall nodded in agreement. "It's been a delight to meet you, Jan. Over and over, the good people in this town have confirmed that I made the right decision."

Jan smiled at the newcomer and then at Bristol and said, "Take your time deciding." Then she headed back toward the kitchen, remembering her pain after Peter had died. She would love him and miss him the rest of her days, but she was so thankful her life had finally moved forward. Buying the tearoom and partnering with Elaine had brought so much joy to her life. And now she was preparing to wed Bob in just a few months—it was more than she'd ever expected. She hoped Marshall would find the same healing that she had.

Once she was in the kitchen, she told Elaine about the newcomer.

"I'll go out and introduce myself," she said, drying off her hands. "Better yet, I'll take their order." She patted the pad in her pocket.

Jan popped the shortbread into the oven, thinking of Marshall losing his wife while he was fairly young too. She guessed he was in his sixties. She didn't remember him from high school, which most likely meant he was at least four years older than she was. But probably more.

Elaine hurried back into the kitchen. "Oh, Marshall's delightful. How wonderful that he's moved back to Lancaster and already found his way into Bristol's book club. He's going to be a great asset around here."

"I agree." Jan unhooked the beater from the mixer and dropped it into the bowl. "Any chance you found out when he graduated?"

"No. I didn't ask." Elaine started the tea brewing.

"Do you remember him?"

Elaine shook her head. "Not at all. I wonder if he had any siblings."

Jan didn't think so, at least not around their ages. "It was nice of Bristol to bring him in."

Elaine plated two mini loaves of sweet French bread with butter and jam. "By the way," she said, "I've been meaning to tell you all day how delicious these are. I snuck one earlier this afternoon."

Jan thought they were pretty good herself but simply said thank you to Elaine. She'd never get used to people praising her baking, not even her cousin.

A few minutes later Jan carried the plates of sweet bread with the little pots of butter and jam into the east parlor.

As they reached the table, Bristol and Marshall were talking books, which wasn't the least bit surprising.

Well, one in particular. *Middlemarch.* The same book Macy was reading.

"The emotions that George Eliot— Shall we call her by her real name?"

Bristol responded, "Why not?"

"All right, then. Mary Anne Evans. Wasn't it a shame that she had to write under a male nom de plume to sell her work?"

Bristol nodded in agreement.

"Anyway," Marshall said, "her characters are so complex, so real. It shows how little we've changed as humans through the centuries. The suffering through self-deception is remarkable. I've known people who have done that to themselves. Yet they never recognized it."

As he spoke, Bristol noticed Jan and when he'd finished, she asked Jan, "Why are you smiling?"

"Oh, no reason." Jan placed a plate in front of Bristol and then the other one in front of Marshall as Elaine arrived with the tea and placed the tray in the middle of the table.

But the truth was, her thoughts were on Macy, who would soon meet Marshall. Yes, Jan appreciated nothing more than a love story. Perhaps Macy would find a love interest yet, or at least a new friend. Either would be most welcome.

She kept herself from sighing, afraid her thoughts about Macy were only wishful thinking. Marshall Taylor was a class act. And Macy, as much as they all loved her, was prickly as could be.

CLOSE TO FIVE, after Jan and Elaine had the tables wiped, the parlors vacuumed, and the kitchen clean, Bob stopped by, asking Jan if she wanted to go for a walk. It would soon be pitch dark, but the moon was full and would be rising over the lake in a short time.

After meeting Marshall Taylor and remembering how crushed and lonely she'd been after Peter died, she wanted nothing more than to spend some time with Bob.

She bundled up in her coat, scarf, gloves, hat, and boots, and they ventured out the front door. First, they stood together on the sidewalk and stared at their new home across the street. The contractors had left and the house was dark, but they held hands and faced it anyway. Jan imagined summer mornings, sitting on the porch with a cup of tea. And summer evenings, sitting with Bob, talking over their day. She couldn't wait for the future they had together.

Finally, Bob tugged on her hand and they began their walk. Jan shared about meeting Marshall Taylor. "Is that name familiar?" Jan asked.

"Taylor is but not Marshall. There were a few different Taylor families around over the years, including an old couple who passed away a couple of decades ago."

"Perhaps they were his parents."

"Maybe so," Bob said.

Soon their conversation shifted to the Snow Globe property and the explosion. Jan filled Bob in on the squatter Elaine and Sasha had found on the property.

"I remember watching Ilene Newton skate over there when I was a girl," Jan went on as her thoughts strayed to the past. "She was several years older than I was, so she would have been in high school while I was in junior high. I thought she was as good as Peggy Fleming at the time."

Bob grinned. "I bet you were too."

"Oh no." Jan laughed. "Although Elaine and I did have a lot of fun whenever we went out there."

The two passed the Bookworm and continued on toward the marina. The wind blew over the lake, reminding Jan of why they liked skating out at the Snow Globe so much. The trees protected the pond from the elements, plus the lights over the skating rink made it all so beguiling.

But the lake was enticing in its own way. She pulled her scarf higher around her neck and then linked her arm through Bob's. "Do you have any thoughts about the Snow Globe property? What Nathan's chances are of actually inheriting it?"

Bob shook his head. "I really don't have any idea. Nathan gave me a call today, just to get my feedback. He doesn't mind if I tell you, but the person contesting the will is simply listed as 'John Doe.'"

"How odd," Jan said.

"Yeah, it really is. I've never heard of it before, but apparently it was the judge's decision. The attorney speculated the judge didn't think the person who contested the will had a chance, and wanted to protect Berl's legacy from a round of stories by the media."

Jan shook her head. "It sounds like some sort of scandal."

"I doubt it's too big of a deal," Bob said. "The attorney figured it will all sort itself out, and there was no reason to challenge the decision."

Jan wrinkled her nose. "Who could be so fond of the Snow Globe that they'd go to so much effort to try to own it? When it really isn't worth much."

"Well, from everything you and Elaine and Nathan have said, it seems a lot of people have positive memories of it. But the big question is, who also feels they have a right to own it? It has to be some sort of relative."

That was exactly why Jan needed to do more research on the Newton family. Surely there were still relatives around who'd rather the property stayed in the family.

Jan and Bob continued on, past the Whisper Art Gallery and along the curve of Chickadee Lake. The moon was over the trees now and shone on the ice-covered lake.

Bob drew her closer, stopped, and whispered, "This will be our last winter together, unmarried."

Jan rose to her tiptoes and kissed his cheek. Yes, she was very grateful for her life, and the future ahead.

CHAPTER EIGHT

On Thursday morning, Nathan called Elaine with the number and name of the snow globe collector who had wanted to buy Berl Newton's collection all those years ago. He was from Portland, and Elaine volunteered to call him since Nathan would be leaving to speak at the conference in Boston.

Nathan also said he'd heard back from the attorney and he still hadn't found the snow globe collection—nor any hints to its whereabouts.

Jerry Kemp was the name of the collector, and Elaine added his name next to *snow globe collector* entry in her notebook, along with his phone number. Then she left a message for him, stating why she needed to speak with him.

After she ended the call, she consulted the rest of the list of people to speak with about the case. She hadn't heard back from Adam Slater, the Snow Globe's neighbor. Nor had she tracked down Berl Newton's grandson, nor the boy's father. The truth was, she hadn't made any progress at all.

She did add Timmy Calkin's name to the list but only as someone familiar with the property.

That reminded her to call Dan about the man, to see if the trooper had any more information. He didn't pick up, so she left a message for him too. Perhaps he wouldn't be able to give her an update, especially if the man had medical problems.

On Friday morning, as she sat in her office and consulted her notebook again, she noted that none of the men had called her back. She circled *Adam Slater*, *Jerry Kemp*, and *Dan*.

Perhaps she'd have to go to Portland and track down the snow globe collector herself. Maybe he would know where Mr. Newton's snow globe collection was kept. Or perhaps she could figure out, from speaking with him, if he might have motivation for contesting the will.

She could hardly justify a trip to Boston to track down Adam Slater, although she was tempted to. If only Nathan had more time while he was in Boston, but he was booked solid with the conference events.

Of course, there was still the issue of Ilene's ex-husband too. She couldn't find anything online that gave his name away. No engagement announcement. No article about their wedding. No divorce decree. It was all very odd.

The ex was definitely moving further up her list, although she couldn't understand why he'd just want the Snow Globe property and not the entire inheritance. Just as she stood, ready to go make a pan of oatmeal for breakfast, her phone rang. A Portland number. She answered it quickly, saying, "Hello, this is Elaine. How may I help you?"

"Jerry Kemp here," a voice said, "returning your call."

Elaine thanked the snow globe collector and then quickly explained what information she was after.

He hesitated for a moment and then said, "I'd rather talk about this in person if you don't mind. You're in Lancaster, right?"

"Correct," she said.

"Could you meet me in Augusta? This afternoon?"

Elaine agreed to. She wished Nathan could join them, but it was impossible. She felt it was more important that she meet with the man sooner rather than later.

After she ended the call with Mr. Kemp, she called Nathan to give him an update.

"I've only ever talked with Mr. Kemp on the phone, never in person," Nathan said. "But tell him hello." His voice grew tender. "And thank you for pursuing all of this. Whatever happens as far as the land being mine or not doesn't matter compared to the safety of those who physically set foot on the property."

She thought about Dan Benson. "But don't you think they've just chalked it up to a teenager making trouble? I doubt they're going to pursue anything more that has to do with the case." She inhaled. "What if the snow globe collection is on the property?"

"Oh, I doubt it's there. Why would Mr. Newton leave something so valuable in the middle of nowhere?"

"Still, we can't rule it out," Elaine said. If it hadn't been catalogued with Mr. Newton's belongings in Florida, then chances were it was somewhere in Maine.

At one o'clock, Elaine walked into a café in Augusta and squinted as her eyes adjusted from the bright sunshine bouncing off the snow to the dim light. A man sitting in a booth to her right stood. He was tall and thin and appeared to be in his sixties, with sandy hair streaked with gray.

"Jerry?" she asked as she approached.

"Yes," he replied. "Jerry Kemp." He stuck out his left hand. After they shook hands, he held up his right hand, which had a glove on it. "Sorry to be rude," he said. "I cut my hand a few days ago on a snow globe, sadly. One of my favorites— it broke in my hand. Taking my glove on and off pulls at the bandage."

"No worries," she said as she sat down across from him. She wiggled out of her coat and pulled her notebook from her purse. Elaine started their conversation by extending Nathan's hello.

"I enjoyed talking with him those few times," Jerry said. "And I've heard such good things about him as an expert in antiques and his work as an auctioneer."

Elaine smiled. Nathan was very good at what he did.

The waitress approached and Elaine ordered a cappuccino, thinking she'd need the extra caffeine to stay awake for the drive home, while Jerry ordered a black coffee.

"Nathan told me that you were interested in Berl Newton's snow globe collection several years ago."

Jerry nodded. "Yes, it's the best collection I've ever seen."

"Where did you view it? In Florida? Or here in Maine?"

"Here," Jerry said.

Relief filled Elaine as she expected to find out where it was in his next sentence. When he didn't elaborate, she asked, "Did he store it on his property outside of Lancaster?"

"Oh, I have no idea," Jerry said. "He showed it to me in a ballroom in Portland, at a downtown hotel. He and his daughter were staying there, and he rented the space for a week or so. I wasn't the only person who viewed it."

"Really?"

He nodded. "I couldn't help but notice the customized cabinets I assumed the snow globes were stored in. All were archival and climate controlled, I'm sure. He was serious about maintaining the collection."

"Does that mean he could have stored them anywhere? A building without heat, for example?"

"Well, as long as it was secure. He wouldn't have just left them anywhere though."

That was true. The waitress delivered their drinks and then Elaine asked, "Any idea how much the collection was worth?"

He smiled and shook his head. "Let's just say I know how much I offered him, which he didn't accept. But you know he didn't need the money. I believe in the end the collection held too much sentimental value for him to sell. He had snow globes from Europe, made during World War II, which you know Berl Newton served in."

Elaine nodded.

"And he had a lot of the old snow globes with churches in them, and ones with skaters, sledders, and skiers. All ones that reminded him of Maine."

Elaine wrote those examples down in her notebook and then asked, "Is that why you wanted the collection?"

"Oh, I've loved snow globes my entire life. Since the first time I saw one as a child."

Elaine thought of Macy's appreciation of snow globes too. She imagined most children—and adults—found them spellbinding.

"They capture the magic of winter. And the sentiments of the past. I began collecting them, cheap ones, as a boy. But then my parents started giving me one each Christmas, and then one for my birthday too, which is on New Year's Eve. Their gifts were a little more expensive and higher quality. Then as an adult, I started collecting antique ones too."

"I've heard many of the original ones were of churches."

"Yes, that's right." He grinned and then took a sip of his coffee. "Do you have time for a history lesson?"

"I'd love one." Elaine wrapped her hands around her cup.

"You may have heard that the first snow globes were paperweights."

Elaine nodded. "But I didn't hear a lot of details."

Jerry Kemp took another sip of coffee, lifting the cup with his gloved hand, and then started telling his story, saying that the first written record of a snow globe, although they were called water globes or glass globes at the time, was at the Paris Exhibition in 1889. They were paperweights, with a globe featuring the Eiffel Tower inside and filled with liquid and pretend snow. They were set on a ceramic base that served as the paperweight. After a time, people began calling them "snowstorms."

Elaine liked that term. It was a little more poetic than water globe or glass globe.

Jerry continued with his story. "Then in 1900 a Venetian surgical instruments mechanic by the surname of Perzy was trying to make light bulbs brighter by putting a globe of water in front of them." Jerry went on to explain that the man added semolina, used in baby food, to add illumination. "He failed in brightening the bulbs, but added a small diorama and, *voilà!* He invented the snow globe and started a family business that continues today."

"Goodness," Elaine said. "That's fascinating."

Jerry nodded. "Isn't it? The Perzy snow globes all featured churches at first and were all hand-painted. They still are, but soon after World War II, the second generation in the family added Christmas trees and Father Christmas and other such scenes. Today the company produces over 350 designs and produces custom snow globes too."

"Did Berl Newton have any of the Perzy snow globes in his collection?"

"Yes," Jerry answered. "I can't remember the exact number, but perhaps as many as thirty."

Elaine blinked. "Wow."

"He had several of the old ones, with the churches. The first snow globe Berl ever purchased, in Austria after the war, was one with a church. There was also the one of the couple skating that he bought for his wife."

"Lovely," Elaine said.

"He even had a few custom made, but he didn't display all of those the day I saw the collection."

"How fascinating," Elaine said. "How did you find out about Berl Newton's collection?"

"At first it was all rumors. At antique shows. And estate sales. I'd hear about this guy who used to live in Maine and had a great collection and at one time had 'the world's largest snow globe.' I did some research and came up with Berl Newton and his old property. It took me a while to track him down in Florida, but I finally did. I wasn't the only one interested in it, and after multiple requests he arranged the exhibit."

"Was it worth it? Seeing his collection."

Jerry gave out a low whistle. "By all means, yes. Although to be honest I've been coveting it ever since. He had globes from Perzy, like I said. One of the Eiffel Tower paperweights. Snow globes from an early American company, located in Philadelphia. He also had souvenir snow globes, some well made with Americana themes—the Statue of Liberty, the Alamo, things like that. Then there were the cheap souvenir snow globes too, that aren't so cheap anymore. Oh, and he also had some custom-made ones with Maine themes, ones that he did display."

"Such as?"

"Oh, Portland Harbor. The Augusta courthouse. And the church in Lancaster, the community one with the steeple."

Elaine's hand went to her chest. "How lovely. That's the church I go to."

"It was one of my favorites of his."

"And those were for sale?"

He nodded.

Those all seemed pretty personal. She wondered what the ones he didn't want to sell were of. Elaine tilted her head. "Why did you want the collection?"

"Good question." He smiled wryly. "Especially after I've confessed to coveting a collection that, I'm guessing, no one has found."

Elaine gave him a questioning look.

"I did some research," Jerry said. "I found out that Berl died and didn't have any heirs. I even researched the will and found out that Nathan is the beneficiary of the property here in Maine and the collection."

Elaine smiled back at him. "You've done your homework." But apparently he didn't know the will had been contested, and she wouldn't share that.

He nodded. "Anyway, why the interest? I have a dream of opening a snow globe museum. Berl Newton's collection would make that all possible. And I'd also love to recreate his World's Largest Snow Globe with the confetti floating down, as a photo booth. Of course, now people could just take a selfie, but I still think it would have an old-fashioned appeal."

Elaine agreed. She'd certainly visit a snow globe museum and relive her delight with the world's largest one.

"Berl Newton was ahead of his time in designing that globe on his property. He had to have used acrylic to make it—and nothing that big had been, that I can find, constructed with the material when he built the first one. I'm guessing he redesigned it several times over the years, and by the 1970s the material was easier to work with. But he definitely had a knack for design."

Elaine mentioned what she'd found out about his building business in Florida, the concrete formula that he'd patented and his work with earth-berm buildings.

"He was intelligent and creative. A real Renaissance man," Jerry said. "When I met him, he was in his early eighties, but he acted as if he were in his sixties."

"What about his daughter?" Elaine asked. "What was she like?"

"A class act. Very devoted to her father. Knowledgeable about the snow globes. Articulate and kind." He paused for a moment. "There was something fragile about her though. She seemed forlorn at times. One of the other collectors, who was a recent widower, asked her out, but she politely declined. Some said she was divorced, but others said she was just separated." He shrugged. "I'm happily married, have been since I was twenty, so I wasn't too concerned with all of that."

Elaine nodded. Jerry Kemp seemed like a good man. They chatted for a while longer, and then she thanked him for meeting with her. He could have told her all of the information over the phone, but a conversation usually went better in person. Finding out there was speculation that Ilene never divorced her husband was information she might not have found out otherwise.

Besides, now she could go visit her mother. Perhaps her mom would remember something about Berl Newton or Lancaster in the old days that would help place another piece in the puzzle. And she'd ask her if she'd kept the old Snow Globe photos.

Jerry said he needed to get going and Elaine said she'd pick up the tab, but he insisted on paying it. After she told him goodbye, she sat for a few more minutes, jotting down more of what Jerry said in her notebook. She wouldn't do it just yet, but she was pretty sure she could cross Jerry Kemp off the list. He seemed like an honest guy, but of course it wasn't implausible that he could have been being manipulative. Perhaps he did know where Berl Newton kept his snow globe collection.

Or perhaps it was already in Jerry's possession. There was no way to know, not at this point. Then again, there was no way he could get away with opening a snow globe museum with a stolen collection.

VIRGINIA MET ELAINE at the door before she even knocked. She swung it open, saying, "I thought I heard a car. I'm so glad it's you."

Her mother wore navy slacks, a yellow top, and a navy cardigan with a paisley print scarf. As always, her short, silvering brown hair was perfectly styled. "Do you have time for a cup of coffee?"

"How about some decaf tea?" Elaine had enough caffeine in her to make it home.

After they made their beverages in the small kitchen, Elaine sat with her mother at Virginia's little table and brought up the old roadside attraction.

"Wasn't that Snow Globe and skating rink fun?" Virginia gushed. "Berl Newton did us all a favor by making such a great family destination so close to Lancaster."

They reminisced about different outings there, the times Jan came along, and the times it was just their family.

"Did you keep the photos taken in the Snow Globe?"

Virginia touched her scarf. "I haven't thought of those photos in years." She stood and started toward the closet. "But they might be in an old album." She rummaged for a moment, pulled out an album, opened it, and then said, "Here they are!"

She returned with an old blue vinyl album that Elaine vaguely remembered from her childhood. Virginia put it on the table, open to a collection of photos taken at the Snow Globe. There was one of the whole family, dated 1970. Elaine's father wore a gray fedora and a wool coat, which Elaine knew was long even thought the photo didn't show that. As a hospital administrator, he always dressed well, even when not at work. Her mother, always the fashionista, wore a red beret, a red coat, and a navy-blue scarf. Elaine, on the other hand, wore an orange stocking cap with a pom-pom on the top. She laughed and, pointing at herself, said, "Why did you let me wear that?"

"Oh, it was lovely," Virginia said. "Your grandmother knitted that for you."

"Well, in that case, it's the cutest thing ever." Elaine laughed again. Nick, her younger brother, wore a brown stocking cap, but without a pom-pom. However, she guessed their grandmother made it too.

The next photo was of Elaine and Jan when they were probably twelve. Both were dressed in matching white ski pants and jackets, without their hoods on. The confetti was all over their clothes and in their hair. They both grinned wildly, as if the photo was snapped midlaughter. Elaine sighed at the memory. Goodness, the years had flown by. "These are wonderful photos."

"Why don't you take them?" Virginia offered.

"Thank you," Elaine said. "I'll include both of them in the Valentine's Day Gala table display."

"Oh, what a wonderful idea!" Virginia clapped her hands together. "You got my letters?"

"Yes." Elaine removed the photos from the album as she spoke. "Thank you."

Virginia grabbed an envelope for the photos, and after they were safely in Elaine's purse, she asked her mother, "What do you remember about the Newton family?"

"Berl was so outgoing. He was a decade or so older than your dad and me, but he knew us by name. He seemed to know everyone in Lancaster, everyone in the county, really." She grinned. "He probably knew half the people in the state."

"Do you think he made much money from the road-side attraction?"

"Well, not by the end. But you know he did so many other things—real estate, design, construction. Those connections most likely led to him moving to Florida."

Elaine hadn't thought about that.

"Oh sure," Virginia said. "You know, people retire early down there and then decide they're too young not to do anything and start investing or building or whatever. Berl partnered with some others from Maine when he moved, and I'm sure they encouraged him to go down in the first place."

That made sense.

"I believe he would have stayed if his wife..." Virginia snapped her fingers and before Elaine could supply Berl's wife's name, her mother remembered it. "Nanette. I think he would have stayed if Nanette hadn't died. It was a tragedy that she died so young. Their marriage was one of those epic ones that people looked up to. In fact, he built the skating rink for her."

"Really?"

"Yes, she loved to skate. And after that he renovated the cabins and added the little church to make it all look like a European village. Then he added the Snow Globe and turned it all into a winter roadside attraction."

Elaine had certainly heard that before. "Did you know much about his daughter, Ilene? Or about her husband?"

Virginia shook her head. "I knew of her, but didn't know her. I saw her skate a few times and I knew, vaguely, that she married, but I don't think the wedding was held around here." Virginia shrugged. "The Snow Globe had closed by then and the family really wasn't on my radar anymore."

That was all Virginia could remember and she quickly shifted the conversation to Jan and Bob's upcoming wedding. And then to Sasha and Brody's. Her mother leaned across the table and asked, "What about you and Nathan? Are you two making any plans?"

Elaine could feel her face grow warm. "Mother," she said.

"Well?"

Elaine shrugged. "We've talked about it, some." She held out her left hand. "But until I have a ring on my finger, there's no reason to put any thought into it."

Virginia reached out and took Elaine's hand. "I'm your mother. I'm only asking because I care."

"I understand, but I can't be thinking about myself right now. I am so happy for Jan." She couldn't let her mother know how often she did think of herself, of how much she had been struggling in the last few weeks not to wonder what her future held, of how much she wanted to trust God with all of this. But this was between Elaine and the Lord.

Virginia stood and stepped to Elaine's side, then kissed her on the forehead. "You're right, of course. I'll put all my thoughts toward Jan and Bob and Sasha and Brody—and my prayers will be directed to the Lord for you and Nathan, until you let me know it's a sure thing."

THE NEXT MORNING, Dan stopped by the tearoom before it opened. Both Archie and Rose were working, so Elaine was able to take a few minutes and meet with him in the dining room. She carried in a tray with some coffee and savory bacon scones on it and sat down beside him.

"I did get your message but wanted to give you an update on Timmy Calkin in person. He gave me permission," he said. "He spent a night in the hospital and was then taken to the VA clinic in Portland. They arranged for temporary housing for him."

Elaine sat back in her chair in relief. "Oh good."

"I wish you hadn't gone back to the property, but I'm glad you found him. Surprisingly he didn't have any frostbite or any other injuries." Dan paused for a moment and took a bite of the scone. Once he'd swallowed, he said, "I couldn't figure how he was keeping warm in the cottage, let alone off in a snow cave. But then he told his VA counselor that he'd lived in the woods for years when he returned from Vietnam during his twenties and thirties. It wasn't unheard of back then for vets to want to get away from it all. Anyway, he knew how to survive, is what I'm trying to say."

Elaine nodded, indicating she understood.

"Physically he's doing fine, but they're doing a psych evaluation on him." Dan wrapped his hand around his teacup. "The man doesn't seem to be in touch with reality, and because of that it's hard to know if the information he's given about the explosion is accurate or not."

"Are you referring to his sighting of a man on the property with a backpack?"

The trooper nodded. "But it's more complicated than that. He lost his glasses sometime in the last month, and his physical examination revealed that he's in desperate need of corrective lenses. That doesn't mean he didn't see someone on the property, but his vision was so bad the doctor said he could have mistaken a tree for a person."

"Oh dear," Elaine said. "Do you know how he ended up at the Snow Globe property?"

The trooper took another a bite of the scone and nodded as he chewed. After he swallowed, he said, "He was evicted from his studio apartment in Waterville last August. After that he couch-surfed for a while, then he caught a ride with an acquaintance, whom I tracked down and questioned. The man thought he was taking Timmy to Augusta, but when they passed the old highway turnoff, Timmy convinced the guy to go by the old Snow Globe property. When he pulled over by the garage, Timmy grabbed his stuff and jumped out, telling the guy to go on."

"Any explanation why he would do that?"

Dan nodded. "The guy said Timmy told him he had a whole bunch of good memories from there, both in the summer and winter."

Elaine exhaled. "Do you think he stayed on the Snow Globe property when he returned from Vietnam?"

"I have no idea," Dan answered. "I asked Timmy but he just shrugged."

From what Elaine had heard about Berl, she didn't think he'd mind.

The trooper drained his coffee and then picked up the second scone to take with him. He stood and said, "I need to get going. Could you pass on this information to Nathan? Tell him to call me if he has any questions."

Elaine assured Dan she would and thanked him for the update.

ROSE'S BOYFRIEND, BRENT, stopped by the tearoom over lunch and Elaine told the young woman to take a break and sit with him. As Elaine hustled to deliver all of the orders, she couldn't help but notice Rose's laughter a couple of different times. There was nothing Elaine wanted more than for the young people she knew to find spouses who would treat them well. Rose and Brent had been dating for a while. Elaine guessed, because he had a young daughter, that they were taking things slowly. But she hoped, in time, they'd marry. She sighed. Perhaps everyone she knew who was single would marry before she did.

Just after noon, when Nathan landed at the Portland airport on his way home from the conference, he called Elaine. She gave him the update from Dan. "That's great," he said. "I have an update too."

"Oh?"

"The attorney called and said a property investor contacted him, asking for my name and number."

"Really?"

"Yeah, he wants to talk to me as soon as possible. Even though the will is being contested."

"What's the investor's name?" Elaine asked.

"Adam—"

Elaine spoke with him. "Slater."

"Duh!" Nathan chuckled. "That's the owner of the back property, right?"

"Yep," Elaine said. "I'm not sure if that makes him an investor or not."

"Well, I'll listen to his pitch," Nathan said. "Although he may be wasting his time."

Elaine agreed. Time, and the court decision in Florida, would tell, but she couldn't help but think Adam Slater sounded as if he could be a scammer. Although she sincerely doubted he'd have any reason to contest the will.

CHAPTER NINE

Just before closing, Rose came back to the kitchen to find Elaine. "There's a man in the foyer, looking for Nathan."

Elaine paused with a bag of Darjeeling tea in her hand. "Oh?"

"I told him Nathan wasn't here so he asked to talk to you."

Elaine scooped the tea into the infuser. She was making it for herself to drink as they cleaned up. Naturally, she'd share it with the others too. She just needed a boost to get her through the rest of the day.

It had turned out to be a busy afternoon at the tearoom, and she had a headache. Not a bad headache, but a nagging one nonetheless, and she hoped to be rid of it by the time Nathan arrived from the airport.

She poured the water into the teapot, and then hurried out to the foyer.

The man wore jeans and a red flannel coat. He held a hat in his hands and looked as if he'd been out shooting hares.

"May I help you?" she asked.

"Are you Elaine Cook?" He spoke with a Bostonian accent.

She nodded.

"I was looking for Nathan Culver. But I figured you might be able to help me." He extended his hand. "I'm Adam Slater. You left me a couple of voice mails."

"Oh, hello." She shook his hand, surprised that he would just drop by. "Yes, I was trying to get in contact with you."

"Sorry I didn't call you back. I thought I might as well just speak with Nathan, but I've left him several messages this afternoon and he hasn't returned them. I figured I'd go ahead and stop in to see you."

"Thank you." She nodded toward the dining room. "Would you like a cup of tea?"

"No, thank you," he said. "But a glass of water would be great."

She showed him the dining room and then said, "I'll be right back. I'll call Nathan and see when he can join us."

The man wasn't anything like what she expected. She was anticipating a suit and tie—not a hunting outfit. If it wasn't for his accent, she'd think he was a local. She called Nathan on the way to the kitchen. He picked up on his car's hands-free device and said he was only about fifteen minutes from Lancaster.

She checked in with Jan after she grabbed her notebook, and then she poured a glass of water for Adam, a cup of tea for herself, and added a plate of lemon tartlets for good measure.

As she entered the dining room she said, "Nathan's fifteen minutes away, but do you mind if I ask you a few questions while we wait?"

"Not if I can ask you a couple too."

"It's a deal," she said, "but I can't answer for Nathan. You might not get the information you're looking for—and will just have to re-ask him." She smiled.

He nodded. "I understand."

She wasn't sure how old he was. Definitely younger than fifty. Perhaps even in his early forties.

"You go first," he said.

"How long have you had your property off the old highway?"

"Three years," he answered. "I built my house two years ago. I work in financing in Boston and needed a place to escape to."

"What made you want to have a vacation home all the way up here?"

"My grandfather used to bring me hunting in this area when I was a boy—we lived in southern Maine. He logged around here when he was a young man." Adam sighed. "We were poor as dirt, so traveling up here was the highlight of my year."

He certainly wasn't poor as dirt anymore. "Why do you want the Snow Globe property?"

He gave her a confused look. "The what?"

"The old roadside attraction property," she clarified.

"Do you mean the falling-down cottages and the larger building that was bombed last Friday night? Along with that odd covered deck along the pond that's ready to collapse?"

Elaine grimaced. The cottages weren't falling down. And the hut wasn't ready to collapse either. She explained about the snow globe and the skating rink, and that the "odd deck" was a warming hut that scores of families in the area had once enjoyed.

"That figures," he said. "I guess I should have known it used to be something way back when."

Elaine nodded.

He sighed. "It's not that I wanted the property so much as I wanted to tear all of those buildings down."

"Oh?"

"They're such an eyesore."

"You don't want to develop the land?"

"No," he answered. "I just want to take it back to its natural habitat. When I bought my property, I was sure whoever owned the other parcel would sell right away."

Adam Slater certainly hadn't turned out to be the villainous character Elaine was expecting. "Did you happen to be at your house last Friday evening? When the explosion happened?"

He shook his head. "I didn't come down until Saturday."

Elaine's eyebrows shot up. "The trooper and Nathan stopped by your place that morning."

"I didn't arrive until afternoon. I noticed that the windows were broken out of the garage building when I drove by, but I figured some kids had vandalized it. It wasn't until the next day, when I stopped in at the Pine Tree Grill, that I heard about the explosion."

"From Bianca and Mel?"

He nodded. "I've never kept it a secret that I was interested in the property. I contacted Berl Newton every three months or so, since I bought my land, about buying his property. He always said the same thing." The man grimaced. "No. Then Mel and Bianca told me Mr. Newton had passed away. I tracked down his will and found out that Nathan was named as the beneficiary of the property. I didn't realize all I needed to do to reach Nathan was return your call." He grinned. "Any chance he'll sell?"

"I can't speak for him," Elaine said. "But the estate isn't anywhere close to being settled. It will be a while." She picked up her pen. "Have you noticed anyone else on the property lately?"

"I'm only here on the weekends, if that," he said. "And for the occasional week when I take vacation time, which hasn't been lately. But I haven't seen anyone, although there were a few times when I've seen smoke coming up out of the trees."

Elaine jotted that down, guessing it was from the fires Timmy Calkin had built in the cottage. "Anything else?"

"Tracks. Snowshoes mostly. Some skis."

Elaine felt her face grow warm. "Actually, my daughter and I skied down the road to your place on Tuesday."

He shrugged. "The road is public."

"How about the trail that cuts up the hill to the snow globe property?"

He grinned. "You're good—that borders the two properties, but the trail is on Newton's land—or Nathan's now."

"Any sight of anyone on your property?"

He shook his head. "No."

Elaine put her pen back down. "Thank you. Do you have any questions for me?"

"No. Well, yes. If Nathan doesn't sell me the property, do you think he'll tear those buildings down?"

Elaine shrugged. "I have no idea what he plans to do." First they'd have to see if Nathan actually was awarded the property.

The front door opened and closed. Elaine stood and peeked out of the dining room. Nathan had stepped into the west parlor. "We're in here!" she called.

As Nathan entered the room, Adam laughed. "You're Nathan Culver."

Nathan seemed puzzled for a moment, but then said, "Oh, I recognize you. From the auction last weekend. And from other auctions in the area too."

The man nodded.

"You collect old Maine items, right?"

The man nodded. "Old hunting equipment. And logging pieces too, some quite large."

Nathan smiled. "I remember now. You bought an old skidder."

"That's right." The man laughed.

Elaine thanked Adam for answering her questions and then excused herself to start cleaning up. She couldn't help but be surprised that he appreciated old things. She'd been so sure, after his response to the buildings on the Snow Globe property, that he had no appreciation for the past. But that wasn't true.

She found herself wondering where he stored all of the equipment he collected. And what he planned to do with it. Perhaps display it on the old Snow Globe property instead of returning it to "nature"?

When she reached the kitchen, Jan sat at the table organizing the photos that had come in so far in the system of boxes and folders Elaine had set up.

"You haven't submitted a photo yet," Jan said.

Elaine wrinkled her nose. She was going to surprise Jan with the photo of them from the Snow Globe, but she hadn't come up with a good one of her and Nathan yet. "Oh, I will," she answered.

Rose filled an order at the counter. "I need to have a couple of Brent and me printed. Unfortunately, I only have ones on my phone."

Elaine understood. She didn't have many photos of her and Nathan either.

"Anything from Macy yet?" Elaine asked.

Jan shook her head. "Hopefully she'll drop something off soon."

As Jan filed another photo away, she said they should all dress up for the Valentine's Day Gala in the Victorian garb they wore for such occasions.

"That's a great idea," Rose said. "And Archie can wear his suit. We'll all look dashing."

Elaine had always loved Valentine's Day. Owning and operating a tearoom with Jan made her love it even more. How wonderful to be able to provide an event for the community.

A half hour later, Nathan stepped into the kitchen.

"How did it go?" she asked.

"Fine. I told Adam the will was being contested and that I had no idea when it would be settled."

They talked some more about Adam Slater, each sharing what he'd said with the other. "He told me he wanted to buy the property to tear the old buildings down and let it go natural," Elaine said.

"Yeah," Nathan responded. "That's what he told me too, but I'm not sure I believe him. He has all of that equipment he's been collecting."

"Where do you think he's storing it now?"

"Not in Boston," Nathan answered. "Maybe in his three-car garage?"

Elaine agreed that was a possibility. "I definitely wonder if he has something up his sleeve."

CHAPTER TEN

On Monday, after Jan finished her baking, she left the tearoom in Elaine and Archie's hands and headed to the *Penzance Courier* office to research the Newton family.

The day was overcast with more snow on the way, and an icy wind blew off the lake. Jan parked in front of the brick building where the newspaper was housed and had been for as long as she could remember. She gathered her notebook and stepped through the front door into the open room, with the exposed brick walls. She expected the room to be drafty with its high ceilings, but it felt remarkably cozy.

Cookie, the receptionist, welcomed Jan. "What brings you here today?"

"I need to look at your index and then microfiche. I'm looking for information on the Berl Newton family and the Snow Globe."

"Really?" Cookie stood and came around to the front of her desk. "I had a man in here researching that same property on Friday."

Jan took a step backward. "Do you mind describing him to me?" Perhaps it was the man who stopped by the tearoom to talk with Elaine and then Nathan.

"In his thirties, maybe close to forty. He wore a beard, and dressed like a Mainer, with a stocking cap and hunting jacket. He had a little girl with him. She was dressed completely in pink."

Puzzled, Jan remembered what Elaine had said about the man who owned the property behind the Snow Globe, but she hadn't described him and Jan didn't actually see him. She didn't think he was married though. Of course, that didn't mean he didn't have a child. Or have someone else's child with him. "Did you get his name?" Jan asked.

Cookie shook her head. "Maybe we should have some sort of sign in, but we don't."

Jan suspected that Cookie usually knew everyone who stopped by anyway and most people would be offended to have to "sign in."

"Well, you know the drill," Cookie said, pointing to the oversized index book on the back counter. "Let me know when you're ready for the microfiche."

It didn't take long for Jan to find multiple entries for Berl Newton. She wrote down the corresponding numbers and then searched the index for Ilene Newton. There were a handful of entries for her.

As Cookie went to collect the reels, Jan settled down at the machine. She decided to start with the oldest first and slowly Berl Newton's story came together, at least the chapters, albeit short ones, that had made it into the *Penzance Courier*.

Jan skimmed through the biographical information about Berl Newton that Elaine had already told her, up until the birth of his and Nanette's daughter, Ilene, in 1955. She competed in ice-skating around the state and graduated high school in 1972. Berl's wife passed away in 1973, and then he closed the Snow Globe in 1976. There was a big double-page spread about that with lots of photographs. Jan wrote down the name of the photographer: Randall Whitworth.

In 1976, there was a short article that Ilene had married a man by the name of Vincent Osborne in Toronto and that the couple were making their new home there. That was definitely new information. Jan jotted down the man's name.

The next mention of Ilene was in 1978, announcing the birth of a son.

Jan reread the sentence and then continued. The boy was named Miles Berl and Berl Newton was listed as the proud grandfather, along with Vincent Osborne's parents. Jan wrote down their names too.

Then in January of 1980, Berl moved to Florida.

After that, there were a couple of mentions in the "Along the Party Line," the gossip column that Jan remembered from her childhood, of Berl Newton when he returned to Lancaster through the years. One time, in 1987, Ilene accompanied him, and she was listed as residing in Florida too. There was no mention of Vincent or Miles after that. There wasn't an obituary for Ilene, nor as Jan suspected, for Berl either.

Jan finished up her notes, tidied up the boxes of microfiche, and then thanked Cookie.

"Did you find what you were looking for?"

"Yes," Jan nodded. "But I have a follow-up question. I noticed photos of the Snow Globe taken by a Randall Whitworth. Do you know if he's still alive?"

"Oh yes. He certainly is," Cookie said. "He comes in here every once in a while to relive the old days." She smiled. "He's in his eighties and lives in a retirement home in Waterville." She took out a slip of paper and wrote the man's phone number down. "He'd be happy to hear from you. He always tells me to send anyone with any questions about 'the olden days' his way."

Jan took the paper and slipped it into her notebook. Then she gave Cookie a big thank-you and a hug and hurried back outside, dashing through the icy pelts of snow as she rushed to her car.

When she reached the tearoom, she hung up her coat and then peeked into the west parlor.

Bristol and Marshall Taylor sat together, sipping tea and deep in a discussion.

"It's so good to see the two of you again! How are you doing? Mr. Taylor, are you settling in?" Jan asked just as she realized she was interrupting. "Oh, I'm sorry," she said. "Don't mind me."

"No worries," Marshall Taylor said. "And please, call me Marshall. We were just talking about the Snow Globe."

"Oh?"

Bristol added, "Marshall was a friend of the Newtons, a close one."

Jan's heart raced. "Is that so?"

He nodded. "Bristol told me a little about what happened out at the Snow Globe property recently. I was in the same class as Ilene and kept in touch with her over the years. I attended her wedding—and a few years ago, her funeral."

"Oh," Jan said, "she really must have been a good friend."

"She was." Marshall's dark eyes grew misty. "She was good at keeping in touch and wrote to me regularly."

"How old was she when she passed on?"

"Well, that was five years ago, so fifty-eight."

Jan winced. "Do you mind if I go get Elaine? I know she'd like to hear the story." The tearoom was quiet and Jan was sure Archie could handle serving on his own for a short time.

"Not at all," Marshall said. He held up his menu and looked at Bristol. "I'm fine with you ordering for the two of us, if you want to let Jan know what we want."

"Great," Bristol said, ordering the maple croissants and Earl Grey tea.

Jan hurried into the kitchen and called out to Elaine. "Dry your hands and start a pot of Earl Grey while I put a plate together. Marshall Taylor was a friend of Ilene Newton, and he's in the east parlor with Bristol."

Five minutes later the cousins sat at the table with their guests, drinking their own cups of tea. Jan asked, "Can you tell us what Ilene was like as a girl?"

"Of course," Marshall said. "She was shy, nothing like her outgoing father. She took after her mother—reserved and quiet. But, oh, how she loved to skate! So did her mother, which is why Mr. Newton turned the pond into an ice-skating rink in the first place. He built it before they ever married, before they even dated, as a way to woo her. He just returned to the area after graduating from the university and Ilene's mother had caught his eye as she skated around the lake. Of course, the complaint of the lake was that it was so windy, so Mr. Newton turned his pond into a rink and built the warming hut. That led to the gift shop and renovating and then winterizing the cottages so people could stay out there and skate and cross-country ski."

Elaine coughed. "The cottages were winterized?"

"Yes," Marshall answered. "We had a class sleepover out there during February of our senior year. I don't know what Mr. Newton did to the cottages, but they were as cozy as could be with just the woodstoves."

"How interesting," Elaine said. "That makes sense."

"Can you tell us about Ilene's marriage? And her son?" Jan asked.

Marshall's demeanor shifted. "Those are both sad stories. Ilene married Vincent Osborne after she graduated from college. They met in Montreal, at a party she'd gone to with her college roommate. He was handsome. In partnership with his father in an import business. Several years older. She fell head over heels in love with him."

Marshall went on to say that he'd been secretly in love with Ilene his whole life, but believed he never had a chance with her and consoled himself with being her friend. When she fell for Vincent he knew his chances were over.

"Did they marry here in Lancaster?"

He shook his head. "In Toronto. Vincent had just opened a branch of his family business there. Everything seemed like a fairy tale, except that her mother had recently passed away. That was heartbreaking for Ilene, but there she was, starting over in a new city with the love of her life." He took a sip of tea, and then said, "At first it seemed her new life was all that she hoped for. While Vincent earned a good living, she took art classes and volunteered. Soon after they married, she became pregnant and it seemed her life was complete."

Marshall explained that Mr. Newton was ecstatic when he became a grandfather. The Snow Globe was closed by then, but he kept the property for the family and loved having the little boy, Miles, come visit. Marshall said that one summer he was in Lancaster at the same time Ilene and Miles were, although Vincent had stayed home. "Miles was a smart, active boy who already loved skating. Ilene invited me out to the Snow Globe and I posed for a photo in the globe with the two of them. She seemed a little sad but assured me that everything was fine."

He had a faraway look in his eyes. "I'm rambling, and I doubt you're terribly interested in my story..."

"No, we are," Jan reassured him.

"Well, then you're only being kind." Marshall met her eyes and smiled. "Anyway, the visit was good for me. Ilene was married and had a child. It was time for me to move on. I returned to Chicago and asked the woman who became my wife out for the first time. A year later, we married."

"Oh, wonderful!" Elaine said. Jan and her cousin both appreciated a good love story.

Marshall smiled. "Yes, it truly was. We were never blessed with children, but we were immensely blessed with each other." He took a bite of a croissant and then said, "Sadly, Ilene wasn't as fortunate. I didn't see her again until our twentieth school reunion. Frankly, I was surprised she came. She'd been separated from Vincent for years and had followed her father to Florida. But Berl had come up to spend time on his property, and so she came with him and attended the reunion."

She confided in Marshall that Vincent had several affairs before she finally left him. At the time she feared that he was turning Miles against her. He was a teenager by then and loved the freedom he had at his father's house and begged to spend more and more time there.

Marshall took a sip of tea and then said, "My wife got acquainted with Ilene on that trip and they became friends too. We ended up visiting Ilene and Berl in Florida, in their beautiful home overlooking the water." Marshall folded his hands together. "One time when we visited, Miles was there. He was surly, as some teens can be. He wouldn't join us at the table or on any of our outings. The next time we visited he'd graduated from college and was traveling in Asia. Ilene admitted that she hadn't seen him for several years, that he didn't keep in touch with her, and stayed with his father if he wasn't traveling. She worried about him."

Marshall continued, saying that later Mr. Newton talked with him about Miles, saying that Ilene wouldn't speak badly about her son, but he'd treated her horribly, blaming her for the breakup of the family and not making the marriage work. "Naturally, she wouldn't speak badly about Vincent to Miles," Marshall said. "I wondered if Mr. Newton was so hurt for Ilene that he'd written Miles out of his will. But I decided to stay out of their family business too, guessing Mr. Newton would pass away first, leave his money to Ilene, and then she would decide what to leave to Miles."

When he didn't say any more, Jan interjected, "But it didn't work out that way?"

"That's right," he answered. "Ilene died from pancreatic cancer a few years ago. It was fast and vicious. Her last wish was to see Miles, but no one could track him down. Mr. Newton got in touch with Vincent, but he said he'd lost contact with Miles too. She died without making peace with her son."

"Oh, how awful," Jan said.

He nodded. "The entire situation made Mr. Newton more angry than ever. He couldn't imagine what would cause a child to treat his mother so badly."

Jan did the math. Mr. Newton would have been in his late eighties by then. How tragic for him to lose his only child— and have no contact with his only grandchild. "What a heart-breaking story," Jan said.

Marshall nodded. "Yes, it really is. I was blessed to have Ilene and Mr. Newton as friends. And I always longed to know Miles's story, but I fear perhaps he died on one of his journeys."

Jan leaned forward. "Really?"

He nodded.

Jan couldn't imagine such heartbreak. "Do you know that Ilene and Vincent divorced, for sure?"

A puzzled look passed over his face. "You know, I always assumed they did, but I never asked." He sighed. "Soon after she was diagnosed with cancer, my wife was diagnosed with ALS. We didn't travel back down to Florida to see Ilene again or for her funeral."

"Oh, I'm so sorry," Jan said. What a horrible way for his wife to die too, and how tragic for Marshall Taylor.

He finished his tea and said, "I have lots of good memories about the Newtons, to be sure," he said. "And several sad ones too. I didn't know Mr. Newton had passed away until Bristol told me. I've been out of sorts with my wife's death and getting ready to move and all. I'm afraid I neglected him."

Obviously Marshall was done telling the story, but Elaine cleared her throat and then asked, "Do you know anything about a snow globe collection that Mr. Newton had?"

He shook his head. "Ilene mentioned it once, but I never saw it."

Jan and Elaine both thanked him for his story and welcomed him, again, home to Lancaster. "We're really glad you've returned," Jan said. "We hope you'll be very happy here."

Marshall smiled sweetly and said, "I already am."

Jan was thankful that the rest of the afternoon went smoothly, because she was ready to clean the place up as soon as possible and try to find more information online about Ilene Newton Osborne, Vincent Osborne, and Miles Osborne. As she thought about them, she couldn't help but be grateful for her own family. What a tragedy to lose your wife, have your only child lose her marriage, and then have your only grandchild turn his back on your daughter and you and then disappear.

After the tearoom closed and Archie had hung up his apron and left, Jan wiped down the kitchen counters one more time. She had a pot of peppermint tea brewing that she'd take up to the sitting room. Hopefully Elaine would join her and they could both get busy on their laptops. There had to be more information on Ilene, Vincent, and Miles Osborne.

As she placed the pot of tea on a tray, her phone dinged. She had a text from Amy. *I have cabin fever. Van is working late. Okay if the twins and I come over for dinner? I have salad I can bring. And bread.*

Jan hesitated for a moment. She'd have to come up with something for dinner. Maybe lasagna. She wouldn't have time to do any research.

She chided herself. Wasn't she just thanking God for her family?

Of course, she texted back. *I'll ask Tara if she can join us. Bob too.* Jan knew Kelly had her karate class so Brian and his family wouldn't be able to come.

Within a minute, Amy texted back, *You're the best! See you soon.*

Elaine was in her office. "Change of plans!" Jan called out. She stepped around the corner and explained what happened. "Do you want to invite Nathan, Sasha, and Brody too?"

"Great idea," Elaine said. "I'll make the lasagna."

Jan had made a batch of caramel brownies for the next day. They'd use those for dessert. Who better to serve them to than family?

CHAPTER ELEVEN

Elaine browned the hamburger and sausage, put the sauce together, grated the cheese, boiled the pasta, and assembled the lasagna. She popped it in the oven by five, and she and Jan had the appetizers of veggies, olives, cheese, and salami out by the time Amy and the twins arrived. After Jan and Elaine both hugged Amy, and patted her growing belly, and heard how the baby girl inside her was growing, they directed the boys to the game closet. The twins picked Twister, which kept them entertained for a good half hour.

Sasha and Brody showed up by six, followed by Nathan, Bob, and Tara. Elaine kept looking for an opportunity to tell Nathan about Marshall Taylor's story, but she was busy with one thing after another. After they'd eaten the lasagna, salad, and French bread, Jan served the caramel brownies with decaf coffee and tea.

They all sat in the east parlor around the fire, enjoying dessert, while the twins sat on the window seat, leaning against the chintz cushions and poking at each other. Finally, Jan pulled a puzzle out of the closet and set it up on a table in the back for them. Eventually the conversation among the grown-ups fell to the Snow Globe.

As they chatted, Amy rested her hand atop her belly. She was only a month away from delivering the baby.

"Jan and I found out more about the Newtons today," Elaine said. Together the women relayed Marshall Taylor's story. After they'd finished, Elaine turned to Nathan. "Does this information seem plausible to you?"

He nodded. "None of that contradicts anything I've heard. But when Berl contacted me several years ago, it was the first time anyone in my family had heard from him since he left except for a Christmas card every year."

Elaine asked. "Berl didn't see your dad when he visited Lancaster?"

Nathan shrugged. "I was out on my own by then, but I don't remember Dad talking about Berl. Maybe he did, and Dad just didn't mention it to me."

When Nathan didn't say anything more about that, Jan asked if Nathan knew of a Randall Whitworth.

"I do," he said. "He's the one who took the photos of Mr. Newton's snow globe collection that Berl sent me."

Elaine sat up straight. Randall might know where the collection was stored. "Nathan," she said, "why didn't you tell me that before?"

He chuckled. "I didn't think of it until right now."

Elaine stood. "Don't say any more. I'm going to go get my notebook—and my laptop."

When she returned, Sasha was asking Amy how she was feeling.

"Well, I'm not nearly as large as I was with the twins, of course, but I still feel as big as a house. I guess I was as big as a barn before." She laughed. "Mostly, I'm anxious to hold this little girl and cuddle her."

Brody had his hand on Sasha's shoulder, listening intently to Amy. Elaine's heart warmed. She wouldn't get her hopes up for a grandbaby from Sasha and Brody any time soon. It would be good for them to have time together after their wedding before they had children. But, still, she hoped they'd start a family sooner rather than later.

She sat down next to Nathan. First she updated the notebook based on what Jan discovered, adding *Vincent Osborne* next to *Ilene Newton's ex*. And then *Miles Berl Osborne* next to *grandson*. Then she jotted down *Randall Whitworth*. Not because he was a suspect but simply because he added to the information of the case. Then she Googled *Ilene Newton Osborne, Tampa, Florida, obituary*.

A small notice popped up from the funeral home. Berl was mentioned as surviving her but there was no mention of a husband or a son. Next she Googled *Vincent Osborne, businessman, Toronto*. An article appeared that stated he'd been charged with embezzlement but the charges were eventually dropped.

She shared the information with the others.

"So we don't actually know if Vincent and Ilene ever divorced, right?" Nathan asked.

"We haven't found information confirming that they did," Elaine explained. "However, Marshall assumed they had."

She glanced around, hoping no one minded she was on her laptop. Sasha was so interested in hearing every detail about

Amy's pregnancy that she didn't seem to notice what Elaine was doing at all.

Elaine typed in *Miles Osborne, Toronto, Canada* and hit enter.

An entry from the *Toronto Sun* popped up, from 1996. He'd been arrested for criminal mischief. Then in 2003, there was a news item that he was missing in Southeast Asia. "Oh dear," Elaine said and then shared the news with the others. The article corroborated Marshall Taylor's account.

"Anything about him turning up again?" Jan asked.

Elaine shook her head.

Nathan leaned forward. "How about an obituary on him?"

Elaine Googled that but couldn't find anything.

Nathan stood and slapped Brody on the back. "Aren't the Celtics playing tonight?"

"I think so," Brody said.

"Let's go up to the sitting room while the girls solve this one."

Brody grinned. "Sounds good to me."

"Ha ha." Elaine shot Nathan a sassy look. He was right. They weren't going to solve this one over the Internet, but it kept getting more and more interesting. Still, she'd probably gotten carried away and neglected their guests.

Amy stood and said she needed to get the twins home, and Tara said she needed to leave too. After telling all of them good-bye, Sasha and Elaine, carrying her laptop, followed Nathan and Brody up to the sitting room to watch the game, and Bob and Jan soon joined them, bringing the plate of brownies.

But it wasn't long until Jan suggested that Elaine see if she could find a marriage for Miles Osborne. "Maybe he married before he disappeared. Maybe there's an ex-wife or something we could contact to see if he ever showed up."

"I'll check." Elaine entered the information and then read the first entry. "Wow!"

"What is it?" Jan asked.

"He did get married—or at least I think it's him. A Miles Osborne anyway. And only four years ago." Elaine glanced up over the computer screen.

Nathan's eyes grew large. "Guess he resurfaced."

Elaine nodded. "He married a Brooke Franklin. It looks as if her family is quite wealthy. They married at a club in Toronto." She turned the screen around so Sasha and Jan could see the photo. Miles was tall and thin and handsome in his tuxedo. The bride wore an off-the-shoulder gown with a long train and veil. She appeared to be younger than Miles.

Jan asked, "Does the article mention his parents?"

Elaine turned the screen back around and then skimmed the article. "No, there's not a mention of either one of them. But his mother would have been dead by then, by a year. However, there's quite a bit about the bride's parents, Beth and Kyle Franklin. Her father works in finance in Toronto." Elaine wrinkled her nose.

"What is it?" Jan asked.

"Oh, I'm just thinking of Vincent Osborne getting arrested for embezzlement."

"Remember, innocent until proven guilty," Nathan said, his eyes still on the TV screen. "And the charges were dropped."

"I know," Elaine said. "It just sounds, from what Marshall said, that the man wasn't always on the up-and-up. I wonder what Miles might have picked up from him."

"The apple doesn't fall far from the tree and all of that?" Jan asked.

Elaine nodded. "Perhaps he married Brooke Franklin for her family's money."

"No need to speculate," Nathan said and then jumped to his feet as the Celtics made a basket just as the first half ended.

Elaine gave him a saucy grin. "Well, Miles and Vincent Osborne are the two main suspects as far as the will goes, don't you think?"

"But not in the explosion," Nathan said, sitting back down. "And there's no crime in contesting a will. Besides, Miles definitely has more right to the property with his family ties than I do, and Vincent would too if he and Ilene never divorced."

"But they treated Berl and Ilene so badly," Elaine countered. "Berl would have left them the property, not to mention his fortune, if he'd wanted them to have it."

Nathan just shrugged and grabbed another brownie. "Jan, these are delicious."

Elaine knew exactly what he was doing. Changing the subject.

She Googled *Brooke Franklin Osborne.* "Oh no."

"What is it?" Jan asked.

"Brooke died five months ago." She skimmed the article quickly. "Her parents are listed as survivors." Funny they were listed first. "Then a son. And finally Miles." She felt sick to her stomach.

"Is there an age for the boy?"

Elaine shook her head. "Perhaps he's from a previous marriage."

She quickly Googled *births, Brooke Franklin Osborne and Miles Osborne.* A notice popped up in the *Toronto Sun* from two years before. A little boy. Aiden Berl Osborne. Elaine read the notice out loud.

"Unbelievable," Nathan said.

Jan clasped her hands together. "I agree."

The response garnered the attention of Brody and Bob too and Elaine caught all of them up on the story.

"How heartbreaking," Sasha said. "I wonder who has the little boy now—Miles or the grandparents."

"Hopefully they're all still in Toronto," Elaine said, "caring for the little one together."

"What did Brooke die from?" Sasha asked.

"Good question." Elaine did some more Googling. No accounts of accidents popped up. She skimmed the obituary again. It was a paid notice, most likely posted by the family. There was no request to donate to a certain charity, like cancer research or anything like that. There was no hint of how she died.

"Is there any information about Miles or Aiden after Brooke died?" Sasha asked.

"I can't find anything."

"Did you check social media?"

Elaine hadn't thought to check there. She logged into Facebook and typed in *Miles Osborne.* Lots of options popped up. She weeded through them, but none of them were the Miles she was looking for. Next she typed in *Beth Franklin.* She found a woman by that name who lived in Toronto. The woman's profile photo was with a man. They both looked to be in their early sixties with silvery hair, tailored clothes, and smiling faces. The woman's page was set to private though.

She couldn't find any social media for any of the others.

Elaine thought again of the little boy. *Aiden Berl.* Why in the world would an ungrateful grandson name his own son after a grandfather he hadn't seen in a couple of decades?

CHAPTER TWELVE

Tuesday morning, once everything was ready in the tearoom but before opening, Elaine left Archie to turn the sign and hurried upstairs. She perched on the sectional in the sitting room and opened her laptop again. It was a beautiful winter day with a completely blue sky. Bright sunshine flooded through the windows, shining light into the sitting room. It was a good thing they kept the tearoom in tip-top shape when it came to cleaning. Today was the sort that would show the slightest smudge on a window and the tiniest dust bunny in a corner.

Elaine searched for an address and phone number online for Brooke and Miles Osborne in Toronto. She dialed the number but it had been disconnected. The address was for an apartment building in downtown Toronto, which she found via Google Earth. It appeared upscale and in a trendy neighborhood, right downtown.

She dialed the number of the property manager but, as she expected, he wouldn't give her any information on Miles.

Next she found a number and address for his in-laws and then one for their family financial business. Elaine left messages at both numbers, and then she searched for Vincent Osborne. She couldn't find a number but found a possible person on Facebook and sent him a message.

As she hit send, her cell phone rang. She answered it quickly. It was Kyle Franklin, demanding why she'd left a message about Miles Osborne. "Do you know where he is?" he demanded. "Is my grandson safe?"

Elaine, using her calmest voice, explained that she had no idea where Miles was or Aiden.

"How do you know Aiden's name?" he demanded.

"From his birth announcement in the *Toronto Sun*," Elaine explained.

"Oh." The man sighed. "I told Beth not to put it in Brooke's obituary. I just thought it would be better not to have his name made public. But I'd forgotten there was a birth announcement in the *Sun*. I think Beth placed that too. Those sorts of things didn't matter to the kids, but they meant a lot to Beth..." His voice trailed off.

"I'm sorry." Elaine stood, feeling uncomfortable. "That's not why I called. I simply want to ask Miles some questions about his grandfather's estate."

"Hold on," the man said. "I have another call I need to take."

Elevator music came on the line and then Kyle Franklin picked up the call again. "That was my wife. She just listened to the message from you on our home phone. I'm afraid you got her hopes up."

"I'm sorry." Elaine turned toward the window again, thinking of the woman in the Facebook photo. "I certainly didn't mean to. I'm simply trying to track down Miles." She wouldn't mention the explosion at the Snow Globe. There was no way it could be Miles, not if he had Aiden with him. And if they were in the area, no one had mentioned a man with a young son.

The man sighed again. "Tell me again, exactly, why you called me about Miles."

At that point Elaine realized she couldn't help but tell him about the explosion, but she started with Nathan getting the notice from the attorney, then finding out the will had been contested, and then the explosion.

"Oh, I have no doubt that Miles is your man," Kyle said. "We've been suspicious that perhaps he'd gone to Maine. His father is probably in on this too. You'd better double-check with that attorney—they've probably contested the whole thing by now. Vincent talked about how rich his father-in-law was several times."

Elaine sat back down, perching on the edge of the sectional. "You've had contact with Vincent?"

"At the wedding. When Aiden was born. At a couple of holidays."

"So he and Miles are close?"

"I wouldn't say close. They're about as different as can be. Vincent is all about money, fast cars, and big houses, even though it's just him."

"And Miles?"

"Yeah. Well. How do I describe Miles? His idea of a honeymoon was backpacking in Chile. Thankfully we talked him into a resort in Bali. He's the kind of guy who'd rather wear flip-flops and shorts than a suit." The man's voice caught. "I do need to give him credit where credit is due. He cared for Aiden, along with Brooke, when she was ill. Although he turned her against us, I'm afraid. Her mother wanted to hire a nurse, but Brooke wouldn't let her. She only wanted Miles to care for her. It was the three of them when she died in their apartment."

"I'm so sorry," Elaine said. "Do you mind me asking what she passed away from?"

"Brain cancer. She was diagnosed right after Aiden was born."

"I really am sorry." Elaine's stomach churned at the thought, imagining if Sasha were diagnosed with such a horrible disease. "When did Miles leave Toronto?"

"We're not sure exactly because he stopped returning our calls, but probably four weeks ago," Kyle said. "Of course, we've looked everywhere we can think of. Vincent hasn't heard from him, or so he says. Your call is the first lead we've had."

Elaine exhaled. "I don't know that it's a lead. There's no way he could survive around here in the wild, especially not with a baby. And there's no evidence he's staying in any of the structures on his grandfather's property, and we haven't heard of any young man with a little boy staying anywhere else in Lancaster or the surrounding area."

"Well, I'd say to expect the unexpected from Miles. He's an odd duck, that's for sure."

Elaine exhaled. The man clearly didn't like his son-in-law. "Why did you suspect he might come to Maine?"

"He talked about it a lot. The property his grandfather had. How much fun he had on it as a child. How much he loved the outdoors, especially in the winter." Kyle's voice grew harsher. "He didn't have a relationship with his grandfather at all, and yet he romanticized his childhood memories with the man and even gave Aiden the middle name of Berl." A bitter tone had entered the man's voice. "And Brooke accepted it."

Elaine wondered if Kyle had expected the boy to be named after him. She could understand his hurt but wasn't sure how to respond.

She opened up her laptop and glanced at the clock: 10:10. She should get downstairs. "Thank you, Mr. Franklin, for your help. I really appreciate it."

"He drives a Subaru with Ontario plates. But be careful if someone approaches him. We truly believe that Miles is unstable. Please let us know if you find him."

"I'll make sure and let you know if anything turns up." She really did want the couple to be reunited with their grandson. After she ended the call, she headed down the stairs to help open the tearoom for the day, her heart heavy for the Franklins.

THE MORNING WAS unusually busy for a Tuesday. Between taking orders, steeping tea, plating food, and delivering the orders, Elaine recalled her conversation with Kyle Franklin. How would she feel if her grandson, Micah, had gone missing when he was two? She couldn't imagine how frantic she would have been. Poor Beth and Kyle. She wondered how they were functioning at all not knowing where little Aiden was.

The more she thought about it, the more she knew she needed to call Dan. She slipped into her office and dialed his number. If Miles, who definitely sounded unstable, was on the property with a two-year-old, he really needed to be found. At the least, the child could be suffering from neglect. At the worst, he could be in real danger. After six rings, the trooper's recorded message started. She left him a quick rundown of her phone call with Mr. Franklin and asked him to return her call or stop by the tearoom.

As she ended the call, her phone dinged. She had a Facebook message.

She looked at it quickly. It was from Vincent Osborne. *Miles is my son. What has he done now?* Elaine cringed. Miles didn't have much of a track record—except that he'd cared for his wife when she was dying. But it sounded as if even that was to the detriment of her parents.

Elaine quickly typed in a message, asking him if he knew where Miles was.

A simple *No* appeared on the screen. Then *Why do you ask?*

She explained she lived in Lancaster and there had been a sighting of a person on the Snow Globe property and she wondered if it could be Miles.

Nothing would surprise me, Vincent wrote back. *Although he'd be a bigger fool than I thought to go there. Just remember, I'm not responsible for anything he does.*

It seemed the man didn't know anything about his son's whereabouts—or at least he wasn't going to tell her. It also seemed he didn't trust Miles either. She ended the conversation by thanking him and then writing, *Please let me know if you hear from him.*

The man responded with, *Ditto.*

She slipped her phone back into her apron pocket and returned to work. She had a bad impression of both Vincent and Miles. What a tragedy that such a good man as Berl Newton would have a grandson who turned out to be such a loser. And poor Ilene too. How sad that when her marriage ended, so did, eventually, her relationship with her son.

Elaine was grateful that Archie helped keep the mood light in the tearoom. As always, he charmed the customers with his accent and impeccable manners. A group of five women, all in their sixties, who had come out from Augusta just to visit the tearoom, joked with him, asking if the tearoom served crumpets.

"My dears," he said, "I'm happy to check to see if we have any today."

Elaine knew for a fact that they didn't have crumpets. And Archie knew that too.

The women laughed and one said, "We were just teasing. I'd rather have a scone with lemon curd."

"And I'll take a raspberry tart," another said.

Elaine headed back to the kitchen. When Archie arrived she asked, "What would you have done if they really wanted crumpets?"

His eyes sparkled. "I get that all the time. They hear my accent and they immediately think 'crumpets.' I called their bluff. If they insisted they wanted crumpets, I would have fessed up." He grinned. "They'll be much happier with Jan's scones and tarts. Crumpets are fine, but they're not nearly as tasty as they sound to Americans."

IN THE EARLY afternoon, Elaine and Jan sat down and shared a pot of tea together. Jan hadn't said much about the kitchen renovation going on in her future house, so Elaine made a point to ask.

Her cousin's eyes lit up. "I'm loving everything about it. The stainless steel appliances, the block tile flooring, the slate countertops. Each component is perfect."

Elaine gasped. "Is everything installed?" Had Jan purposefully not been talking about the house to spare Elaine's feelings?

"Nearly. You'll have to come over soon."

Elaine nodded. "I'd like that."

Next, they talked through the Valentine's Day Gala. The big day was coming soon. So far they'd given away all of the invitations and had collected a large number of photos and a handful of letters.

"I'm positive we'll have enough to decorate the place," Jan said.

Elaine nodded. She was sure of it too. She'd ordered the glass tabletops, and they were scheduled to arrive any day.

As they chatted, Sasha stepped into the kitchen, a large manila envelope in her hand. "I brought photos," she said, a broad smile on her face. She pulled out a small stack. Elaine stepped to her side and Sasha handed her the pictures, one by one. The first was a studio photo taken when Sasha was two. She wore a purple print dress and sat on Elaine's lap. Sasha's head was tilted toward her mother's, with an adoring expression on her face.

The next photo was of Sasha and Ben, with the sunset behind them. The photo was taken when they lived on Oahu, when Sasha was six. She had a white plumeria flower, with a yellow center, in her hair and wore a pink sundress. Ben wore his army uniform and had a big smile on his face. The next photo was of Sasha and Jared at her high school graduation. Her brother had his arm around her in both a proud and protective manner. The fourth photo was of Brody and Sasha after a run last summer, taken on the tearoom deck with the Chickadee Lake behind them. Both were red faced and sweaty, with expressions of pure joy on their faces as they stood with their arms draped around each other.

"Aww," Elaine said. "I love all of these."

Sasha smiled. "The four loves of my life. I've been so blessed."

Elaine nodded, loving the Valentine's Day photo idea of including more than just sweethearts. It really did encourage people to think about all the positive relationships in their lives. She just hoped Macy would agree—and contribute a few photos too.

As she gave Sasha a hug, Archie stepped into the kitchen and said to Elaine, "Trooper Benson is here to see you."

As Elaine released her daughter, Sasha's eyebrows shot up. "Ooh, has something happened with the case?"

"Maybe," Elaine said and motioned for Sasha to follow her out to the entry.

After she greeted Dan, she offered him a cup of tea.

"No, thank you," he said. "I'm on my way to the Snow Globe property, but I wanted to speak with you first."

Elaine nodded.

"I got your voice mail about this Miles Osborne. Berl Newton's grandson, right?"

"Yes."

Sasha asked, "What?"

"I'll tell you in a minute," Elaine said.

Dan continued. "And his in-laws wonder if he's here?"

Elaine wrinkled her nose. "It's not that they have any proof. It's just that he disappeared around four weeks ago, with their grandson, and they have no idea where he is. They believe it might be a possibility. I wouldn't have thought it could be except for Marshall Taylor's story about how well insulated the cottages are, and the fact that Timmy Calkin was able to survive in one for a couple of weeks."

Dan nodded. "Well, we searched the cottages once but I think this warrants another search. I still have the key."

"Could Sasha and I go with you?" Elaine couldn't get the thought of little Aiden Osborne out of her head.

The trooper hesitated for a moment and then said, "You can come out to the property just in case we do find a child. It would be helpful to have you there. I'll contact the attorney on the way and ask for permission again."

He nodded at both Elaine and Sasha. "I'll meet you out there."

As he left, Elaine asked Sasha if she had time to go out to the property.

"Of course," she answered. "And you can fill me in on the details on the way."

Elaine did just that as she drove, telling Sasha about the phone call with Kyle Franklin and the messages from Vincent Osborne.

"Wow," Sasha said. "Miles having a little boy and being on the run really complicates things, doesn't it?"

Elaine agreed.

When they reached the property, Dan had parked in front of the old gift shop and was still sitting in his vehicle.

Elaine parked beside him and realized he was talking on the phone. Once he hung up and climbed out of the car, Elaine and Sasha joined him. The sunshine made all the buildings seem more inviting than they had on the night of the explosion or even the afternoon Elaine and Sasha had found Timmy Calkin. The temperature was just above freezing, the warmest it had been in weeks. However, another storm was predicted soon.

"Mr. Marner gave me permission to look around," Dan said. "He was surprised to hear that Miles Osborne may be in the area."

Elaine's face grew warm even in the cold. "His parents-in-law are grasping at possibilities. There's no evidence he might be here. I simply thought it would be worth checking again, just in case."

Dan agreed. "I hope he's here. I hate to think that the child might be in danger."

Elaine nodded. "And there's one other thing we should look for. Berl Newton's snow globe collection. We expected that it would turn up in Florida, but it turns out no one knows where it is. It seems probable he left it in Maine."

Dan shook his head. "I don't know where he would have kept it out here. Nowhere is really secure and although the buildings have had some maintenance done on them, I can't imagine him keeping something so valuable here. But I'll keep it in mind."

The trooper said he wouldn't allow Sasha and Elaine into the buildings, but they stood in the doorways as he investigated each one, starting with the gift shop. It still housed shelves, although they were all empty, and a counter. A window seat was built into a nook in the far corner. One wall had a row of cupboards, which were all locked. Dan turned toward them. "Nathan and I chose not to break into these, but considering the current circumstances I'm going to attempt to pick the lock. Mr. Marner gave me permission to do so."

He took a tool from his belt and bent down, wiggling it into the keyhole on the cupboard. After a couple of minutes the lock released, and he slid open the door. He knelt down and pulled out a souvenir snow globe. "The cupboard's full of them," he said. "And it's definitely not the collection you're looking for."

"Anything else in there?" Elaine called out.

He shook his head and walked over to the doorway with one of the snow globes and handed it to Elaine. She looked at it as he searched the rest of the building.

It was made out of cheap plastic with a skating rink inside with "lights" over the top, which were blobs of plastic painted yellow and strung on black strings. Several pine trees were positioned around the rink. *World's Largest Snow Globe* was printed on the base of the souvenir.

Elaine handed it to Sasha, who shook it. As the snow-like flakes fell, Elaine clasped her hands together. No matter how cheap the snow globe was, it was still enchanting.

"Nothing here except the snow globes," Dan said as he took the souvenir and returned it to the cupboard. "I'll check the garage again next."

There was no one in there either, and nothing new. Next, he went through the cottages one by one, finding nothing. As they walked to the last one, the sun was beginning to set but Elaine could see well enough. The back of the building, under the snow, seemed to have an odd shape to it. Perhaps a wood-shed or something covered with snow. Or maybe just a hill. The snow was rounded over the top of whatever was there.

As Dan went into the last cottage, the one past where Timmy had been staying, Elaine trudged through the snow toward the back, sinking down with each step.

Sasha yelled, "Mom, what are you doing?"

"Just curious," Elaine called back. She thought through what she remembered of the cottage Timmy had been stay-ing in. There was a door at the very back, which Elaine had assumed was a closet.

The farther she went, the deeper the soft snow became and she was soon falling through up to her thighs.

She trudged back around to the front door again, where both she and Sasha peered inside.

"Did you open that door before?" Elaine asked, pointing.

"It's just a closet," Dan said, but he opened it anyway and looked inside.

"Is there another door?" Elaine asked.

He shook his head.

"Do you mind looking closer?"

He pulled out his flashlight and turned it on. He waved it around and then said, "There's a panel." He put his flashlight back on his belt and then fiddled with something. After a minute, he pulled a piece of wood away from the back wall of the closet.

He pulled his flashlight out and waved it around again. "Hey," he said. "There's some kind of room back here."

Elaine stepped into the cottage with Sasha right behind her.

"Wait," the trooper called out. "I need to make sure it's safe first."

They froze in the living room.

After a pause he said, "There's a bottle of bleach and drain cleaner. Go back outside. I'm coming out."

They waited for him next to the nearest cottage, the one Timmy had been staying in.

When Dan came out he had his phone to his ear and was speaking into it. "That's right. The old Snow Globe property. I took another look and found a few interesting items in the back room of a cottage. The same ingredients that were used to create the recent explosion on the property."

He ended the call and met Elaine's eye. "You probably heard…"

"Yes." She swallowed hard. Someone had stored the ingredients on the property. Perhaps they planned to set another explosion.

"That's not all I found," the trooper said, "although I'm waiting to investigate more once the chemicals are removed from the building—and once we know the place isn't rigged." He paused as if searching for the right words.

"Go on," Sasha said, her voice a little high.

"There are cabinets in the room. Rows of them."

"As if for a collection?" Elaine asked.

"Perhaps."

Sasha stepped forward. "What's in them?"

"Nothing," Dan answered. "They were all completely empty."

Elaine gasped. "Empty?"

He nodded.

Elaine sputtered. "But there was something in them? Before?"

"I can't be certain, but it seems most likely." He shrugged. "I doubt if they were custom made for nothing."

Elaine's heart dropped. *The snow globes.* How long had it been since they'd been taken? And who in the world took them? And to where?

CHAPTER THIRTEEN

As Jan neared Waterville, she mulled over what Elaine had told her about the hidden room they'd found the day before. Once the chemicals had been removed, Dan had allowed Elaine and Sasha into the area. Elaine said the cabinets were all climate-controlled and had been alarmed. If they had, in fact, housed the snow globe collection, which seemed very probable, whoever took them either knew how to disarm the system or else knew the password.

She slowed as she entered the city limits. Mr. Whitworth lived in an adult care home not far from downtown.

It didn't take her long to find the old ranch-style house with a ramp up to the front door with heaps of snow piled on either side of it. She parked out front and then walked through the tunnel up to the front door. A middle-aged woman, who wore slacks and a heavy sweater with her hair pinned in a bun, answered. Jan introduced herself and told the woman that she'd spoken to Randall Whitworth the day before and he'd agreed to see her.

The woman smiled. "I'm Amanda. And, yes, Randall is expecting you. Come on in." She led the way through the foyer and into a living room. "He's back in the family room. We've been getting ready for you all morning."

"Really?"

The woman smiled. "You'll see."

Jan did see—as soon as she entered the family room. An elderly man sat at a large table with boxes of photos around him, all labeled. He had gray hair, sagging cheeks, and a big smile.

"Mr. Whitworth?"

He pushed up against his walker and stood. "Call me Randall. You must be Jan."

She nodded as she shook his hand. "I'm so pleased to meet you. Thank you for being willing to talk with me."

"I'm glad you came." He smiled again. "There's nothing I like better than talking about history."

Amanda took Jan's coat and then left the room.

"You're interested in photos of the World's Largest Snow Globe, right?"

Jan nodded.

"That's what I thought. I pulled—well, Amanda did—those photos out. That's pretty much all I brought with me when I moved here, all my boxes of photos. I have bookcases in my room filled with them..." His voice trailed off, and he sat back down. He motioned to the chair next to him. "Have a seat."

Jan sat down.

"I have everything arranged, chronologically."

The photos matched the story that Marshall Taylor had told the week before in the tearoom. How Berl built the rink for Nanette, and then created the Snow Globe to attract more visitors. He loved building around the place. Renovating the garage. Converting the store into a gift shop. Renovating each of the cottages so that they were winterized and people skiing or wanting to skate for several days at a time could rent them. Adding the little chapel.

Randall had photos of Berl with a hammer in his hand. Nanette skating on the rink, wearing a fur hat. The gift shop. There were photos of Ilene as a little girl on the ice. And then photos of scores of people skating. All were black-and-white.

Randall scooted the next stack, also black-and-white, over to Jan. The top one was of the World's Largest Snow Globe. "It really was remarkable," Randall said. "First the concept. Who hasn't imagined themselves inside a snow globe with all of that magical snow sifting down?"

Jan agreed.

"I don't know how he ever fathomed he could do it or how he came up with the design."

Jan picked up the stack and started going through the photos. They were all black-and-white too. "Do you mind if I snap some pictures of the photos with my phone?" she asked.

"Go ahead," he answered. Then he said, "I used to do all sorts of photography for Berl. Real estate photos to start with." Randall leaned forward so he could see the photos Jan was leafing through, which was a series of Berl, Nanette, and Ilene in front of the gift shop. "Family photos. The roadside attraction photos. Over the years, Berl and I became friends and he confided in me."

Jan put down the stack and picked up another. "How about his snow globe collection? Did you ever photograph it?"

"You know about the collection?"

Jan nodded. "There's a local collector who saw it several years ago. In the ballroom of a hotel in Portland." She wouldn't add that it was mentioned in the will. Or that it was missing.

Randall reached for one of the boxes. "Yes, I was at that showing. It's the last time I saw Berl—he invited me because of all the work I'd done for him over the years. He used some of the photos I'd taken, copies of these." Randall smiled as he held the box in his hand. "Berl had a remarkable collection. He first saw snow globes in Vienna after World War II had ended, when he was part of the Allied Occupation Forces."

"Fascinating," Jan said. She knew the story, but Randall seemed so happy to be telling it that Jan didn't say anything.

"For forty years the Austrian company only put churches in the snow globes." He took the lid off the box and pulled out the top photo, handing it to Jan.

It was of a snow globe with a quaint European church with a double steeple, just like the little chapel Berl had built, with evergreen trees on either side of it.

"That's the one that started his collection. He brought it home with him," Randall said. "Nanette was enchanted with the snow globe and so he bought one for her as a wedding gift." He pulled the next photo from the box. It was of a couple ice-skating on a frozen pond, surrounded on three sides by trees. The woman wore a long coat and a red scarf that trailed behind her. The man wore a black top hat. It was absolutely enthralling.

"That's how the collection started and in just a few years, it inspired Berl to build the World's Largest Snow Globe roadside attraction. Soon the place drew more visitors in the winter than it did in the summer."

Randall took more photos from the box and spread them across the table. "Once he built the gift shop, Berl and Nanette displayed their snow globes on the top shelves, with a sign that said Not For Sale. Then they began carrying snow globes to sell, the cheap souvenirs. But they continued to add to their collection, even traveling together to Vienna to buy more."

The photos on the table were of a variety of snow globes. Scenes with villages, more churches, snowmen, Santa Clauses, a ballerina, children sledding in the snow, a Victorian house that reminded Jan of the tearoom, a cathedral.

Then a photo of the souvenir snow globe Mr. Newton used to sell in his gift shop, just like what Elaine had described that Dan found in the old gift shop.

"Berl continued to buy snow globes when he traveled, which included a couple of more trips to Europe and also New York and Boston too. He'd branched into building, developing new supplies and experimenting with different types of structures. He was hired as a consultant by several firms, which led to more trips. He brought more and more home and soon it was obvious he couldn't keep them in the gift shop." The man stopped.

"So where did he store them?"

The man shrugged. "I don't know. He'd have me come photograph each new one at his house. But I didn't see the collection displayed there. Sure, there would be one or two here and there. A couple on the mantel in the living room, for example. I assumed the collection was stored somewhere in the house but didn't know for sure."

"Where was their house?"

"Up past the church. It burned years ago, after Berl sold the property."

"Oh goodness," Jan said. "That's too bad."

Randall nodded. "It was such a loss to our community when he moved, but after Nanette died, it pained him to stay in Lancaster. Their house. The roadside attraction. All of it reminded him of her." He began collecting the photos of the snow globes. "But, honestly, he'd outgrown Lancaster. He had contacts with a couple of different builders in Tampa. It offered opportunities for him not available here, in both real estate and in building."

"What do you know about his daughter? And her son?"

"Ilene and Miles?"

Jan nodded.

"I knew Ilene from the time she was a baby. The last time I saw her was the last time I saw Berl. In Portland, at the hotel you mentioned. I asked her about Miles and she simply said he was fine. She didn't offer any details." Randall shrugged. "From what I understand, Ilene divorced her husband and moved to Florida, to join her dad." He opened another box. "I know at one time Berl was over the moon about his grandson, although it seems later there was quite a bit of conflict in the family."

He pulled out a photo from the box. "When Miles was a child, Berl had this snow globe custom made. It was right before he moved to Florida."

Randall slid the photo over to Jan. The interior of the snow globe was the World's Largest Snow Globe roadside attraction, including the rink with a woman skating on it, the little church, the gift shop, and a couple of the cottages. Out in front was the figure of a little boy.

"Is that Miles?" Jan asked.

Randall nodded. "Yes. It's probably the most valuable of all the snow globes. Berl had it custom made in Vienna."

Jan felt sick to her stomach, thinking that the family had, at one point, been cohesive and loving and happy. How sad that things had fallen apart.

Randall took the rest of the photos out of the box. "I have photos here of townspeople skating at the Snow Globe. Would you like to look?"

"I'd love to." Jan took the stack, eager to relive some fun memories instead of dwelling on the pain of the Newton family.

She shuffled through the stack, looking at photo after photo of children, teenagers, and parents enjoying themselves. She recognized a few of the people. Classmates from elementary school. The older siblings of neighborhood kids. A few people, who were adults at the time, whom she remembered from childhood. As she neared the end of the stack, she flipped to a photo of two girls.

She laughed. "That's me. And my cousin Elaine." She turned toward him. "This is absolutely precious."

Randall grinned. "Would you like to have it?"

She held the photo to her chest. "Are you sure?"

He nodded as she flipped to the next photo. Her free hand flew to her chest. "May I have this one too?"

CHAPTER FOURTEEN

Just as the tearoom closed for the day on Thursday, both Sasha and Tara stopped by on their way to Augusta.

"I was going to have dinner with Grandma," Sasha said. "And she suggested I bring Tara with me."

"That's wonderful," Elaine said as she balanced a tray of dishes.

"I was hoping Mom had some extra treats we could take with us." Tara tugged on her beaded earring. "I'd planned to get something made last night but ran out of time."

Elaine laughed. "I'm sure she does." As she followed the girls into the kitchen, she thought of all the years she and Jan had together growing up. But then as adults they'd hardly seen each other for years. It was the opposite for Sasha and Tara. She hoped they'd have a long and beautiful friendship as they shared their grown-up years.

A few minutes later, Tara and Sasha left, taking a tray of cream puffs with them. Once Elaine and Jan had finished cleaning up, Jan left to meet Bob over at their new house to inspect the contractor's work. They were nearly done and wanted to sign off soon.

It wasn't long until Nathan stopped by too, saying he had e-mails to catch up on but hoped he could hang out with Elaine while he worked. As he set up his laptop in the sitting room, Elaine brewed a pot of tea. Then she grabbed a few files to go through before snatching the tea, a plate of scones, and some cups and joining Nathan.

It was less than a week before the Valentine's Day Gala, and Elaine checked through the list of tickets that had been sold. Pastor Mike and Sarah weren't on the list and neither was Macy.

Elaine hadn't decided on a photo of her and Nathan yet to add to the many that had been collected. Secretly, she hoped he'd submit one but she knew he probably wouldn't. And she wouldn't hold it against him. He had a lot to keep track of at the moment.

Macy hadn't submitted a photo either. She and Jan had tried to be inclusive, but perhaps they hadn't tried hard enough.

Elaine filled each of their teacups with English afternoon tea and pushed the plate of scones closer to Nathan. "Have another one," she said.

He patted his belly. "I'd better not."

She had a pot of soup on the stove for dinner, but they didn't plan to eat until later, when Jan and Bob could join them.

As Elaine stood to go brew another pot of tea, Nathan's cell phone rang. She figured it was a work call and continued on down to the kitchen. When she returned, Nathan was just ending the call.

"That was the lawyer," Nathan said. "He said that the appeal to contest the will has been denied."

Elaine sat down, wondering if that meant there would be more trouble out at the Snow Globe. Or less.

"And he gave me some inside information."

"Oh?"

Nathan nodded. "It was Miles Osborne who contested it." His face was as serious as Elaine had ever seen it.

Elaine leaned back in her chair. "Does Mr. Marner have any idea where he is?"

Nathan shook his head. "I asked him if there was a way I could talk to Miles. I really feel I should, but Mr. Marner doesn't have any information about him. I'm surprised, frankly, that Miles didn't contact the firm handling his grandfather's estate directly."

"I can see why he wouldn't. He's gone on the lam with his son. He doesn't want to be found."

Nathan sighed and held up a slip of paper. "Mr. Marner did give me the name of an appraiser—a Cal Knoll—who knows the value and the location of the snow globe collection, plus Mr. Marner said there were a few pieces down in Florida. He'll go ahead and have those boxed up and ship them to me. He expects everything to be settled in a couple of days."

"What did he say about the empty cabinets in the cottage out on the property?"

Nathan ran his hand through his hair. "That it sounds like we have a real mystery on our hands." He smiled. "He said he wished he could help us, but that there's nothing more he can do."

Elaine nodded. At least the legal details of his inheritance would soon be resolved. And surely they'd find the collection at some point. "Any idea what you'll do with the property?"

Nathan shook his head. "I haven't really thought about it, to be honest. I figured whoever was contesting it had more of a right to it than I did..."

"But now that we know it was Miles, why would he just want the property and the collection? And not all of the money?"

Nathan grimaced. "That might be the true mystery."

"And one we'll never solve." Elaine sat back down. "Does knowing that change your thinking in any way about him being a suspect as far as the explosion? Do you think it's likely that he was or might still be on the property?"

Nathan shrugged. "I have no idea," he said. "I know you're worried about the little boy, and I don't blame you, but we really have no evidence that Miles Osborne has been anywhere near Lancaster, let alone on the old Snow Globe property."

Elaine shivered. Hopefully they'd know the truth sooner rather than later.

"I'd better call the appraiser, Mr. Knoll." Nathan held up the piece of paper again. "Before business hours are over."

As Nathan dialed the number and then put the call on speaker, Elaine turned her attention back toward the list of tickets that had been sold for the Valentine's Day Gala as the phone rang. They had thirty-eight coming so far. Nineteen couples. She knew Macy wasn't on the list, but she hoped perhaps another single person was. And she still hoped Macy might be.

Just as Elaine expected Nathan's call to go to voice mail, someone answered with, "Hello. Knoll's Appraisals. How may I help you?"

Nathan explained who he was and that an attorney from Florida, Andrew Marner, had given him Cal Knoll's name and number.

"Hello, Mr. Culver, I've been expecting your call."

"Great!" Nathan responded. "Mr. Marner said that you'd be able to tell me where the snow globe collection is and together we could assess whether it's in a safe place or if it should be transported to my warehouse."

"The containers are safe, but I'm not so sure about the building. How about if I meet you out there tomorrow."

"Where is there?" Nathan asked.

"The Newton property."

"The old roadside attraction?"

"Yes," the man answered.

"What building are they in?" Nathan gave Elaine a concerned look.

She frowned.

"The last cottage before the side road," the man said. "I met Berl Newton there several years ago. He'd built a hidden room in the slope of a hill off the back of the cottage years and years ago. The cabinets were fireproof and alarmed."

"They *were* alarmed," Nathan said.

"No, they *are*," the man replied. "It's quite a clever system. You'll be impressed when you see it."

"I'm afraid there's been a change in the location of the collection," Nathan said. "The cabinets are empty, as of two days ago."

BY THE TIME Elaine and Nathan met Mr. Knoll, along with Dan, out at the Snow Globe property, it was past nine o'clock. Dan turned his flashlight on and by the beam she could see that Mr. Knoll was probably in his sixties. He wore a stocking cap and a ski jacket. He'd insisted on coming all the way from Portland, convinced that there had been a mix-up. He couldn't fathom that Berl Newton's collection had been stolen, and was sure some sort of mistake had been made.

They all trudged to the last cottage and then the trooper unlocked the door and shone his flashlight, all the way to the back closet.

"Yes, this is it," Cal Knoll said. "The room is built into the side of the hill."

The trooper opened the closet door and then removed the panel. He stepped through first, followed by Cal, Elaine, and then Nathan.

Cal whistled. "Yep, this is where they were. Any idea how long they've been gone?"

Dan shook his head. "I've checked with the security company. Someone deactivated the system a few days before the explosion."

Cal stepped up to one of the cabinets. "He designed these and then had them custom made years ago. I think he felt as if he was getting away with a big deception. That no one would be so foolish as to guess he'd store it in such an obvious place."

Elaine crossed her arms as if she could protect herself from the loss. Oh, how she'd been looking forward to seeing the collection, especially after Jan had shown her the pictures on her phone of the photos Randall Whitworth had taken of it. She truly did long to see the snow globes herself, including the one of Miles on the grounds of the Snow Globe Village as a child.

"Well, it's just unbelievable," Cal said, looking around the room again. "I'm guessing it was someone who knew the collection was here."

"Do you think he ever moved the collection down to Florida?" Elaine asked. Perhaps someone down there had taken it.

"Oh, no," he answered. "I'm sure he didn't."

Elaine stepped out of the shadow into more of the light from the trooper's flashlight. "So perhaps they've been here since the early 1970s?"

"I can't imagine that either," Cal said. "But perhaps. He was eccentric. And very proud of this property and what he'd made here." He shrugged. "I guess it's not unheard of that he might keep a valuable collection here for all of this time."

"Maybe he didn't rent this cottage out," Elaine said.

Cal shrugged. "Perhaps, but I don't have any idea. I met him here several years ago. At that time I don't think any of these cottages were being rented out."

Elaine couldn't help but think of Vincent Osborne. His marriage to Ilene was breaking up around the time Berl

Newton moved to Florida. Would the man have had knowledge about where the collection was housed?

"It definitely looks as if there's been a burglary," Dan said. "I already made a report and alerted Mr. Marner, since he's the executor of the will."

Nathan nodded.

Elaine was pretty sure he rued the day that he read the letter from Mr. Marner telling him Berl Newton had left his property and snow globe collection to him. Now he was the benefactor of a crime.

AFTER CHURCH ON Sunday, Jan asked Elaine if she'd present the complimentary tickets to the Valentine's Day Gala to Pastor Mike and Sarah with her. "After everyone else has left," she said. "With Bristol's help, we've raised enough money for the weekend away. Bristol is taking care of the gift certificate for it. And if you give the tickets to Pastor Mike instead of Sarah, he will probably accept them."

Nathan was talking to Bob at the back of the church and didn't seem to be in a hurry.

Elaine said she would and then asked Jan what plans they had for the day. "We're heading over to Augusta to watch the twins so Amy and Van can go out for the afternoon."

"Oh, that's so nice," Elaine said.

"Hopefully they go to a movie so Amy can get a nap." She laughed.

Elaine remembered those days when she was pregnant with Sasha and trying to keep up with Jared.

As the crowd thinned out, Jan and Elaine got in line to greet Pastor Mike and Sarah. Elaine had the tickets in her hand and once everyone else had passed by, except for Bob and Nathan, they approached the couple.

Elaine extended the tickets to Pastor Mike. "We know you two are busy, but we are cordially inviting you and Sarah to our Valentine's Day Gala as our guests," she said.

"Meaning, it's complimentary," Jan added.

Sarah glanced at Pastor Mike and took the tickets. "How kind of the two of you." She genuinely sounded grateful.

"Is it actually on Valentine's Day?" Pastor Mike asked.

Jan nodded. "Starting at 5 p.m. For high tea."

"Did we have anything planned?" Mike asked Sarah.

She appeared a little hurt but said in a sweet voice, "Not that I know of."

"Nothing with the kids?"

She shook her head.

"Okay." Pastor Mike smiled at Jan and Elaine and then said, "May we let you know?"

Elaine and Jan said, "Of course" in unison and then laughed.

"And no worries if you have something else planned," Elaine said.

"But we'd love to have you join us," Jan added.

Sarah sighed. "We can tell you now—"

Elaine braced herself, fearing the answer. Was something going on?

"We don't have anything else planned," Sarah said. "Unless there's an emergency, we'll be there."

"Great!" Elaine beamed at the two of them, but after she told them goodbye and then went and found Nathan, she couldn't help but wonder what the conflict was with the couple. Even though they'd both been gracious, it was obvious there was tension between the two.

Hopefully the tea wouldn't be one more stressful obligation in their busy lives.

As she and Nathan walked to his Cadillac, Elaine hoped the weekend away for the Ryders would make up for any inconvenience.

"How about sandwiches for lunch?" Elaine asked as they drove to the tearoom.

Nathan patted his belly and grinned over at her on the passenger side. "Sounds good to me."

It would be nice to have the house to themselves for a relaxing Sunday afternoon. That didn't happen very often.

A couple of minutes later, as Nathan pulled up to the tearoom, Elaine pointed to a Range Rover parked out front with Ontario plates. Her heart raced as a man who looked to be in his sixties climbed out of it. A woman in the passenger seat stayed in the car. The man wore a trench coat and an ivy cap.

"May I help you?" Elaine called out.

"I'm Kyle Franklin. I'm looking for Elaine Cook."

Had they driven all the way down from Ontario just to see her? It was an all-day drive, twelve hours or so. "I'm Elaine," she answered, squinting to see if she recognized him from the profile photo on his wife's Facebook page.

As he stepped toward her, she could see he had a pink stocking cap in one hand and a photograph in the other. "We were just out at the Newton property and found this." He held up the cap.

Nathan climbed out of his car, and he and Elaine walked toward the man. Nathan introduced himself and they all shook hands, and then Kyle showed them the photo. It was of a clean-cut man, around forty, and a child with blond hair.

"That must be Miles and Aiden," Elaine said.

The man nodded.

She pointed toward the stocking cap. "Where did you find it?"

"In front of one of those run-down buildings."

"Which one?"

He shrugged. "The bigger one."

"The garage? Or the gift shop?"

"Aren't they all abandoned?"

"They are now, yes. But the explosion was in the garage a few weeks ago. I just wondered if perhaps the hat had been there since then. It snowed a lot the day after and perhaps now, with the melting, it was uncovered."

"I wouldn't know." The man appeared stressed. "All I know is we found a child's cap out there and we're looking for our grandchild."

"Well," Elaine said, "we searched through all of the buildings, just last week. For the second time." She turned toward Nathan.

"That's right. And Trooper Dan Benson has searched the property thoroughly."

"We'd like to take a look," Kyle said. "To see if there's any hint of Aiden beyond this photograph. We need to see the insides of the buildings ourselves."

"Of course you do," Elaine said, turning toward Nathan. "Would it work for us to go out there now?"

Nathan nodded. He now had the keys to the place because Dan had turned them over once he had the go-ahead from Mr. Marner.

"Great." Kyle took a step backward. "We'll meet you there."

By the time Elaine was settled back in Nathan's car, Kyle Franklin had taken off, the gravel from the edge of the road flying out from under his wheels.

Elaine buckled her seat belt, wondering about Beth Franklin not getting out of the car. Nevertheless, she'd have a chance to meet her soon enough.

When Elaine and Nathan reached the property, the Franklins had already parked in front of the gift shop. There was a second vehicle, a white Suburban with a Massachusetts license plate, parked beside the Range Rover. Kyle Franklin was standing beside a man, talking. Beth Franklin was still in the Range Rover.

Nathan joined the men, but Elaine went around to the passenger side of the Franklins' vehicle. A woman with silvery hair, cut in a perfect bob, turned her face toward Elaine. She stared for a moment and then opened the door.

"I'm Elaine Cook."

The woman nodded. "Beth Franklin."

"Pleased to meet you," Elaine said. "Although I'm so sorry about the circumstances, especially about your daughter." Elaine paused for a moment. "And your grandson's disappearance."

"Thank you," the woman said. "It's all been an ordeal, as you can imagine."

Elaine teared up as she met the woman's gaze. Elaine knew what grief was, and she knew what it was like to have had a loved one go missing. Thankfully Avery had been found. She nodded toward the buildings. "Will you be joining us?"

The woman said she would. "I was just waiting until the last possible moment to step into the cold."

The men had started toward the gift shop so it seemed as if it was time. Beth scooted out of the vehicle.

"Who's the man with your husband?" Elaine asked.

"A private detective we hired after Miles and Aiden disappeared. His name is Leonard Scott. He's from Boston."

"Oh." Elaine tried to hide the surprise in her voice, but it made sense that they'd hired someone. She would have done the same thing. "Has he discovered anything?"

The woman pursed her lips. "I can't say... Not yet, anyway."

The women started walking toward the three men. "Our daughter and then Aiden were all we had. I know she would have wanted us to raise him. We're still in disbelief."

The men had stopped at the door of the gift shop while Nathan unlocked it.

Beth pointed toward her husband. "Look at how his shoulders are stooping. He's aged so much in the last several months."

Elaine wanted to give the woman a hug, but that seemed too forward.

Nathan had the door open and the men entered.

Elaine explained that the building used to be a gift shop as they stepped inside. Nothing had changed inside. Or in the garage.

Nathan headed toward the little church and Elaine quickened her step. She hadn't been able to look inside of it yet and was excited to do so. Nathan unlocked the door and, after looking inside, held it open for her. She stepped over the threshold. It had six small pews, three on each side. An altar, a pulpit, and seven stained-glass windows—three on each side and one straight ahead. They were all scenes from the Bible. Jesus as a baby in Mary's arms. Jesus as a boy at the temple. Jesus as a carpenter. Jesus with a lamb. Jesus on the cross. And Jesus ascending to glory. Obviously, Berl Newton was a man of faith.

"Anyone in there?" Kyle called out.

"No. It's all clear," Nathan answered.

"We'll wait out here then." Kyle's voice had decreased in volume as if he'd already walked beyond the chapel.

Elaine stepped out and said, "What a lovely building."

Nathan nodded. "I think it's my favorite on the property."

They didn't find anyone in the cottages as they trudged through them, one by one, either. The private investigator had lots of questions. Nathan told him about Timmy Calkin squatting in one of the cottages, emphasizing that he was the only person found to be on the property.

The investigator asked about the owner of the property down the lane, and Nathan told him about Adam Slater too.

When they reached the last cottage, Elaine thought about the snow globe collection, but she didn't mention it to Beth. She didn't want to complicate the situation. The collection had nothing to do with the Franklins.

Nathan unlocked the door and then led the way inside. There was no "ladies first" when they were looking for something nefarious.

A noise caught Elaine's attention, but at first she just thought it was one of the men. But then Nathan said, "It's coming from the back room."

He hurried toward the closet.

"Be careful!" Elaine called out, wishing they'd called Dan to accompany them. She hurried around Beth, wanting to be by Nathan's side.

By the time she reached the closet, he had the panel off and was stepping into the hidden room, followed by the private investigator.

"What are you doing?" Nathan's voice demanded from inside.

"Is it Miles?" Kyle yelled.

The investigator answered. "It doesn't appear to be . . ."

Elaine followed Kyle through and then froze as Beth stepped to her side. The investigator had his gun pointed at a man, who definitely wasn't Miles.

Jerry Kemp, the snow globe collector, stood facing all of them, his arms held high.

CHAPTER FIFTEEN

The first thing Jerry Kemp said was, "The gun isn't necessary, I can assure you." Elaine almost believed him. Almost. Except that he'd deceived her.

"Jerry." She stepped forward. "You said—"

"Wait." Nathan put his arm out to stop her. "You know this guy?"

"Yes. It's Jerry Kemp, the collector from Portland you told me about. He's the one who wanted to buy the snow globe collection."

"Snow globes?" Beth's voice trembled. "Miles loved snow globes."

Nathan pulled out his phone.

"Whoa," Jerry said to Nathan. "What are you doing?"

"Calling the state police."

"There's no need for that," the man said. "I can explain."

"You told me you had no idea where the collection was stored," Elaine said. "Yet here you are."

"And obviously I didn't take the collection," Jerry retorted. "Because why would I come back to an empty room?"

Elaine put her hand on her hip. "Maybe you're covering your tracks?"

"It doesn't matter why you're here," Nathan said. "You're trespassing." And then he said, "Hello? Dan, can you come out to the old Snow Globe property? We have a trespasser, who may have information on a burglary."

"What is he talking about?" Beth asked.

Elaine just shook her head and said, "Long story."

Once Nathan ended the call, he turned to Kyle and said, "Would you please take the ladies outside? And then direct the trooper to this cottage."

Kyle nodded and Elaine led the way back to the cottage and then out the front door. Once they reached the outside, she told the Franklins about Berl Newton's snow globe collection, their search for it, the hidden room, and then the empty cabinets.

"Why would he store an expensive collection in a hillside?" Kyle asked.

"Well, it seems he wanted to keep it in Maine. And people have said he was rather eccentric, so perhaps he liked it being in an odd place, where he figured no one would ever expect to find it." Although Jerry Kemp had figured it out.

They stood in the cold until the trooper arrived. They were glad to see that it was Dan. Before Elaine could introduce him, Kyle stepped forward, his hand extended. "Good to see you again, Trooper Benson."

Puzzled, Elaine asked, "You've all met?"

"We stopped by the state police office in Augusta yesterday," Kyle explained.

Dan nodded in agreement and said, "It's good to see you two again," as he shook Kyle's hand. Then he greeted Elaine too.

Elaine quickly explained that Nathan and a private investigator, hired by the Franklins, were holding Jerry Kemp in the back room of the cottage.

Dan's eyebrows shot up. "He's a little late to the party, it seems."

Elaine nodded.

"I'll take him in for questioning," the trooper said. "And see what we can find out."

He turned toward the Franklins. "Have any clues turned up?"

Kyle shook his head. "Just the hat. There's no trail of Miles accessing any of his accounts, not since he withdrew cash and left Toronto. Four weeks is a long time to live off that amount."

Dan said, "He's traveled the world, right? He could be anywhere."

"Possibly," Kyle said.

Dan gave the man a sympathetic look and said, "Well, good luck." He headed into the cottage and a few minutes later he returned with Jerry Kemp in handcuffs.

Once they'd left, Elaine asked Kyle and Beth if they'd join them back at the tearoom for sandwiches. They hesitated for a moment, but then Kyle accepted the invitation for both of them. Elaine extended it to the private investigator too, but he said he'd rather roam the property, if that was all right.

Nathan said it was, and Elaine told the Franklins they would meet them back at the tearoom soon.

AN HOUR LATER, as they ate tea sandwiches and salad in front of the fireplace in the east parlor, the Franklins shared more about Brooke's marriage to Miles. She was ten years younger than Miles, and they were shocked when she started dating him.

"We didn't know much about him," Kyle said, "but after doing some research we were even more concerned. He'd led the life of a vagabond—not what we wanted for our daughter and future grandchildren."

Beth folded her hands around her teacup. "After he graduated high school, he traveled the world. Europe. Asia. Africa. South America. And also attended university and like his grandfather, got a degree in engineering, between his travels. Basically he was a bit of a flake. At some point his relationship with both of his parents became strained, although we never could figure out the exact details. He would still see his father from time to time, and he did come to the wedding and to the hospital after Aiden was born, but they're not close."

Elaine gathered that from Vincent Osborne's message.

Kyle took over the narrative for a moment. "Anyway, when Miles met Brooke he was working as a designer for a manufacturing company."

He didn't sound like a flake to Elaine, but perhaps the Franklins weren't disclosing everything about him.

Beth continued, saying that after Aiden was born and Brooke was diagnosed, Miles took a leave of absence from his job to care for both them. "We thought it was a little odd—it seemed a husband should care for his family financially. After she died, Miles seemed to think he was the only one who could take care of Aiden and didn't plan to go back to work anytime soon. We offered to help, but he refused." Beth swiped at her eyes. "Brooke wouldn't have wanted that, not at all. She had no idea how unhinged he was becoming before she died. She'd be sick to know Miles ran with Aiden." She lifted her napkin from her lap and dabbed at her eyes.

Elaine reached over and patted the woman's shoulder. "I'm so sorry."

"We're just praying that we can find Aiden before it's too late. That's why we hired the investigator and why we came down ourselves."

Elaine said that she completely understood.

It turned out the couple had spent the night before at Green Glade and would stay the next several nights there too. "We won't leave," Kyle said. "Until we're absolutely sure Miles and Aiden aren't here."

As Elaine filled everyone's teacup, she asked, "Do you have any other leads where Miles might be?"

"We went through their apartment and found his travel journals. My assistant has been contacting people mentioned in those, but if he's not here, he could be anywhere in the world." Kyle sighed and took the pink hat out of his pocket again.

"If they are somewhere else, I hope it's warm." Beth shivered in her cardigan. "I can't bear the thought of Aiden being out there in the cold."

Elaine nodded. They had to find that little boy. She stared at the hat for a moment. Someone had mentioned a child in pink. Jan!

"I just remembered something." She told them about the receptionist at the newspaper in Penzance mentioning that a man had been in the office to research the Snow Globe and he had a little girl with him, all dressed in pink. "It's the *Penzance Courier* office," she said. "Take the photo of Aiden in tomorrow morning. Cookie is the receptionist's name."

"We will," Kyle answered. Then he said that they planned to go to Portland the next day. "And check at the airport. We couldn't locate Miles's or Aiden's passports in the apartment. Perhaps they came down here for a time and then moved on."

Elaine wondered if perhaps Miles stole the snow globe collection and planned to sell it to finance a trip overseas. But then again, it didn't sound as if he were destitute. Surely he and Brooke had saved some money. "What about his apartment? Did you clean it out?" Elaine regretted asking the question as soon as it tumbled out of her mouth. "I'm sorry," she said. "It's none of my business."

"No. That's fine," Kyle said. "Actually, Miles and Brooke lived in an apartment that belongs to us." He shrugged. "We plan to leave it as it is for now. Of course, once we find Aiden—"

Beth finished his sentence. "—he'll move in with us."

THE NEXT DAY the Franklins stopped by the tearoom on their way to Portland, and Macy accompanied them. Elaine was surprised they hadn't left earlier and asked how they were doing.

"We hardly slept," Beth answered. "We thought a strong cup of tea would help get us going this morning."

Elaine knew Macy offered tea and coffee at Green Glade, but she was thankful the couple stopped in. She seated them in the west parlor and then handed them menus.

"We did go by the newspaper office," Kyle said. "And the receptionist—" He turned toward Beth, but she shrugged.

Elaine provided the name. "Cookie."

"That's right." Kyle took the photo out of the inside pocket of his coat and put it on the table. Miles and Aiden smiled up at all of them. "She thought there was a strong possibility it could be them. The man wore a beard and appeared older. And the child was all dressed in pink with her hair in pigtails. The woman was so convinced it was a little girl..."

"I'm convinced it's Aiden," Beth said. "Who else could it be?"

Elaine agreed. Why would anyone else be researching the Snow Globe?

Seemingly changing the subject, Kyle said, "Macy told us some more about the Newton family. We're hoping for the rest of the story as we eat."

"Definitely." Macy seemed pleased to be able to offer them information they were interested in.

Elaine returned a few minutes later, interrupting Macy in the middle of telling about Ilene's love of ice-skating. Elaine took their orders as the front door sounded. She turned to leave just as Marshall Taylor appeared in the archway to the parlor.

She greeted him with, "Oh, good morning! Come on in!" She quickly introduced him to Macy, saying that he had joined her book club.

"Bristol mentioned you," Macy said. "I'm pleased to meet you."

Then Elaine introduced him to the Franklins, telling Marshall that they were the in-laws of Miles Osborne.

Marshall's eyes grew wide.

Then Elaine quickly explained to the Franklins that Marshall had been a friend of Ilene Newton's from the time they were children until she passed away.

Kyle rose quickly and shook Marshall's hand. "Won't you join us?"

"Oh, I don't want to intrude."

"No, we insist," Beth said.

Elaine was afraid that Macy would feel displaced, but she had a pleasant expression on her face. "Yes," she said. "Please do. We'd all like to hear more about Ilene Newton."

Elaine handed Marshall one of the menus in her hand but he said he had no need for it. He quickly ordered the bacon scone. "I've been craving one since last week," he explained. "Oh, and a pot of English breakfast tea too, please."

When Elaine returned with the tray of teapots and cups, the Franklins were telling their story to Marshall. When she returned again, this time with the scones and pastries, Marshall was telling them about Ilene.

Beth murmured, "She sounds lovely."

Marshall continued talking as Macy watched him intently.

Elaine continued on with her work. Finally, the Franklins asked for the bill. They wanted to pay for the four of them and then be on their way. "I doubt anyone at the airport can help us," Kyle said. "But we thought we'd show Miles and Aiden's photos around and see if anyone remembers them."

"Well, it certainly can't hurt," Elaine responded.

The couple told Macy and Marshall goodbye and then followed Elaine to the cash register. They were soon on their way to Portland.

However, Macy and Marshall stayed for quite a while. Elaine filled both of their teapots as they chatted away. They knew some of the same people and families from back when, even though Marshall was a decade older. One time when Elaine came into the parlor, Macy was actually laughing.

Eventually the two got up to leave and Marshall said he'd pay for their extra pots of tea.

"Refills are on the house," Elaine said.

As they reached the foyer, Marshall said the Valentine's Day Gala looked like fun. "Are you sure single people are welcome too?"

"Absolutely," Elaine said. "Our hope is that everyone will join in the fun."

"And you still have openings?"

She nodded. "May I sign you up?"

Marshall turned toward Macy. "Are you going?"

She nodded. "I plan to, although I haven't formally responded yet."

Elated, Elaine reached for the list on the counter. "I can sell you tickets right now if you'd like."

"Wonderful." Marshall smiled at Macy. "Please give me the honor of paying for yours too."

Macy blushed. "I can get mine."

"Please, I insist." Marshall tipped his head in a genteel manner.

Macy seemed flustered but finally said, "All right." Then she added, in a whisper, "Thank you."

Relieved, Elaine completed the transaction with Marshall and then motioned toward the display of photos. "Remember to bring a picture in. We'd love to add them to the collection."

Macy didn't respond, but Marshall said, "What a wonderful idea. I'll look through my albums."

Marshall held the door for Macy as they left. Elaine stepped to the window and watched as they headed toward Green Glade, chatting away as they walked side by side.

ROSE AND ARCHIE both came in at noon so that Jan and Elaine could concentrate on getting everything ready for Valentine's Day the next day. Sasha, who had the day off from her job as a trainer, came in to help Jan with the baking and truffle making. As they all worked in the kitchen, their conversation fell to the Snow Globe property and Miles and Aiden Osborne.

"I just can't imagine what the Franklins are going through," Elaine said as she washed the Desert Rose set of china for the next day.

"What if Miles *is* on the property?" Sasha asked.

"It's been searched, over and over."

"The back part of the property too?"

"Yes, Dan and the other officers searched it that Saturday, after the explosion"—Elaine plunged her hands back into the dishwater and began washing a platter—"but that was before we knew about the hidden room built into the hillside."

Sasha took a tray of Linzer heart-shaped cookies out of the oven as she asked, "What are you getting at?"

Elaine rinsed the platter as she answered. "Think about the room built into the hillside. They didn't find that on their initial search. What if there's another structure like that?"

Jan rolled more dough. "Maybe someone should check that out."

"Maybe we should, Mom," Sasha said.

Elaine took a deep breath. What if Aiden Osborne was stuck in some odd structure with his father out in the forest?

"We're in good shape to be ready by tomorrow," Jan said. "I'll get Rose to help in here while Archie sees to the tearoom."

"Let's go," Sasha said. "While the sun is still shining."

"Are you sure?" Elaine asked Jan, but she was already drying her hands and ready to go.

CHAPTER SIXTEEN

Elaine followed Sasha as they skied past the gift shop into
the deep snow toward the warming hut and the pond.
Sasha had to break the trail as they went, which was no easy
feat, but she plowed ahead with Elaine struggling to keep up
behind her. They crossed the pond and aimed for the trees on
the edge of the property line. Their plan was to ski back and
forth as far as they could go before the sun set. If they didn't
find anything, they planned to come back on another day.

Soon they reached the trees and turned west. Sasha would break
trail up a hill, and then down, relying on gravity to help make it go
faster. When they reached a gully where the creek flowed through,
they turned around and headed back toward the old highway.

Elaine wondered if they were crazy to think they could find
something on the property. It wasn't quite as bad as a needle
in a haystack, but with so many little hills covered with trees it
could be next to impossible. Unless there was an actual hobbit
door in a hillside. But considering how well Berl Newton had
camouflaged the hidden room, she doubted he would have
designed something so obvious they could easily find it.

As she moved her right arm and left leg forward, she breathed a prayer that if Miles was hiding on the property with Aiden, then they'd find them.

They kept skiing until they could see the road and stopped.

"How are you doing?" Sasha asked Elaine.

"All right." She was getting warm but the sun was lowering and it would soon be freezing again.

"Want to do one more down and back?"

Elaine nodded. But after that they'd have to head back to the tearoom.

The hills seemed steeper on this pass, but Elaine wasn't sure if they actually were. Perhaps she was just running out of energy. Sasha got pretty far ahead of her, reached the end, and turned around, coming back twenty feet away from Elaine. When Elaine saw her coming, she crossed over and met Sasha. Elaine caught her breath and then Sasha started off and, once again, Elaine fell behind.

As she struggled to go faster, she thought she caught a whiff of smoke. She stopped and breathed in deeply. It was definitely smoke, coming from burning pine.

Elaine didn't want to yell for Sasha and scare off whoever lit the fire. She could still see her ahead, traveling up a knoll. Elaine waved frantically but of course Sasha had her back to her and couldn't see her gesturing.

Finally, Sasha reached the top and turned around. Elaine motioned frantically for Sasha to return and then held her finger to her lip in a *shh* motion. Sasha squinted and Elaine realized that the sun was right behind her, making it harder for her daughter to see. She was grateful when Sasha started down the hill anyway.

When she grew close, Elaine whispered, "I smell smoke."

"And I saw smoke from the top of the hill. To the south."

"Let's go see what we can find," Elaine said.

"How about if you text Nathan first? And ask him to call Trooper Benson?"

"Good idea." Elaine speared her pole into the snow and retrieved her phone from the pocket of her coat. Then she took off her glove and texted Nathan with the information, including approximately where they were and the request that he call Dan. After she received a response of *Wow! Okay!*, she stashed her phone, resituated her glove, and grabbed her poles, ready to go. Then Sasha led the way through the trees.

The smell of smoke grew stronger and as they came out of a grove, Elaine could see the smoke too. It was coming from the top of a snow-covered hill. There was no sight of any kind of door, but perhaps it was on the other side. Sasha must have thought the same thing, because she stepped back into the trees and slid along, heading west. Elaine followed.

Sasha then moved to the south, still staying in the trees. Finally she stopped behind one. Elaine stopped too. Sasha pointed to the hill. Snow was piled high in front of it, but behind the bank they could see the top of a wooden door.

SASHA AND ELAINE stayed put as the sun fell lower and lower behind the trees. Elaine hoped that Dan would arrive soon. Elaine checked her phone. The first text said that Nathan had reached Dan, then that both were on their way.

Then it seemed to take forever for them to arrive. Elaine could barely stand the thought of being so close to Aiden Osborne. She was tempted to text Beth and Kyle, but refrained from doing so.

Finally Elaine said, "Maybe we should knock on the door."

Sasha shook her head and whispered, "They'll be here soon."

Elaine was growing chilled and was tempted to clap her hands together, but she didn't want to make any sound. And she didn't want to let go of her poles in case she needed to take off skiing. Although it wasn't as if Miles wouldn't be able to catch her if he wanted to, even if he had Aiden on his—

She gasped.

"What is it?" Sasha whispered.

"Do you remember Timmy said he'd seen someone with a pack on the property? It was probably Miles with Aiden in a baby backpack."

"Oh, Mom, you might be right." Sasha grimaced. "Can you imagine a baby living out here all this time?"

Elaine shook her head. "Not at all, but we'll soon find out—hopefully." But it would be better if Miles and Aiden were here in the forest rather than far away in Katmandu.

The sun disappeared behind the trees and the woods began to darken. Elaine's toes numbed and her face stung from the cold. She pulled her scarf over her mouth and nose. Just as Elaine was about ready to suggest that they head back to Sasha's car, a beam of light shone through the trees.

Sasha quickly skied toward it as Elaine held her breath, hoping it was Nathan and Dan and not someone else—perhaps Miles Osborne.

Would he be armed? With Aiden on his back?

A few minutes later Sasha returned, with Dan and Nathan right behind her. Both were out of breath. Once the trooper caught his, he asked if they'd seen anyone.

"No," Elaine said. "Just the smoke coming out of the hill."

Nathan sniffed the air. "It hangs down in this little valley. We couldn't smell it up above."

Perhaps Adam Slater couldn't smell it over at his place either.

Nathan turned toward Dan. "Shall we go knock on the door?"

"How about if Sasha and I do?" Elaine whispered.

"No." Nathan's voice was firm.

"Hear me out, please."

Nathan crossed his arms, his poles still in his hands.

"Whoever it is, chances are he won't shoot at us if he's armed. We'll simply say we're lost and see how he reacts. If he matches the photo, I'll lift up my pole. Then you two can step out of the trees, and you"—she met Dan's gaze—"can question him."

"No," Nathan said again.

"Actually," Dan said, glancing first at Elaine and then at Nathan. "It's not a bad idea. I'm the only one with the weapon. If he does—and I'm not saying it's Miles—come out with a gun and I'm at the door, I won't have the advantage. If my uniform alarms whoever opens the door, that wouldn't be good either. Elaine and Sasha won't set off any red flags. Well, besides that they're knocking on a hidden door at dusk in a dark woods, but you know what I mean."

"So we'll stay back here, in the trees?" Nathan didn't sound happy about the idea.

"Yes," Dan said. But then the front door started to move.

"Come on." Elaine tugged on Sasha's sleeve. "Go before anyone comes out too far. I'll follow you."

Sasha led the way with Elaine struggling after her. They reached the snow bank and then went around it. The door was open a crack.

"Hello!" Sasha called out. "Can you help us?"

For a long moment nothing happened. The door stayed partly open but no one stepped out.

"Anyone there?" Elaine called as they slid closer.

Finally it opened. A man with a full beard, wearing a stocking cap and a down coat, stood staring at them. "What are you doing here?"

"We're cross-country skiing." Elaine squinted at the man. Was it Miles? It was hard to tell with the beard.

The man pointed toward the east. "The road is that way."

Sasha nodded.

"Are you hurt?" he asked.

Elaine shook her head, not sure why Sasha had nodded that she knew which way the road was. She'd assumed they would claim they were lost. "We're all turned around," Elaine blurted out. "We've been going back and forth all afternoon." She wasn't lying, not exactly.

A child's voice called out, "Daddy!"

The man turned around. "Hold on a minute. I'll be right there."

Elaine leaned to the side to see inside the structure. By the light from a lantern, she could make out a cozy living place with a couch, a small kitchen, and a woodstove, like the ones in the cottages. A child, wearing a pink down vest, toddled around a corner. "Daddy!"

"Buddy..." The man turned back toward them. "I can lead you to the road if you need—"

The child had on a pink hat and pink jacket but the man called her—or him—*buddy*. It seemed Miles was trying to disguise Aiden, to make people believe the baby was a girl. She focused on the child. Strands of blond hair showed under the hat, and the child had brown eyes, just like in the photo. Elaine was sure it was Aiden and that the man was Miles.

"That would be great if you could help us." Sasha quickly introduced herself and then said, "This is my mother, Elaine."

"Nice to meet you," the man said, but he didn't offer his name.

Instead he turned back to the child. "We're going to go out. Let's go grab your coat and pack."

The child squealed and ran back into the earth-berm home.

Elaine hoped Nathan and Dan could hear what was going on and would follow them. If they confronted Miles closer to the road, with Aiden on his back, it would be better than back here in the woods.

The man followed the child and a few minutes later they both returned with a child pack, dressed for going outside. In no time the man strapped on his snowshoes, grabbed a flashlight, wiggled the child into the pack, and then strapped it on his back.

"Thank you so much," Elaine said as he stepped out and pulled the door shut behind him. She raised her pole, indicating that the man matched the photo. Then she turned to Miles. "We really appreciate your help."

"I'm happy to." He took off up the hill at a fast pace, swinging the flashlight from side to side.

Sasha stayed near him, of course. She asked about the home in the hill.

"It's been in my family a long time," he said.

"Are you living there?" she asked. "Or vacationing?"

Already Elaine couldn't hear his answer, but when she reached the top of the hill and turned around, she could make out Nathan and Dan not far behind her.

The plan was working perfectly. She had to admit that Miles wasn't the ogre she'd expected, but she'd known enough unstable people in her life to understand that a person could present himself, or herself, in the best possible light for a time, especially to strangers.

She continued on, keeping Sasha and the man in her sights as she skied as hard as she could, swishing her arms back and forth. It was completely dark now and the moon was rising over the treetops. It wasn't full, but at three-quarters, it definitely helped.

Every once in a while she could hear Aiden cry out in delight about something. A tree branch swaying in the evening breeze. The hoot of an owl. The twinkling stars.

At one point the child yelled, "Faster, Daddy! Faster!"

Elaine's heart raced. Hopefully the Franklins would have their grandson back soon.

Sasha waited for Elaine a few times, which forced Miles to also. When they neared the road, he stopped and said, "You're a hundred yards from the buildings. Just keep on going and you'll find your car."

They both thanked him as Dan and Nathan came up over a knoll.

The trooper boomed, "Miles Osborne?"

The man spun around. "What's going on?"

"I'm Trooper Benson with the Maine State Police. I need to question you about the explosion in the old garage on this property."

Miles shook his head and a resigned expression settled on his face. "There's not much to tell, eh?"

"But you know about it?"

"I do."

Elaine caught herself before she could gasp.

"You need to know anything you say can be used against you."

"I understand that." He sighed. "I need to talk to an attorney."

"And I need to take you in." As Dan spoke, a vehicle approached and then turned toward them.

"As long as my boy can go with me."

As the vehicle came to a stop it was obvious it was the Range Rover. Kyle hopped out and shouted, "You found them!"

Elaine watched Miles's face to see his reaction, but he wasn't giving away even a hint of emotion. His face was as stoic as could be.

Now Beth was out of the vehicle too. "Aiden!" she called out.

Aiden bounced in the child pack and said, "Look, Daddy! Gigi. And Gramps."

"Yep," Miles said. "I think they've come to visit you."

Aiden waved.

Miles turned toward Dan. "We'll need Aiden's car seat. My Subaru is hidden not too far from here."

"I'm afraid I'll have to call Children's Services to come pick him up," Dan said to Miles. "Or you can let him go with his grandparents."

"No," Miles answered. "It won't take me long to clear all of this up. I need my boy to stay with me."

Kyle was a few feet away now. "We'll take him. We have a car seat with us. Clothes and diapers. A few of his toys."

Miles shook his head.

"Then I'll go ahead and call Children's Services," the trooper said. "And have a social worker meet us at the station."

"And then what?" Miles asked.

"It depends on what happens once we're done questioning you. If we keep you for the night, your child—"

"His name is Aiden," Miles said.

Dan nodded. "Aiden will go stay with a foster family."

Miles shook his head. "No, I don't want that."

"I'd recommend the grandparents," Dan said quietly. "Not that the foster family wouldn't keep him safe, but if you don't want to unsettle him further by placing him with strangers, that's the thing to do."

An expression of pain passed over Miles's face. Finally he said, "Beth and Kyle will be required to stay in Lancaster, right? They can't take him back to Toronto?"

"Yes," Dan said. "Of course."

For the first time, Miles turned toward his in-laws. "I need to know where you're staying. I'll come get him tonight. As soon as I'm done."

Elaine thought for a moment that Kyle was going to protest against that, but then he said, "All right. We're staying at the Green Glade Cottages."

But Beth protested. "At least wait until the morning. We haven't seen him for so long."

"No," Miles said. "I'll come as soon as I clear all of this up, hopefully before he's asleep." Then he turned toward Dan. "Just give me a minute with Aiden." Miles slid the pack off his shoulders and pulled the little boy out, holding him in his arms. "Hey, buddy," he said. "I need to go talk with the nice policeman for a little bit. So you're going to go with Gigi and Gramps, all right? And then I'll come get you."

"No." Aiden stuck out his lower lip. "Go back. You and me. Okay?"

Miles shook his head. "Not right now. But we'll do that later. I'm going to carry you over to Gramps's Range Rover and put you in your car seat, okay? They'll feed you dinner and play with you." Miles shifted Aiden up and then held him with one arm while he picked up the baby pack in the other. Then he started toward the Range Rover. Kyle and Beth began walking alongside them.

"May I leave the baby backpack with you?" Miles asked. "And my snowshoes? I'll need them later."

"Of course," Kyle said.

Elaine was impressed with how amiable everyone seemed to be as she skied back to Sasha's car. Nathan spoke with Dan, but Elaine couldn't hear what he said.

Aiden began to whimper as Miles put the baby pack in the back of the Range Rover.

Elaine watched Miles hold the little boy as he took off each of his snowshoes and put them in the back too. Then he started toward the back seat.

Elaine took her skis off, and then Sasha strapped them and hers on top of her car while Elaine watched Miles tell Aiden goodbye. The boy seemed to be all right until Miles put him in his car seat. Aiden began to cry. Beth ran around and climbed in the other side, so she'd be sitting beside him.

Elaine could no longer see Aiden, but she could hear him scream, over and over, "Daddy! Daddy! Don't leave me!"

Sasha gave Elaine a horrified look, and Elaine felt as if her heart might break. Miles bent down, probably to fasten Aiden into the seat, and then stood back up and closed the door. The screams were now muffled, but Elaine could still hear the boy.

Dan directed Miles toward his SUV. It was obvious Nathan wasn't going with them and would ride with Sasha.

"Let's get going." Sasha climbed in the driver's seat.

Nathan nodded and unstrapped his snowshoes. Once he stashed them in the hatch, he climbed into the backseat. Dan took off first and then Kyle, followed by Sasha.

Elaine wondered if Aiden was still screaming.

"That was awful," Sasha said.

"It doesn't mean Aiden isn't safer with his grandparents though," Elaine said.

"What do you mean? It's obvious Miles is great with him. I hope Trooper Benson lets him go tonight so he can get Aiden back right away."

"Sasha."

"Remember, Mom—innocent until proven guilty."

"But he just confessed," Elaine said.

"Well, we didn't hear his explanation." Sasha was following the Franklins quite closely. "Maybe he had a good reason."

Elaine shook her head. "Didn't the man try to blow Nathan and me up? There's no good reason for *that*."

"You're right." Nathan answered instead of Sasha. "And that was horrible. But he didn't confess to causing the explosion. He said he knew about it, not that he'd caused it. Maybe it was an accident. He deserves to be heard."

CHAPTER SEVENTEEN

The next morning Jan rose early. Once she had a bowl of oatmeal and poured herself a cup of tea, she got right to work to finish up the baking for the Valentine's Day Gala that evening. As she worked, she thought about Elaine's account from the night before.

Miles and Aiden Osborne had been the man and "little girl" in the newspaper office, looking at microfiche about the Snow Globe.

Elaine had been unsettled the previous evening, and so was Sasha. But each one for different reasons. Jan sympathized with the grandparents too, but was surprised that Miles Osborne didn't seem to be the man they'd all expected.

Who knew how it would all work out? Jan said a prayer, asking God to reveal the truth. She wanted Miles Osborne held accountable for what he did, and for the Franklins to be able to see their grandson. That would be justice. But she knew they would have to leave all of it to the Lord, especially the final outcome.

Elaine came down a few minutes later, appearing as if she hadn't slept at all. As her pot of English Breakfast steeped, she stared off into space. Once the tea had steeped, she poured it into a cup with a little bit of milk.

After she took a long swig, Jan laughed and said, "Can you talk now?"

Elaine winced. "I can try."

Jan wiped her hands on her apron. "I've made a list of everything we need to do."

"Great," Elaine said. "Rose will come in at nine and Archie at eleven. Sasha will come in then too. She's on sandwich duty."

Jan nodded. The high tea needed to have a large number of assorted sandwiches—crab and cucumber filling, egg salad, ham and Brie, salmon spread, and pesto chicken—along with other savory items, to fill their guests. Jan would be making ploughman cheese scones—filled with diced apples, bacon, and chutney, along with mini bagels with salmon spread and sausage rolls.

"I'll go ahead and do the tables now," Elaine said.

"Great," Jan answered. "The sooner that's done, the better." She wished she could help. Going through the photographs, valentines, and love letters had been a delight. She couldn't wait to see all of them under the glass. She stopped a moment. Actually, it wouldn't take long to arrange everything under the glass.

"I'd like to help." Jan put the tray of cranberry hazelnut tartlets in the oven, set the timer, and then said, "I have some time. Let's do this."

Jan led the way into the dining room, where all of the photos had been spread out across the big table in groups. All of the glass toppers that had been delivered the day before were waiting by the individual tables in cardboard boxes. Jan had put on the fresh red tablecloths the night before.

She picked up the photos, cards, and letters for table number one in the west parlor while Elaine picked up the stack for table number two.

As she arranged photos for table after table and then placed glass on top of each one, Jan soaked in the stories. She came across Amy and Van's wedding photo and one of them with Max and Riley when the twins were only a week old. What an amazing time that had been! Then photos of her son, Brian, with his wife, Paula, and their daughters, Avery and Kelly, from five years ago. There were photos from Tara of her and Jack too. What a blessing all of her children and grandchildren were! Bob had brought in a photo of him and Jan from the day they became engaged with Jan flashing her ring. She placed her free hand to her heart. She couldn't be any happier.

There were also photos from Dan's family that his wife had dropped off, and photos of Archie and his wife, Gloria, and his sister, Geraldine, and of Rose and Brent and Emma too, along with photos from many townspeople, including Cookie down at the newspaper office, who sent some of her and her new husband, Arne. The list went on and on.

However, there was nothing from Macy, nor from Pastor Mike and Sarah either.

As Jan worked, someone knocked on the front door. Jan quickly went to see who was there.

It was Bristol with a white envelope in one hand and a plastic sleeve in the other with a few photos in it. Bristol held up the sleeve. "Am I too late?"

"No, come on in," Jan said.

"I only have a minute and I know you're busy, but here's the card and gift certificate to the B and B in Portland for Mike and Sarah." She handed that to Jan. "And"—she held up the sleeve again—"here are a couple of photos of Mark and me, plus one with Greg. As I was going through our photos, I came across one of the Ryders on their first day in Lancaster, at the church." Bristol pulled that one from the sleeve and held it up. "Isn't it precious?"

The photo was taken on the steps of the church. Pastor Mike and Sarah looked like kids, and their children were just babies. Asher was maybe six, Leanne a preschooler, and Caleb was around nine months old, tucked in Sarah's arms. All were smiling, even Caleb. The doors to the church, behind them, were wide open and every member of the family looked as if it were the happiest day of their lives, even the baby.

"This is wonderful," Jan said. "Thank you so much. And for the ones of your family."

Bristol smiled. "It was so much fun looking through the old photos."

Jan was thankful she had, and that she'd pulled one of the Ryders too.

After Jan included the photos under the glass at the table in the east parlor where the Ryders and Bristol and Mark would sit, she returned to the west parlor and slipped in the two photos from Randall Whitworth at the table where Nathan and Bob would sit, hoping Elaine wouldn't notice them until the tea had started.

Then she returned to the kitchen to pull the tartlets from the oven.

Just after she had gone out to flip the Open sign, Elaine came into the kitchen and said, "You'll never guess who showed up."

Hope rose in Jan. "Pastor Mike and Sarah?"

"No." Elaine shook her head. "The Franklins."

"With Aiden?"

Elaine nodded.

"Would it be weird if I went out and said hello? I'd love to meet the little guy."

"Oh, I think that would be fine, but let's get the order filled and take it out together. They want a lemon curd scone, a bacon cheddar scone, and the healthiest thing we have for Aiden."

"I have the strawberries for tonight, plus some grapes and canned peaches," Jan said. "I'll serve him a fruit cup. And one of the sausage rolls."

As they worked, Rose came into the kitchen with another order. "I have four tables in the west parlor already. It's a good thing Archie will be in soon."

Jan agreed and quickly assembled the fruit cup. Once they had the order for the Franklins and Aiden filled, Elaine carried the tray with the tea and cups, and Jan carried the food. Just as they stepped into the parlor, Jan heard footsteps on the porch. In no time, the entire place would be full.

Aiden was a lovely child with his blond hair and big brown eyes, but he looked miserable. His eyes were red and his face blotchy, although he was pointing at an old-fashioned valentine under the glass and seemed concerned about the cupid.

"Where's baby's daddy?" Aiden asked, pointing at the cupid.

"The baby is fine," Beth responded. "He's an angel."

"With his mommy?" Aiden asked.

"Yes, that's it." Beth patted his head. "His mommy is close by."

Jan quickly told Beth and Kyle hello and then introduced herself to Aiden. He tucked his chin down and wouldn't make eye contact.

"He's a little shy," Beth explained, "but very happy to be with us." She patted his leg. "Aren't you, Aiden?"

He squinted and shook his head.

Beth sighed. "He really is fine. We had a wonderful evening last night and he went to bed without a whimper."

That was hard to believe, but there was no point in challenging the woman.

Jan told Aiden it was nice to meet him. He ducked his head again. As she turned, she saw Marshall Taylor standing in the archway to the parlor.

"Hello," she said to him. Elaine and the Franklins echoed her greeting.

Marshall waved to all of them. "Did you find the child?"

"Yes." Kyle beamed. "Come meet Aiden."

Marshall shuffled across the room, weaving around the tables. The little boy ducked his head again. Marshall squatted down beside his high chair. "Hello, Aiden," he said. "I'm Marshall Taylor. I went to school with your grandmother, and I knew your daddy when he was a boy."

"Daddy?" Aiden looked toward the foyer. "Daddy!"

"Oh dear," Marshall said. "I'm sorry."

Beth put her arm around Aiden's shoulders. "We're hoping to take him back to Toronto today."

"But you can't," Elaine blurted. "Dan, I mean Trooper Benson—"

Kyle interrupted her. "We talked with him this morning. He's looking into it."

"What's going on with"—she lowered her voice—"Miles?"

"He's been arrested," Beth said. "Right now, just for trespassing, but I'm sure a charge for setting a bomb will also soon be included. It's a very serious offense."

Jan was surprised about that. "Trespassing? Are you sure?"

"It's not his property." Beth seemed to be losing patience.

Jan felt sick to her stomach. She'd never met Miles, but she was beginning to feel sorry for him. However, Nathan was obviously okay with the charge. "Does he have an attorney?" Jan asked.

"Well," Beth said, "he's in all sorts of financial trouble. Apparently he hasn't been able to hire one yet."

No doubt he'd soon be assigned a public defender then.

Kyle reached over and took Beth's hand. "This will all sort out. We told Trooper Benson we'd be here and asked if he could meet us. Hopefully he can."

"I'll let you eat in peace," Marshall said. "Thank you for letting me meet Aiden."

Beth nodded and Kyle said, "Good to see you again."

"How about a table by the fire?" Elaine asked Marshall as Jan started toward the archway.

"Actually," he said, "I just stopped by to drop off some photos." He handed Elaine the envelope. "I hope you can still use these."

Elaine murmured, "Thank you." Jan stopped, hoping to look as Elaine pulled the photos out of the envelope.

"One photo is from Macy. She asked that I bring it with me. Could you put it at the table we'll be sitting at with our book club members?"

"Of course," Elaine answered. She held up a photo of Macy with her son, Shane, and daughter-in-law, Zale.

"Wonderful!" Jan said.

And then Elaine held up a portrait of a middle-aged man and a woman, dressed in formalwear.

"Is that you?" Jan asked Marshall.

He nodded. "And my late wife. On our twentieth anniversary."

"How lovely," Jan responded.

"Thank you." He turned to leave, calling out "See you tonight!" over his shoulder.

Jan took the photos straight to where Marshall and Macy would be seated, while Elaine greeted a group of four people who just came in through the front door. After Jan positioned the photos, she returned to the kitchen.

A few minutes later, Elaine came in with an order. "Dan just arrived," she said.

"And?"

"He told the Franklins if they want to keep Aiden with them until Miles is released, they must stay here."

"What did they say?"

"That their daughter wanted them to have custody."

"Do they have that in writing?" Jan asked. "In a legal document?"

Elaine wrinkled her nose. "Probably not. Don't you think they would have brought that information with them if they did?"

Jan agreed. "When will Miles get out?"

"Dan isn't sure. The prosecuting attorney claims he's a flight risk."

"Has he done more than trespassing and causing the explosion?"

"There have been some break-ins out that way. He's their main suspect."

Jan locked eyes with her cousin. "What do you think? Is the man a thief? And a threat to his child?"

"Well, he was a threat to Nathan and me." Elaine shuddered. "And if he had Aiden on his back when he set and detonated the bomb, then yes, I'd say he could be a threat to Aiden." She shuddered again.

"What is it?"

"I don't know." Elaine was beginning to feel conflicted. "He seemed so eager to help Sasha and me, only to have us trick him. His wife just died and now he's separated from his son. He seems so—"

"Vulnerable?" Jan offered.

"Yes. I mean, the Franklins do seem nice and everything, but they also seem used to getting what they want."

Jan could see that. "But remember, their daughter just died. And Aiden is all they have. I can only imagine how I'd feel if Amy died and Van ran off with the twins."

Elaine nodded. "I thought about that too. But Sasha told me I was 'overidentifying' with the Franklins."

Jan smiled. "That sounds like something my girls would say too." She turned back toward the counter. "I'm going to dip the strawberries in chocolate so I can help Sasha with the sandwiches when she arrives."

Elaine nodded. "And once Archie is here, I'll start pulling all of the serving dishes."

"We can do this," Jan said. "Regardless of the heartache around us, we'll make this the best Valentine's Day yet."

THE HOURS PROGRESSED at a rapid pace as they all worked together to fill the orders for the day and keep up with preparations for the Valentine's Day Gala.

But, just after two o'clock, a delivery woman stepped into the entryway with a dozen red roses. Elaine greeted her on her way into the west parlor.

"I'm looking for Elaine Cook," the woman said.

"That's me." Elaine's heart raced. "You can leave them by the cash register." She thanked the woman and quickly delivered the order and then returned to the roses, placing the tray on the counter.

First she opened the card—an old-fashioned one with a lacy motif. *Dear Elaine,* Nathan had rewritten. *You truly are my valentine. Looking forward to seeing you tonight! And to the years ahead too. Love, Nathan*

She put the card back into the envelope and breathed in the sweet smell of the roses. She held her breath for a long moment and then exhaled. As much as she wished for more of a verbal commitment from Nathan, she had to be content with the card and the roses. They both spoke volumes. She felt the same way about him. For the stage she was in life, he was her valentine too. And *the years ahead*... held the promise she needed to be content until he was ready to propose.

She grabbed the vase and hurried up to her room with the roses.

As soon as three o'clock came around—they were closing an hour early to set up for the tea—Rose switched the sign to Closed while Archie started vacuuming and Elaine began wiping all of the tabletops with glass cleaner.

Sasha finished up the rest of the sandwiches and then started arranging them on the serving platters while Jan arranged the sweets.

"Brody will come as soon as he's off work," Sasha said. "So by four or so. He'll help us get the candles arranged and lit."

"Great!" Jan answered. "Brian and Paula will come early too, along with Tara and Jack. Amy and Van will only come for the tea—their babysitter isn't available until 4:30. And they're bringing your mom."

"Oh, that's great," Elaine answered.

One by one, Jan, Elaine, Rose, and Archie all changed into their Victorian clothes. Jan wore her sapphire gown that matched her eyes, while Elaine wore her emerald-green gown with her lace-up boots. Rose's gown was gold taffeta, embroidered with red flowers, and Archie wore his Victorian cut-away, charcoal herringbone suit with the teal vest.

Once they were all back downstairs, Sasha took a photo of the four in front of the fireplace in the west parlor. As soon as they'd finished posing, Jan said, "Okay, troops, let's get the food served up and get this show on the road."

Brody, dressed in a suit and tie, lit the tea light candles all around the tearoom while Sasha ran upstairs to change out of her workout gear and into her dress. Jack and Tara helped with the candles while Brian and Paula helped load the sandwiches onto serving trays.

JAN TOOK THE dipped strawberries out of the fridge, wondering when Bob would arrive. She knew he had a hearing in Augusta, and she hoped he wouldn't be late.

Four thirty passed and Sasha returned to the kitchen, wearing a long cobalt-blue dress.

"Wow," Jan said. "You look gorgeous." Then she opened up a cupboard and pulled out a manila envelope. "Will you go slide these under the glass of table number four in the east parlor, please? Where Nathan is going to sit." As she handed Sasha the envelope, she said, "Don't peek until you get to the table. And don't let your mom see."

Sasha's eyes lit up. "I'll do my best."

At four forty, while the water heated to begin brewing the special Valentine's blend—black tea with rose petals and a hint of chocolate—Jan toured the tearoom, starting in the entry where the string quartet was warming up. Then she went from the east parlor, to the west parlor, to the dining room. Bathed in candlelight, the entire place had a romantic, Victorian ambiance. The red tablecloths, covered with the photos, valentines, and love letters under glass with a single votive candle in the middle, provided just the right splash of color, while adding to the old-fashioned feel.

Jan stopped in the east parlor and glanced at Bob and Nathan's table. Sasha had slipped the photos under the glass, just as she'd asked. Hopefully Elaine would notice them once Nathan arrived.

She stepped closer to the table. There were two photos that hadn't been there earlier. Old ones, although they were both in color. She squinted and then squealed. "Elaine! Where did you find these?" But as soon as she yelled, she realized she was calling Elaine over to the table with the photos she'd had Sasha plant. She didn't want Elaine to see them yet.

Too late. Elaine stood in the archway, grinning. "Aren't those great! Mom had them."

Jan grinned, glancing down at them. "The photo of your family is great. And the one of us in our matching white ski pants and coats is priceless."

"I know, right?" Elaine laughed. "We sure thought we were something." With that she continued on, back to the kitchen. Whew! Elaine hadn't seen the other photos.

Jan glanced back down at the pictures. They *were* something. Two beautiful girls with their entire lives together. She was so thankful she'd shared those younger years with Elaine— and now the last three years too.

She left the table and stepped into the entry, where Archie was serving as the maitre d'. As the guests arrived, he would escort them to their designated tables.

Jan clasped her hands together. Everything was perfect.

Miles and Aiden Osborne and Beth and Kyle Franklin hadn't entered her thoughts since that morning. But now her mind drifted to them. She shook her head. There was nothing they could do to help any of them now.

Just as she started back to the kitchen, Bob walked through the front door.

"Wow." He grinned. "You look beautiful!" He opened his arms and she fell into them, breathing in the scent of his aftershave mixed with the wool of his coat.

"Happy Valentine's Day," he said, as he released her.

"To you too," she answered.

Bob hung up his coat and then she showed him his table in the east parlor, pointing out all the photos. He was thrilled with them, and Jan noticed other guests poring over the photos at their tables too. She told Bob goodbye and then said, "I'll join you when I can."

"Great!" he beamed. He understood how these events worked, and she was grateful he and Nathan would sit together, along with Virginia. They could all keep one another company during the evening while Jan and Elaine made sure the event ran smoothly.

As she left, she wished she could tell Bob about Miles Osborne and get his opinion, but that would have to wait until later. There were too many people around to tell him about the night before or about the Franklins coming in that morning. But she wanted his legal opinion on what Miles Osborne's rights were as far as his son. And when he thought the man might be released from jail.

CHAPTER EIGHTEEN

Elaine glanced at the clock in the kitchen: 4:55. She feared
Nathan had been delayed.

Sasha helped Jan arrange the hors d'oeuvres trays while
Elaine poured hot water into each of the teapots.

Jan took the trays out to Rose and Archie to pass around.
When she returned, she said, "Nathan's here. At his table. Go
say hello while I finish the tea."

Relieved, Elaine hurried out. When she reached Nathan,
she thanked him for the flowers and the card. He smiled, said,
"You're welcome," and then pointed at the photos under the
glass. She glanced down.

"Have you seen the photo I brought in?" he asked.

She squinted in the dim light. "You brought in a photo?"

He nodded and pointed. It was of the two of them along
the shore of Chickadee Lake, taken the summer before. Their
faces, kissed by the sun, were both beaming.

"We look so happy," Elaine said.

"We are so happy, aren't we?" Nathan asked.

Elaine nodded. She was. And also sometimes confused. But no one ever said love was easy.

Nathan pointed to a black-and-white photo. "Where did this come from?"

"Jan got some pictures from Randall Whitworth. It's probably one of his."

"How interesting." He was leaning over the table now and squinting. "Because this looks an awful lot like you and maybe Jan." He chuckled. "And I swear, this could be you—and me!"

Elaine stepped closer. The first photo *was* of her and Jan skating. And the second one was of her skating, with a boy coming around the curve toward her. She squinted. "Are you sure that's you?"

Nathan began to laugh. "Yes. Isn't that something?" He put his arm around Elaine and drew her close. "I'm guessing these are Jan's surprises."

"I'm thinking that too." Elaine leaned against him, as he pointed out the photos from the Snow Globe that she'd contributed—well, that her mother had.

As Nathan pulled her even closer, Jan stopped in the doorway. "What do you think?" she asked, pointing to Randall Whitworth's photos.

"That you're quite sneaky."

Jan beamed. "Didn't I do good?"

"You did." Nathan laughed again.

Jan tilted her head toward the entryway. "Amy, Van, and your mother are here. And Pastor Mike and Sarah just arrived too."

"Oh good. I'll come say hello."

"And then we'll start serving the tea and food."

"Perfect." Elaine lifted onto her tiptoes and kissed Nathan on the cheek.

He put his arm around her waist and gave her a quick kiss.

Relieved that all seemed well, she followed Jan out into the entryway. First she greeted Van and Amy, who looked darling in an ivory maternity dress with a heart-shaped brooch, and then gave her mother a hug, telling her that Nathan and Bob were expecting her.

Pastor Mike and Sarah were talking with Archie. Sarah wore her hair in a French braid crown, wound around the top of her head, and was dressed in a long pink chiffon gown with a white faux fur jacket. Pastor Mike wore a navy-blue suit with a pink bow tie. Both looked smashing—but also very serious for what was supposed to be a fun evening.

"We have a table for you in the west parlor. The two of you will be sitting with the poetry readers and Bristol and Mark," Elaine said.

Sarah shot Pastor Mike a look and Elaine feared they'd rather sit alone. But the Valentine's Day Gala had too many people attending to offer private tables. "I'll show you," Elaine said. Behind her, Archie greeted Macy coming in the door. Elaine waved to the woman but continued on with Sarah and Mike. Bristol, Mark, and Marshall Taylor were already seated at the table.

Marshall rose and extended his hand to Pastor Mike and then to Sarah. The man was dressed in a tailored suit and expensive shoes and seemed as genteel as ever. Sarah seemed to warm to him as Pastor Mike pulled out her chair. As Elaine stepped back, Archie led Macy to the table. The men stood for her and then Marshall pulled out her chair.

Elaine hesitated for a moment and watched Macy greet everyone at the table. Then she pointed to the photo of her with her son and daughter-in-law under the glass. Pastor Mike and Sarah commented on it and then spotted the photo of their family on the church steps.

"Oh, look at that!" Sarah said. "We were so young."

Pastor Mike gazed at his wife with affection, even though he said, "And so happy." He put his arm around her.

For a moment she leaned against his shoulder and chuckled. "Back then, I never thought I'd say this. But things were less complicated then, weren't they?"

Pastor Mike nodded and pulled her closer.

After they sat down, Marshall pointed to the photo in front of him. "This is my wife and me." His eyes grew a little misty. "This is my first Valentine's Day since she passed away."

All of the people at the table offered their condolences as Elaine headed back to the kitchen, passing Archie and Rose coming out with trays of teapots.

As the music from the quartet played, the four served the rest of the tea and then Pastor Mike stood in the entryway and prayed a blessing on all who were in attendance and thanked the Lord for love, friendship, and community.

Next, Elaine and the rest of the crew delivered the trays of food to each table—platters of tea sandwiches, fruit, sausage rolls, and savory scones. Elaine spoke with their guests as she served them. Sasha and Brody. Amy and Van. Tara and Jack. Brian and Paula. Pastor Mike and Sarah, and everyone at their table.

And finally, Nathan and Bob and Virginia.

It was a privilege to serve each one of them.

Elaine, Jan, Rose, and Archie, replenished the trays of food and pots of tea as everyone visited. Each time Elaine sashayed through the west parlor, it seemed that Pastor Mike and Sarah seemed more relaxed.

Once everyone was done with the savory course, the servers passed around the tiered trays of sweets—including the chocolate strawberries, Linzer cookies, shortbread, tartlets, and truffles, along with more of the special blend of Valentine's Day tea.

While the guests enjoyed their desserts, the poetry readers began their performance, taking turns in the east parlor, the west parlor, and the dining room. Marshall read poetry by John Keats, Bristol read William Wordsworth, and Macy read Elizabeth Barrett Browning. They rotated around, reading several poems at a time.

Everyone seemed to enjoy the poetry and, of course, Jan's delicious creations.

Once the dessert course was winding down, Jan stood in the archway of the west parlor and announced that she had a special gift, on behalf of the community, to present to a very special couple.

"These two people give selflessly to our community," Jan said, "often at the expense of their own relationship and family. They visit the ill, make sure those who need food receive it, listen to our problems, and most importantly, pray for and love all of us, whether we attend their church or not."

Elaine turned her attention toward Pastor Mike and Sarah, who locked eyes with each other for just a moment.

Jan continued. "We have a gift certificate for a weekend away in Portland for Pastor Mike and Sarah. They have an anniversary coming up, their twentieth, and we want them to be able to celebrate with a getaway." Jan smiled. "And the church board has arranged for a pastor from Augusta to cover the services for the weekend you choose to go."

Jan gestured toward them. "Come on up."

Pastor Mike led the way and Sarah followed. Jan hugged each of them and then handed the card to Sarah. "Thank you," she said. "We're all so grateful for both of you."

"Thank you," Pastor Mike and Sarah said in unison.

Pastor Mike smiled and then said, "It's an honor to serve the people of Lancaster. We're so thankful that God led us to this community."

Elaine pressed her hands together, thinking of all the people she knew who had been led to Lancaster. She couldn't imagine what her life would be like anywhere else.

Everyone enjoyed another cup of tea and chatted more, going from table to table to look at the photos, letters, and valentines. Elaine loved how the images and words from the past drew everyone together.

Reluctantly, the guests began to ready themselves to leave. Many sought out Jan and Elaine to thank them for the wonderful evening. Elaine wasn't surprised that Marshall did, but she was surprised when Macy approached her.

"What a nice evening," she said. "Well, the tea wasn't as hot as I like it but"—she smiled wryly—"besides that, everything was perfect."

"Thank you for reading for us."

"Of course," she said. "All of it was lovely. It meant a lot to me to be included."

Elaine reached for the woman's hand and squeezed it. "I'm so glad you had a good time." She doubted Macy could comprehend just how grateful she was for that.

Marshall and Macy left together. Although Elaine was sure he would walk her home, she was also certain Marshall was still mourning his wife too deeply to be interested in another woman. But she did expect that he would be a good friend to Macy as they shared their love of literature and the history of Lancaster too.

AMY AND VAN, Virginia, and Paula and Brian left with the other guests to start back to Augusta, while Sasha, Brody, Tara, and Jack stayed to help clean up. Once the dishes were all in the kitchen, Elaine insisted they go as well, along with Archie and Rose too.

"It won't take Jan and me long to clean up," Elaine said, knowing Nathan and Bob would help too.

As Jan and Elaine put away the leftover food, Nathan and Bob started in on loading the dishwasher. As they all worked, Elaine shared about the Franklins coming in with Aiden that morning.

When she'd finished, Bob asked if Miles had an attorney.

Elaine answered, "Last we heard, no."

Bob turned to Nathan. "I'd like to find out his story—I could drive to Augusta right now. Mind if I talk with him?"

"Not at all," Nathan said. "In fact, I'd like to go with you." He reached for Elaine's hand. "How about it? Would you like to join us?"

As if they needed to ask!

Nathan drove and Bob sat up front with him, while Elaine sat alone in the back seat. Jan stayed at the tearoom to finish the cleaning and to get ready for the next day.

The night was clear and moonlight sparkled on the snowbanks alongside the road. It was 9 p.m. by the time they reached the jail, just across the river, in downtown Augusta. The building was made of stone and over a hundred and fifty years old.

Nathan parked in the lot, and the three of them walked along the sidewalk to the wide stairs leading to the front door. When they entered, Bob spoke with the officer at the counter while Nathan and Elaine slipped into the waiting room.

A few minutes later another officer came out. Then Bob disappeared down a hall for fifteen minutes. When he returned, he said that he'd spoken with Miles and he wanted to talk with Elaine and Nathan, if they were willing.

"Is that all right?" Elaine asked.

Bob said that it was. "Bail is low, but for some reason all of Miles's accounts are frozen. So he can't get out. Or hire a lawyer."

Elaine and Nathan followed him down the hall and showed their identification before they were scanned with a metal detector. After that, they stepped into a room where an officer sat with Miles at a large table.

"We'll be fine," Bob said to the officer. "I'll shout if we need anything."

The officer seemed reluctant to leave, but he did as the three settled into chairs around the table. Miles looked exhausted with dark circles under his eyes. His hair, which had been covered in the woods by his hat, was darker than his beard, and a little shaggy.

"Look," he said. "I'm really sorry about the explosion. I never meant to scare the two of you like that, much less threaten your lives. I never even meant for there to be an explosion. I mean, of course at first I did. Otherwise I wouldn't have hauled the bag of fertilizer into the garage."

He leaned forward. "There was someone hanging around the property. I thought maybe he'd been sent to find me, and I just wanted to scare him off. I found some diesel fuel in the garage and then the fertilizer in the garden shed, which I moved into the garage. But I didn't set it off, and realized it was a stupid plan no matter what. I couldn't leave Aiden alone in the berm-house and I couldn't mix it with him on my back. And an explosion would only draw attention to me anyway." Miles shook his head. "I don't know what I was thinking."

Nathan cleared his throat. Elaine guessed he was confused about the bomb being made from bleach and drain cleaner, not fertilizer and diesel. She exhaled. Obviously no one had told him what actually exploded—or else he was playing dumb and trying to pin it on someone else.

Miles frowned. "I was going to move the fertilizer back to the garden shed the next day so the two ingredients would be far away from each other. And then that night there was an explosion. I feared someone had been injured so I put Aiden on my back and snowshoed up. The building wasn't on fire so

I figured it wasn't as bad as I feared. I saw two people walking around and although they seemed upset it didn't seem as if they were badly injured."

Elaine thought of Miles watching them, when they had absolutely no idea he was there—with Aiden.

"Once the state trooper arrived, I left," Miles said, "hoping the man who had been hanging around the property would leave too."

"Did he?" Nathan asked.

Miles shook his head. "Mostly—there turned out to be two. One was younger. The older one was old and slow and seemed confused."

Elaine didn't interrupt to explain about the private investigator Kyle and Beth had hired or about Timmy Calkin.

"Did you see anyone else on the property?" Nathan asked.

"Besides the two of you, I presume?"

Nathan nodded.

"And the state troopers?" Miles asked.

Nathan nodded again.

"The neighbor guy was around some. And I saw tracks from two people skiing on the property, which I'm guessing now were you"—he nodded toward Elaine—"and your daughter."

Elaine affirmed his guess.

"There was a vehicle parked on the lane going down to the neighbor's earlier in the day of the explosion. A white Suburban that nearly blended in with the snow."

"Any idea who it belonged to?" Bob asked.

"At first I thought it was the old guy who'd been hanging around, staying in the last cottage, but after a while it became pretty clear he didn't have any resources." He shrugged. "So I don't know. Maybe it belonged to the first guy."

Again, Elaine bit her tongue, thinking about the private detective, Leonard, and the vehicle he drove.

Nathan folded his hands together on top of the table. "Do you know where the snow globe collection is?"

He nodded.

"Will you tell us?"

"Sure." Miles's eyes lit up. "It's in the back room of the earth-berm house. Aiden and I moved it there before the explosion. We used a sled and had to pack the globes in bubble wrap and boxes that were in the room. It took several days. I don't know why Grandpa didn't store it there in the first place. It's a much safer location."

Elaine leaned back in her chair. "What did you plan to do with it?"

Miles exhaled. "Nothing. I mean, I'd planned to move the cabinets too but then there were so many people around that I didn't dare." He rubbed the side of his head. "I really enjoyed the collection as a child—playing with the less valuable ones is one of my favorite memories. But what could I do with it? Except enjoy it for a short time. It doesn't belong to me, right?"

Everyone was silent for a moment. Elaine felt a little sick at her stomach.

Bob cleared his throat and then asked, "Can you tell us more about the conflict with your in-laws?"

Miles ran his hand through his hair, started to say something, and then stopped. Then after hesitating again, he said, "I know this has been a really difficult time for Beth and Kyle, and I'm sorry that my actions added to their stress. But I was afraid if Aiden and I stayed in Toronto, I would lose custody of my son."

Bob put both hands flat on the table. "Did they have reason to claim you were an unfit parent?"

"From their perspective, I guess they thought so. But more importantly, they had an entire legal team going after me. Once they froze my assets, I couldn't even hire anyone to help with my defense. Then when they evicted me from our apartment—"

Elaine gasped. "What?"

"They own it." He shrugged. "They were appalled that I hadn't gone back to work after Brooke died. I planned to, honestly, but I thought it would be best for Aiden for me to find a job that would allow me as much time with him as possible."

Elaine wasn't sure what—or whom—to believe.

"It was their apartment. They had every right to do what they wanted, but it seemed to be another step to control me." He rubbed his hand through his hair again. "Foolishly, Brooke and I had all of our savings invested through their firm. What I didn't realize was that Kyle's name is on all of them so he could invest them more easily, and he froze them after I fled. Thankfully I'd taken out quite a bit of cash when I left, but I've used nearly all of that now."

Elaine couldn't imagine Kyle doing such a sneaky financial move. He seemed so nice.

"Why would he do that?" Bob asked.

"They wanted me to take a job in their firm and move into their guest house so that Aiden would be closer to them. I didn't want to do that. We'd had a lot of issues with them all through our marriage. It would have been stifling to both Aiden and me to live near them like that. Once I started saying no to them, they started reacting. It was subtle at first, but then their attorney approached me, asking me to sign a document giving them guardianship of Aiden. They were claiming that it was Brooke's desire, that she was afraid of me and didn't trust me to raise our boy."

He went on to say that he refused to sign over his rights. He reached out to his father for help, but he refused, saying it would be best for the Franklins to raise the boy. Then his father said he'd been trying to get ahold of him because he had a plan to help Miles. He had a Google alert on Berl Newton and the old man had died a few weeks before. Vincent had tracked down the man's will. He explained that all of his assets were going to charities except for the Snow Globe property and collection. Those were going to a Nathan Culver. Vincent had already talked with his lawyer about contesting the will.

Elaine couldn't keep biting her tongue. "Were your parents still married? Or did they divorce?"

Miles laughed, mirthlessly. "That was the million-dollar question. I asked my father that many times in my teens and twenties. What I didn't realize was I should have asked my mother. Anyway, he finally gave me an answer after Grandpa died. Yes, my parents did divorce soon after they first separated. Neither ever remarried, and I think my father wanted me to think that they hadn't divorced, most likely so it would appear he had some claim to Grandpa's money. I think, when he approached me about contesting the will, he believed I could get the inheritance—and then share it with him."

Miles went on to say that he told his father he didn't want anything of his grandfather's, although if life had turned out the way he wanted, he'd like the Snow Globe property and collection.

"He took that literally and had his attorney meet me on the way out of town with the paperwork to contest the will. Actually, it contested the entire will but I crossed out everything but the property and collection, initialed it, packed our passports and other things, and then left town. I cleared out my checking account so I had some cash, though I didn't know where we were going. At first I thought we'd go to Asia or somewhere else I'd been years ago, but then I thought of the Snow Globe property. No one would think I'd be crazy enough to hide out in the woods in Maine, right? Especially since few people knew about the earth-berm house. I figured that would be the perfect place." He sat up straighter. "And the truth is, being here has been good for me. I was horrible to my mom and grandfather. I feel their love here in Maine, and their forgiveness. I don't want to do to Aiden what my dad did to me—turn him against his maternal family. But the best thing for Aiden is for me to raise him." He slouched down a little. "But any hope of me keeping custody of Aiden is probably looking worse and worse. Brooke would be heartbroken for us."

Elaine's heart raced, thinking of the young wife and mother dying so young. How heartbreaking for all of them.

"So you absolutely didn't intentionally set off an explosion?" She was careful with her words.

"That's right," he said.

Bob turned toward Elaine. "Do you think Timmy Calkin could have set it?"

"I don't think so," she said. "He didn't seem to want to scare anyone—plus he didn't seem with it enough to pull something like that off."

Bob clasped his hands together. "Let's hope the truth prevails." Elaine guessed he was thinking of the bleach and drain cleaner bomb too—either Miles was a pathological liar or else he was innocent, and she was certain it was the latter.

Bob looked straight at Miles. "I'll think about all you've said and get back to you tomorrow if I think I can help you."

"Thank you," Miles said. "I'll pay you once I get my finances sorted out." He met Elaine's gaze. "And, again, I never dreamt that the fertilizer and diesel were close enough to explode. I'm really sorry my actions ended up scaring you so badly. That was never my intent."

Again, Elaine believed the man. Her heart sank at the trouble she'd caused him, based on her assumptions. Which were fueled by Beth and Kyle.

CHAPTER NINETEEN

Elaine couldn't stop yawning the next morning. They hadn't arrived home until nearly midnight, and then it had taken Elaine forever to fall asleep. She kept turning Miles's story over and over in her head. Then her thoughts would turn to Aiden.

And to the bomb. Nathan said he would talk with Dan Benson about Miles's story as soon as he could.

Now, as she turned the tearoom sign to Open, her thoughts fell on the little boy again. There was no way he could understand where his father was.

Halfway through the morning, Nathan came into the tearoom with a large manila envelope in his hands. "Do you have a minute?" he asked.

Elaine nodded. "We can talk in the dining room." She hurried back into her office and grabbed her notebook. She wanted to make sure and update the information she'd been collecting.

Nathan said he had something to show her, but first he wanted to tell her about his conversation with Dan. "He said Miles told him the same story about the fertilizer and diesel fuel."

"How about Miles's recollection of the SUV? Did you mention that to Dan, and that Leonard Scott was driving one the first day we met him?"

Nathan nodded. "Dan is looking into that."

She added *Leonard Scott* to her list of suspects.

As they sat down at the table, Nathan pulled a paper from the envelope. "Mr. Marner sent a fax this morning. He came across a document in Berl's papers that specified why he wanted me to have the property and the collection."

"That's great," Elaine said.

He nodded and then began reading from the papers. *"I bequeath my beloved property in Maine and my snow globe collection to Nathan Culver, the son of my best friend from childhood. It may seem to some like an odd thing to do, but I remember how much he liked the property as a child and how inquisitive he was. That is the sort of person I would like to steward the property from this point forward, until Nathan sees fit to bequeath it to someone else. As far as the snow globe collection is concerned, Nathan values old things. Some of the snow globes in the collection are glamorous—and some are kitsch—but I know Nathan will value them all. I hope he will accept my gift in the spirit that I'm giving it, keep the collection safe, and perhaps develop the property into some new endeavor to bless the people of Lancaster."* Nathan stopped reading, raised his eyebrows, and met Elaine's gaze. "I think he's overestimated me. I don't really have any desire to develop a piece of property."

"I wonder what he had in mind," Elaine said.

"There's no indication of that in the document," Nathan answered.

"Well," Elaine said, "give it some thought. There's no hurry."

Nathan nodded.

"I thought of something," she said. "Last night, when I was tossing and turning."

"What's that?"

"I should have said I thought of *someone*."

"Who?"

"Jerry Kemp."

Nathan slapped his forehead. "I forgot to give you the update. Nothing came of all of that. He said he'd just stopped by, for old times' sake, and found the cottage door unlocked. There was no evidence that he forced his way in, so no charges were pressed."

"Okay," Elaine said. "But that wasn't what I was thinking of."

Nathan tilted his head in a questioning manner.

"He had gloves on, right, when we saw him that day?"

Nathan nodded. "But we all did."

"When I met him for coffee he had a glove on one hand. He said he'd cut his hand on a snow globe, and taking off his glove pulled on the bandage."

"Do you think he's lying? That he burned it in the explosion instead?"

"I don't know," Elaine said. "Maybe he'd been around the place before." She wasn't ready to take him off the suspect list. "Is there an inventory on the snow globes?"

Nathan nodded. "I have it right here. We can see if they are all there, once we gain access to them." He paused for a moment as if he were thinking. "And I have another update."

"Oh?"

"Adam Slater called this morning. He said he'd heard the estate had settled and he wanted to make me a formal offer, but he also wanted to apologize for lying."

Elaine gasped. "What?" And then she laughed at herself. If he'd caused the explosion, he'd hardly confess.

Nathan smiled. "It's not the way it sounds, believe me. He does want the property for his logging collection, which is currently stored in his three-car garage. Once he knew we were all sentimental about the cottages and everything, he thought maybe he could keep them. Rent them out during hunting season, that sort of thing."

"So you think he wants to start a new roadside attraction?"

"Yeah," Nathan answered. "Except I don't think he realizes how little traffic actually goes by on that particular road."

"So are you going to take him up on the offer?"

Nathan shook his head. "No—or at least not yet, anyway."

Elaine leaned toward him. "What do you want to do next?"

"Go back to the jail. Bob's there, and he asked me to return. Would you come with me?"

"I'll ask Jan." Business was slow and Elaine didn't think her cousin would mind, although she felt as if she'd been slipping away from work quite a bit lately.

Jan was fine with the proposition. Rose had just arrived and business was definitely slow.

A HALF HOUR later, Elaine and Nathan were walking back up the steps of the Augusta jail. As they entered the front door, the crying of a child echoed in the old building. Elaine stepped into the waiting room. Aiden Osborne sat in the middle of the floor, his head thrown back as his cries shifted to screams. Kyle stood near the boy with a stuffed giraffe in his hand while Beth sat in a chair nearby with her arms crossed. Next to her sat their private investigator, Leonard Scott. As the man turned his head toward Elaine, she noticed an injury on his forehead that had scabbed over. When they'd met him at the Snow Globe, he wore a stocking cap. She guessed he'd had the injury then too because it looked as if it was a few weeks old.

"What happened?" Elaine asked him, touching her own forehead.

"I ran into a branch, in the woods," he said. "It looks worse than it is."

Elaine smiled at him. The wound didn't seem to be from a scrape. It was more like an abrasion, one that had been quite bad when it first happened. She turned her attention toward Aiden and knelt on the floor next to him. "What's the matter?"

Aiden dipped his head down, put his hands up to his face, and continued to cry.

"He's been like this since last night," Kyle said.

Beth shook her head. "He's just throwing a tantrum, that's all. Once he figures out he can't get his own way, he'll stop."

At that, Aiden began wailing again. Over the little one's cries, Nathan asked the Franklins what they were doing there.

"Our lawyer is trying get us temporary custody of Aiden so we can return to Toronto," Kyle answered. "He's meeting with

Miles and his attorney right now, asking if we can all consult with a mediator. I think the district attorney is with them too and the trooper who arrested Miles."

"Oh." Elaine glanced at Nathan.

Nathan's eyes lit up. "So Trooper Benson is in there? And Miles's lawyer? Right now?"

"Apparently," Kyle answered.

Beth sniffed. "I don't know how Miles was able to afford a lawyer."

"Excuse me." Nathan stood. And then to Elaine, he said, "May I speak with you in private?"

"Yes," she whispered, following him to the foyer.

"I should have talked this through with you earlier, but I'm wondering if we should drop the charges against Miles." He stopped. "Could we discuss that?"

She shook her head. "We don't need to talk about it. I'm in complete agreement."

Nathan exhaled. Elaine felt relieved too. Miles hadn't turned out to be the monster his in-laws had portrayed him as, not at all. She absolutely believed he didn't cause the explosion—and it seemed clear Aiden belonged with his father, not the Franklins.

When they went back to the waiting room, they found it empty. Beth and Kyle had apparently taken Aiden on a walk to try to calm him down.

She and Nathan watched as people paraded up and down the hall. It wasn't long until Jerry Kemp walked past with his attorney. Then Leonard Scott came out with a man dressed in a suit and tie. They both sat down in the waiting room. Neither spoke, but the man pulled out his phone and started texting. After a while he put it away and took out a manila folder that he began leafing through.

"Are you all right hanging around longer?" Nathan whispered to Elaine.

She nodded. She wouldn't miss all of this for anything.

The man took his phone out again and answered it. "I'm not sure where they are," he said. There was a long pause and then he said, "I'll tell them to come back ASAP."

He ended the call and began texting. Elaine guessed he was sending a message to Kyle or Beth. She guessed he was their attorney and that he'd come down from Toronto—or perhaps they'd hired a local one—to sort everything out.

"I only did what they told me to," Leonard said to the man.

"*Shh,*" the man said as he slipped the phone back into his pocket.

"Well, mostly. It seemed like a—"

"Hush." The man opened the manila folder again. Leonard slouched in his chair, took a stocking cap out of his pocket, and pulled it down over his head.

Ten minutes later the Franklins came back into the waiting room. Aiden was asleep, draped over Kyle's shoulder. "What's going on?" Kyle asked the lawyer.

"The district attorney wants to speak with you."

"You said you'd take care of everything."

The man shrugged. "You didn't tell me how complicated it all was."

"You go," Beth said to Kyle. "I'll stay out here with Aiden."

"No, they want to speak with both of you." The man stood. "I'm going with you, of course." He turned to Leonard. "Don't do anything stupid, which means stay right here."

Leonard nodded. His expression wasn't defiant anymore. It was downright pathetic.

Neither of the Franklins acknowledged Elaine or Nathan. It was as if they were invisible.

"How odd," Elaine said.

Nathan nodded, taking Elaine's hand. "Are you hungry?"

"A little," she said, "but I don't want to miss anything."

He squeezed her hand. "Neither do I."

It wasn't long until the Franklins came out, without Aiden. Beth was crying and Kyle had his arm around her. They didn't stop in the waiting room or say a thing to Elaine or Nathan. Or to Leonard Scott.

Elaine stood. "Should I go after them?" she asked Nathan.

"It's up to you," he said.

She hesitated. They wouldn't be happy that Nathan had dropped the charges.

Hurrying after them, she called out, "Beth! Kyle!" just as they made their way out the door. She continued after them and then called out again as she reached the steps.

They were at the bottom but turned and looked up at her. At least they stopped.

She hurried down the steps. "Are you all right?"

Beth shook her head. "Miles is being released, and taking Aiden."

Kyle kept his arm tightly around Beth as she asked, "Why in the world would Nathan drop the charges against Miles?"

"It seems improbable that he set the explosion. He didn't even know what kind of ingredients were actually used in the explosion."

"So you think, in the two times you interacted with Miles, that you could make that judgment?" Beth spit out. "While we, after knowing him for years, are wrong? He was lying, pure and simple."

Kyle drew her closer. "Sweetheart..."

She pulled away abruptly and glared at her husband. "We just lost our grandson!"

"I'm really sorry," Elaine said. "For all of your heartache and troubles. And I'm praying that it will all be sorted out."

"Thank you," Kyle said, but Beth just shook her head.

"Will you go home now?"

Kyle nodded. "As soon as we collect our things at Green Glade."

Elaine told them goodbye and started to walk away, but as she did Kyle called after her. "Could I give you the car seat for Aiden? Otherwise Miles will have to buy one to get him back to their car. And we have the baby backpack, and Miles's snow-shoes too."

"Thank you," Elaine answered. Those were all things Miles needed. At least Kyle wasn't being vindictive.

A few minutes later she lugged the items up the stairs of the jail and into the waiting room, where she found Bob talking to Nathan.

Both told her hello and then Bob said, "I was just saying that Leonard Scott confessed to causing the explosion. He said the Franklins had sent him down to see if he could find any trace of Miles, and he suspected Miles was on the property. When he saw the diesel and fertilizer, he wondered if Miles was planning an explosion. He couldn't figure out how to make that sort of bomb, but he did know how to make a bleach and drain cleaner one. He hoped that would detonate the fertilizer and diesel too, setting off a large explosion. He hoped to draw the law to the site, and they would flush out Miles for him."

"Didn't he see that Nathan and I were there?" Elaine asked.

"Yes," Bob said. "Which he figured was all the better. He was going to call it in anonymously, as someone who was just driving by. But once you were there, he hurried to mix the ingredients, figuring it would come better from the two of you."

"But we'd looked into the garage. The burlap bag and gas cans weren't anywhere near each other."

"He pulled it over next to the fuel."

"Oh." Goodness, it sounded as if they were fortunate the entire place didn't blow.

"Leonard was out behind the garage when he detonated the bleach and drain cleaner bomb. A big splinter of wood hit the side of his head."

"What about the bleach and drain cleaner Dan found in the hidden room?"

"Yeah, Leonard found that room, and stored more bleach and drain cleaner in there."

"Was that before or after Miles moved the collection?"

"After," Bob answered. Then he continued. "The night of the explosion, he parked his SUV on the side road and left before Dan, and then the explosives unit, arrived. The snow covered up his tracks. However, he made it clear the Franklins never asked him to do anything destructive. That was entirely his idea, and I'm guessing he's telling the truth about that. They were very upset with what he'd done."

Elaine felt relief at that, at least.

"Any other questions?" Bob asked.

"What about Jerry Kemp? What did he have to say?"

Bob shook his head. "He'd found the snow globes before Miles did, and one did break on him. One of the old ones with a church in it. So he wasn't lying when he said he'd been cut by a snow globe."

Elaine shook her head. "And what was he planning to do the day we found him?"

"He says he was just taking another look. That he wanted to make certain he was ready to make an offer to Nathan."

"Do you believe him?"

Bob shrugged. "Wasn't he driving a hatchback?"

"That's right," Elaine said. "He hadn't brought a truck big enough to cart the whole thing off."

Bob nodded. "That's what the DA surmised too. They're allowing Jerry to go but depending on what we find out after we go over the snow globe collection, they may haul the man back in," Bob said and then looked directly at Nathan. "Would you give Miles and Aiden a ride back to the Snow Globe property so we can go over the inventory and try to settle this, if you have the time to do it now?"

"I do." Nathan glanced at Elaine. "Want to come along?"

"Definitely."

"I'll meet all of you there," Bob said. "But I thought I'd stop by and see if Jan can come with us. We'll bring enough snow-shoes for all of us."

"Thank you," Nathan said, "and take your time. I imagine Miles hasn't had much to eat today. We'll feed him and Aiden before we get on our way."

CHAPTER TWENTY

After dining in a café a few blocks from the jail, they all started back to Lancaster and then on to the Snow Globe property. Both Miles and Aiden immediately fell asleep. Aiden's head leaned against the car seat toward his father, and Miles was as close to Aiden as his seat belt allowed, with his hand resting on the boy's leg.

Elaine and Nathan stayed silent, not wanting to disturb them. As Nathan drove, she took her notebook out from her purse and looked at her list one more time. Slowly she crossed off everyone's name—except for Leonard Scott's. Instead she circled his and noted that he'd caused the explosion. That mystery was solved. Now they just needed to figure out whether the snow globe collection was intact or not.

When they reached Lancaster and Nathan slowed, Miles stirred and then woke up. "That was fast," he said.

"You must be exhausted," Elaine said.

He yawned. "Yeah."

"What's next?" Nathan asked. "Will you return to Toronto?"

"Not after this," Miles said. "I'd wanted to maintain a relationship with Kyle and Beth, and I still hope we can—but it will take some time. They did say they'd give me sole access to my financial accounts—after Bob told them he had a friend in Toronto who would help me pro bono if they didn't."

Elaine was grateful for Bob's help. Where would they be without it?

Soon they were out of town. When Nathan turned onto the old highway, Aiden awoke. As they approached the property, he clapped his hands together and squealed, "Goin' to Daddy's trees!"

"Well, buddy," Miles said, "we are going back to the forest, but it's not mine. It belongs to Nathan."

"Nathan's trees?"

"Yep, that's right. We'll get our stuff together and move on to another destination."

Elaine glanced at Nathan. He kept his eyes on the road, but his expression seemed troubled. As they approached the property, Bob's car came into view. As they parked beside it, both Jan and Bob waved.

They all slipped into their snowshoes and then Miles tucked Aiden into the backpack and wiggled his arms through the straps. As they all started, Aiden called out, "Goin' to Daddy's house!"

Clearly he hadn't understood what Miles had explained in the car. But how could he?

"Sorry," Miles said. "Clearly Aiden believes in squatter's rights."

They all laughed.

"The technical term is adverse possession," Bob said. "Especially when the squatter has some sort of historical claim on the land."

Elaine sighed at Bob's words. Nothing was simple about the situation.

But Miles smiled. "Don't worry. We won't be making a claim. It's yours fair and square, Nathan." He tugged on Aiden's foot that was kicking back and forth. "We'll gather up our things. We don't have much, but I'm relieved there are so many of you to help pack it out."

"Of course," Jan said. "It's the least we can do."

They spread out along the trail, with Elaine and then Nathan taking up the rear. When they reached the knoll above the earth-berm house, Elaine watched as the others made their way down. Miles led the way with Aiden waving his arms back and forth. Next on the trail were Bob and then Jan.

By the time Elaine and Nathan reached the earth house, Jan had her snowshoes off and was holding Aiden while Miles took his snowshoes off.

Soon they were all ready to traipse into the house. "It's small," Miles said. "But we should all fit."

Miles lit two lanterns that sat on the table and then took Aiden back from Jan. Elaine had glimpsed the interior the night they'd tricked Miles, but it was bigger than it had appeared from the door. Besides the living area and small kitchen, a hall led to a single bedroom and a bathroom.

"The toilet is an early compost model, or what used to be known as a waterless toilet," Miles explained. "Grandpa really was ahead of his time."

He asked Nathan to carry one of the lanterns and head down the hall to the last door. "This is the storage room," Miles said, as Nathan opened it. "I don't know why Grandpa didn't move the snow globes down here in the first place."

Aiden squealed with delight as Nathan held the lantern up and the light bounced off the snow globes. Bookcases lined the narrow storage room and hundreds of snow globes sat on the shelves. The room was just wide enough that if Miles stayed in the middle, Aiden couldn't reach the snow globes.

"Grandpa built this room to be climate controlled and watertight. Hopefully it still is. I did intend to bring the cabinets, like I said. Now you'll have to haul all of the snow globes back out."

Nathan nodded in agreement but didn't say anything.

"Here, I'll take the lantern," Bob said to Nathan. "So you can look through the inventory."

"Thanks." Nathan passed the lantern to Bob and then said to Miles, "I'm going to try to figure out which snow globe broke."

"Oh, I know," he said. "It was an old one. With a church, from Austria, I think."

"That's what Jerry Kemp said too." Nathan watched Miles as he stepped to a shelf.

"I found it on the floor in the collection room." Miles picked up a few items from the shelf. "The church, trees, and base didn't break, so I saved them after I cleaned up the glass." He held up the pieces.

"Oh dear." Elaine stepped closer. The church was white with a high steeple. "It could have been nearly a hundred years old."

"I honestly didn't think of that," Miles said. "I was just so relieved that my favorites were all right."

"Which ones are those?" Nathan asked.

He pointed to one of two skaters. "My grandfather told me that was my grandmother's favorite. I never met her, but my grandfather never got over her death. I know she was a wonderful person."

His voice choked a little and Elaine thought of his own wife dying so young, much younger than his grandmother had.

"And this one." He pointed to the one with the little boy standing in the snow, with the skating rink behind him. "The boy is me. Grandfather had it custom made." Miles picked it up, shook it, and put it back on the shelf.

Aiden laughed as the snow fell and then shouted, "That's me!"

The snow globe was beautiful, and Elaine couldn't help but be touched that Berl Newton had commissioned a snow globe to be made for Miles. Although he'd never given it to him. She thought of Miles giving his son the middle name Berl. He really had loved his grandfather.

Elaine glanced from snow globe to snow globe. One of a Victorian house, that looked similar to Tea for Two, caught her attention. It was painted white with red trim, and the hedges around it were heart shaped.

Nathan caught her eye and smiled. She looked at the next one, a stone church, as Nathan glanced at his inventory list and then back at the snow globe. Then he took out a pen from the inside of his coat pocket. "It'll take a while to go through the list."

"I'll help," Miles said. "I'll just get Aiden occupied with some toys and be back." His face reddened as he took a snow globe from the shelf. It was a cheap souvenir one from the gift shop.

Aiden squealed in delight. "Mine!"

"Yep, buddy. This is the one for you." He turned toward Nathan. "I took it from the gift shop. Sorry."

Nathan just shook his head and smiled as Miles handed the snow globe to Aiden.

"Maybe he'll let us watch him." Elaine reached out to the little boy and, surprisingly, the boy fell into her arms. She and Jan backed out of the room and then took turns reading books to the little boy.

He seemed fine as long as his father was close by. After a while he climbed into Elaine's lap and cuddled as she read, still holding the snow globe, and then fell asleep. Elaine held him gently, comforted by the weight of the little boy against her.

Finally, Miles came out and lit the burner on the small propane stove. He smiled at the three of them on the little couch and then said, "How does some tea sound?"

Both women said that sounded good.

"It won't take me long to pack," Miles said. "We'll get going before it starts to get dark."

Elaine sensed that he was dragging his feet as he pulled down mugs from a cupboard and a teapot.

"Tell us about this place," Elaine said.

"It was *the* big secret," Miles said. "As a kid, I was beside myself that when we all visited Maine, we had this getaway to come to. We came in both the summer and the winter. We'd pack our perishables and clothes, but besides that the place was always ready for us."

He continued, saying it was like camping out, but better. "It was Grandpa's big experiment to see if an earth-berm house would work."

"How old were you the last time you came?" Elaine asked.

"I was a teenager. I'd spent part of the year with my dad for the first time, which was hard on Mom and Grandpa. I think they hoped I'd be my old self, but I wasn't. I was rude and annoying." Miles poured the hot water as he spoke. "I do remember seeing the snow globe collection in the back room of the first cottage. Grandpa had the room built and then moved all of the snow globes there before he left for Florida. He said he wanted all of them in one place. I remember as I looked at them, I felt like a little kid again. Safe. Loved. But by that evening I was ranting and raving again." He placed a towel over the teapot. "I was a handful, that was for sure."

"What happened after that?" Elaine asked.

"I stopped going down to Florida. I ended up saying some pretty mean things through the years. I wish there'd been someone else to help me see what a horrible person I was being—my dad sure didn't call me out on it. I think it was hardest on Grandpa to have me hurt his only child, his daughter, the way I did. I'm pretty sure Mom forgave me, but I doubt Grandpa ever did."

Elaine asked, "Why's that?"

"Well, I'm not saying this shows the value of a person's love or anything like that, but I think it can be an indication of their forgiveness. Grandfather didn't leave me anything."

"But your mother did?"

He nodded. "That's the money in the accounts the Franklins froze."

"What?" Elaine had assumed that had all been their daughter's money.

"Brooke invested it for us." He shrugged. "And trusted her father to manage the accounts. *C'est la vie,* right?"

Elaine nodded but as she looked up she was relieved both Nathan and Bob were standing in the hallway and had heard what Miles had said.

He really wasn't the loser the Franklins had portrayed him as.

Aiden continued to sleep in Elaine's arms as the others crowded around and drank their tea. Nathan said that all of the snow globes were accounted for—Jerry Kemp had only broken the one and hadn't stolen any of them. He texted the DA as he spoke to let him know.

When he'd finished his tea, Miles said he'd pack up their things while Elaine held Aiden.

"Not so fast," Nathan said. "I have a question for everyone first. If each one of you were in my shoes, what would you do with this property?" He glanced toward Bob. "You go first."

"I'd renovate the entire property back to the glory days. Fix all the buildings. Open up the skating rink. And build a new giant snow globe." He smiled. "I don't know if it would still be the world's largest, but that wouldn't matter."

"Thank you," Nathan said. "How about you, Jan?"

"I'm with Bob," she said. "This was one special place way back when. I'd love to see families from Lancaster coming back out here again."

Nathan acknowledged her words and then asked Elaine.

"All along, I've thought it would be great to renovate it," she said. "But the more I think about it, the less sure I am. Families are so busy now with sports and clubs and those sorts of things. I don't know if coming here would be a priority." Aiden stirred and she paused for a moment, but when he stopped, she continued. "Berl saw a need for that time and met it. What's the need now that needs to be met?"

"There are lots of needs," Jan said. "But I'm not sure what this property can do. I've always seen this place as more of a want than a need."

Nathan smiled at her answer and then asked Miles what he would do with the property.

"I've actually put some thought into this as Aiden and I've been snowshoeing around here," Miles said. "I'd turn it into a camp for at-risk kids. I'd have both summer and winter camps, with no more than thirty kids at a time. I'd add a hall for meetings and dining and renovate the cottages, but I don't think it would take too much work. If I'd had a camp like that to come to as a teenager, I think it would have helped."

"How would you keep it running, as far as finances go?" Bob asked.

"Grants," Miles said. "Plus, I have the money from my mother. I'd put a portion aside for Aiden's college and all of that, but I can't think of a better way to use it. Perhaps I could help spare other families what mine went through."

Elaine thought it sounded like a lovely idea—except that Nathan owned the property.

Miles stood. "We've stayed too long. Aiden and I need to get going."

"Where will you go?" Elaine asked.

"I'll stay in town until I figure out a plan."

"No." Nathan stood. "You'll stay right here. I don't know if you can pull your dream off or not, but I'm going to do everything I can to give you a shot at it."

"What do you mean?" Miles ran his hand through his hair.

"I'm going to deed the property to you," Nathan said. "And the snow globe collection too."

Miles sat back down, a little hard. "No," he said. "I can't take all of this from you."

"But I want you to have it," Nathan said. "You can sell the collection to help finance your dream. We all know a buyer who'd love to purchase it."

Elaine couldn't help but smile at the reference to Jerry Kemp, but the joy inside of her was because of Nathan's selfless act.

It made sense that Miles should have the property, but it was the grace that Nathan had shown him all along that truly touched her. Nathan had been generous in his view of Miles, allowing for the possibility that the man wasn't the monster the Franklins portrayed him to be, even when Elaine was convinced of his guilt.

Nathan had been an agent of grace in all of this.

"I'll talk with my attorney," Nathan said, nudging Bob. "And he'll figure out the transfer. The property will be yours with no obligation. You and Aiden can live here. You can turn it into a camp for at-risk youth. Or you can sell it."

Miles's eyes grew misty. "I can't thank you enough, and not just for your generosity but for your trust in me too." He glanced from Nathan to Bob and then to Jan and Elaine too. "Thank you, all of you."

ELAINE AND NATHAN didn't speak much on their way back to the tearoom, driving in Nathan's Cadillac, quite a distance behind Jan and Bob. It had started to snow by the time they reached the Lancaster town limits. When Nathan finally stopped in front of the tearoom, big fluffy flakes were coming down.

As he put the car into park, he said, "I have something for you."

"Oh?"

He nodded. He hopped out of the car, hurried around to the back, and then returned with a small, square cardboard box. "It's actually from Miles—and me." He chuckled a little.

Bursting with curiosity, she opened the box and then pulled out an item in bubble wrap. As she unwrapped it, she realized what it was. The snow globe with the Victorian house inside.

She held it to her chest and met Nathan's gaze.

"Miles and I both saw you admiring it," he said.

"Thank you." She'd never forget this Valentine's week. She felt closer than ever to a future with Nathan. She shook the globe and as they both watched the snow fall, she said, "I'm so thankful for you. Especially for your good character and most recently for the grace you showed Miles."

Nathan shook his head. "That property wasn't meant for me. If Berl had a chance to know Miles now, he would have left him the land. Anyone would have done what I did."

"I'm not so sure." She shook the globe again and then turned her head toward the tearoom, the windows lit by lamplight, and the snow falling all around it.

She turned back to Nathan.

"Let the globe be a reminder of God's grace to all of us," Nathan said. "And of this season in our lives."

He leaned toward her then and their lips met. His felt as soft as the falling snow as he drew her closer. She wasn't sure exactly what was ahead for them, but she knew love and grace—and God's timing—would be at the center of their journey.

She was sure a happy ending still awaited her.

ABOUT THE AUTHOR

Leslie Gould is the #1 best-selling and award-winning author of thirty novels, including ten with Guideposts. She teaches college writing and enjoys research, studying church history, and traveling all over the USA (and the world, when she can!). She and her husband, Peter, have been married for thirty-four years, live in the beautiful Pacific Northwest, and are the parents of four adult children.

JAN'S LEMON TARTLETS

Ingredients

For the tart dough:

1⅓ cups (166 grams) all purpose flour

1 stick (115 grams) cold unsalted butter, cubed

¼ cup granulated sugar

pinch of salt

1 egg yolk

For the lemon curd:
(makes extra, about 1½ cups in total)

⅓ cup lemon juice, about 2 lemons

2 large eggs

1 egg yolk

½ cup sugar

2 tablespoons chilled unsalted butter, cut into ½-inch cubes

1 tablespoon heavy cream

¼ teaspoon vanilla extract

pinch table salt

Berries for serving (optional)

Instructions

Make the tartlets:

1. Cut the butter into the flour until the mixture resembles coarse breadcrumbs.
2. Stir in the sugar, then add the egg yolk until combined. Use your hands to work the mixture into a dough.
3. Roll the dough out on a floured surface.
4. Cut the pastry into rounds with a cookie cutter and press into mini muffin tins.

5. Bake at 350° F for 20 minutes or until golden. Set aside to cool.

Make the lemon curd:
1. Heat lemon juice over medium heat until hot but not boiling.
2. Meanwhile, whisk eggs and yolk in a medium bowl. Gradually whisk in the sugar. While whisking, slowly pour hot lemon juice into the eggs. Return to saucepan and cook over medium heat. Stir constantly with a wooden spoon until mixture registers 170° Fahrenheit and coats the back of a spoon.
3. Remove pan from heat and stir in butter. Once melted, stir in cream, vanilla, and salt. If the curd didn't come together and thicken, simply return to heat and cook a bit longer, stirring constantly, until it thickens.
4. Curd can be stored in an airtight container in the fridge for up to a week, just cover with plastic wrap to prevent it from drying out.

Assemble the lemon tartlets:
1. Spoon the lemon curd into each tartlet shell.
2. Top each tartlet with a berry (optional) and serve.

READ ON FOR AN EXCITING SNEAK PEEK
INTO THE NEXT VOLUME OF TEAROOM MYSTERIES!

Tea and Promises
BY SUSAN PAGE DAVIS

Elaine Cook walked into the kitchen carrying a loose-leaf notebook. Her cousin, Jan Blake, didn't look up from her latest cooking project. The stand mixer whined as she beat a white mixture in a deep glass bowl. Elaine set down her notebook and fixed herself a cup of orange spice tea while she waited.

After a minute or two, the mixer slowed and stopped.

"Hi," Elaine said. "What are you making?"

Jan pushed up her glasses. Her denim apron had collected a few white spatters, and her face bore a determined look. "Icing. I'm fixing petits fours for the wedding reception."

"Why don't you have the baker do that?" Elaine asked. Jan's wedding to Bob Claybrook was just over two weeks away.

"Haven't I told you what they're charging?"

"More than we charge?"

"Well, about the same, but I just can't convince myself to pay someone that much when I can do it myself. Besides, they wouldn't be as good as ours."

Elaine smiled and sat down on a stool at the opposite side of the work island. "Ours are pretty good. Why would you change the recipe?"

"I'm just looking for something a little different," Jan said. "I think this batch may be the one."

"I hope you wrote down everything." Elaine realized that remark was unnecessary. Jan approached her recipes as a scientist would a formula. She measured precisely and noted the differences made by any changes she put in place.

"Oh, I did."

"How many batches have you made?" Elaine asked.

"This is only the third. It would be serendipitous if I struck the right combination so soon."

"*Mmm.*" Elaine smiled. If she were the one getting married— and she pushed down a little pang at the thought—she would hire someone else to do everything and relax and enjoy herself. "Are you sure you should take this on? That seems like so much trouble. Remember how crazy you went testing all those scone recipes a few weeks ago?"

"Ha! I do. I admit, I went a little overboard. But it's no trouble." Jan smiled. "You know I love doing this."

"I know." Elaine nodded. This was one of Jan's ways of relaxing. After much discussion, she had agreed to have a caterer provide most of the food for the reception, and a highly praised baker would make the wedding cake. But Jan still had to bake something.

"Okay. Well, we got a few more RSVPs this morning, and I thought we should look through the list." Elaine opened her notebook.

"Thanks for mentioning it. Last night, Bob did give me a couple more names he wants added."

Elaine nodded. "All right, but these last-minute add-ons are making the list pretty long."

"I know. Sorry. These are business connections, and he said they probably won't come, but he wanted to ask them."

Elaine resigned herself to a small amount of chaos. "Okay. But with all our old friends and family—and we both have large families—not to mention the church folks and Bob's colleagues—"

"And all the other merchants on Main Street," Jan added. "I understand. But it's hard to say no."

"It is." Elaine turned to her list of guests Jan wanted to include. "Have you heard from April and Alfred?" The elderly cousins living in Florida had a question mark beside their names.

"They won't be able to come, but they were tickled that we invited them." Jan picked up a clean table knife and scooped it through her icing. She lifted the knife and eyed it critically. She took a graham cracker from a package nearby, smeared the frosting on it, and took a bite. She chewed for a moment with her eyes closed.

"Nope. Almost, but not quite." She frowned and opened her eyes.

"Let me try it," Elaine said.

"Help yourself." Jan slid the pack of graham crackers toward her. Elaine took one, and Jan handed her the knife.

"*Mmm.* That's terrific," Elaine said. "What's not to like?"

"I don't know. Maybe it's just a tad too dry?"

"You might never find the exact proportions."

Jan shrugged. "I'll know it when I taste it."

Elaine looked down at the bowl of icing. "So what do you do with the reject batches?"

"I put it on cupcakes for Rue to serve her guests at the B and B. I offered her a special price."

"I see. Well, if we want to get Bob's late invitations out, I'll need the addresses."

"I left a note on your desk," Jan said.

Archie Bentham, one of their servers, came into the kitchen. "Do we have any lemon tarts left?"

"We certainly do." Jan pointed to the counter.

"Can I help you get your order ready, Archie?" Elaine asked.

"Thank you. Two lemon tarts and a serving of macadamia cookies. I'll fetch the tea." Archie's British accent was pronounced this morning. He nodded at her open notebook. "Is that the guest list?"

"Yes," Elaine said. "I've got you and Gloria, and Geraldine, checked off, along with Rose and Brent and Emma." Elaine expected that their other employee, Rose Young, would marry her young man soon and officially become little Emma's stepmother.

"We'll all be delighted, I'm sure," Archie said.

"We're getting down to the wire," Elaine told him. "Most of the people on the list have responded, but we still have a few question marks."

The wall phone rang, and Jan answered it. "Tea for Two, Jan Blake speaking. Oh, hi, honey."

Elaine smiled as she prepared the pastries for Archie. Bob called Jan several times a day from his law office in Waterville, and they got together nearly every evening. Elaine supposed she and Nathan Culver weren't much different—except they weren't officially committed. Nathan stayed in close touch with Elaine, but not with the frequency of Bob's calls, texts, and e-mails to Jan. But, after all, Bob was the groom, and the couple was moving into the house he had recently purchased, right across the street from the tearoom. Jan and Bob had myriad things to talk about.

Rose came in with a tray of dirty dishes, and Archie carried out his tray with a teapot and the plates Elaine had readied.

Jan hung up the phone. "Bob's adding another lawyer and his wife."

"What?" Elaine stared at her in mock horror.

"Kidding," Jan said. "He was just asking me if I wanted anything at the market."

"Oh. Good. Because I was going to suggest we move your reception to a bigger venue. Like maybe the Civic Center. This house will not hold two hundred people, and neither will our church's fellowship hall."

Jan just smiled.

"How many are on the list?" Rose asked.

"I don't know exactly, but it's over a hundred and counting," Elaine said.

"We've tried to keep it down so we can get married in our church," Jan assured her.

"That's fine," Elaine said. "I think we're okay at the church, so long as you don't add any more. But the reception—I mean, you wanted everyone to be able to sit down, and you know it's going to be a squeeze."

"Now who needs to relax?" Jan asked. "We've been over all this. It will work."

"Yes, you've planned it down to the last square inch," Rose reminded Elaine.

"Using the dining room and the extra tables in the parlors," Jan began, "it'll work. And not everyone we invited will come."

"True, but we won't know the exact number until the last minute," Elaine said. She thought about it. "It will be a little crowded, but—"

"But not too bad," Jan said, dumping a measuring cup full of flour into a clean bowl. "I wish it would be warm enough to use the porches."

"It won't be," Elaine said. "People who have winter weddings in Maine should know better."

Jan chuckled, but Elaine went on.

"You know it's usually not warm enough to sit outside until late May. And you guys picked a date in the middle of winter! For all you know, there'll be a blizzard the day of the wedding."

"No, Bob checked the Farmer's Almanac," Jan deadpanned.

Elaine threw her hands in the air. "They print that thing a year in advance. That's not a reliable weather report."

Rose turned toward them with a big smile. "Relax, you two. Everything is going to be beautiful. Putting the buffet and gift table in the entry and moving the counter is genius."

"Thank you," Jan said. "That was my idea."

Elaine nodded. "Brian is getting a crew together to move furniture around the day before. And you're right. If we counted right, we should be able to seat close to a hundred people, even though the tearoom normally only seats forty."

"And we're not doing a sit-down dinner," Jan reminded her as she cracked an egg. "With a buffet going, everyone doesn't have to sit down at once. People will be standing around talking and moving from group to group."

"Of course. And the head table will be in the east parlor, for the wedding party." Elaine's head was spinning from all the planning and calculating she and Jan had done over the past few weeks.

"And a couple of reserved tables for family," Jan said.

Rose situated a teapot carefully on her tray. "Of course. You've got to have places where Amy and Elaine's mother know they can sit down when they're tired."

"Well, I'm glad you changed the tea on Friday to the party room at Green Glade," Elaine said. "Having it here, and then the reception on Saturday too, would have been way too much."

"Yeah, that was one of our better decisions," Jan admitted. "It was so kind of Macy to offer to host the tea."

"The men will have to move the furniture after closing time on Friday, won't they?" Rose asked. "I mean—you are keeping the tearoom open half a day on the Friday before the wedding, right?"

"Oh, you're right," Jan said.

"Don't worry," Elaine said in soothing tones. "The guys will come after the rehearsal. You're having a tea instead of a rehearsal dinner, so the evening should end fairly early. Let Brian organize the moving crew."

"And I'll help your girls decorate," Rose said. "It will be so much fun."

Jan smiled. "I hate that Bob and I are causing such a commotion and so much work for everyone. But I love that we're having the reception here, and that everybody is so willing to join the craziness and make it happen."

"It's going to be great," Elaine said.

The wall phone rang again.

"I'll get it." Elaine strode to the phone. "Tea for Two, Elaine Cook speaking." A moment later, she pushed the mute button and turned to Jan with apprehension. "It's the florist. Can you talk to him?"

Jan was by now deep into mixing up cupcake batter so she could use up the extra frosting. She set down a wooden spoon and wiped her hands on her apron. "Did he say what he wants?"

"It seems there was a storm in Florida that killed some of the flowers you wanted."

"Don't they grow them in greenhouses?"

"I don't know, but if he can get everything you specified, it will be expensive."

"Okay, let me talk to him." Jan took the receiver from her. "Hello?"

Elaine's phone rang, and she smiled as she looked at the screen.

"Must be Nathan," Rose said, placing the last serving dish on her tray. "Catch you later." She headed back out to her station in the west parlor.

Elaine would have been happy if the call came from one of her children or grandchildren, but Rose was right about Nathan. When he called, she felt a certain energy and joy.

"Hi," she said into her phone. She gave Jan a little wave and walked slowly out of the kitchen and around the corner into her office.

"I've cleared my afternoon," Nathan said. "Still want to go shopping?"

"I'd love to," Elaine replied. "It's getting crazy around here. And we need to nail down what we're giving Jan and Bob for a wedding gift."

"Right. We've sort of left it till the buzzer, haven't we? Can you meet me for lunch, and we'll go from there?"

"Sure."

Nathan named a restaurant a few blocks from his auction business, and Elaine hurried upstairs to change her clothes. An outing with Nathan was just what she needed. He was her old childhood friend, but he'd become much more to her since she'd moved back to Maine. Love had found them both, but they'd moved slowly in the relationship as Elaine sorted through her grief for her late husband, Ben, who had passed away only three years ago. In some ways it felt like just yesterday, in others, it felt like a lifetime. Jan's upcoming wedding had given Elaine plenty to think about, and she knew that if Nathan proposed to her now, she would say yes. But would he ask her?

It was a tantalizing question, and she felt a bit giddy as she walked toward him in the restaurant half an hour later. Yes, she was definitely ready.

He rose, smiling, as she approached and pulled out her chair for her. Before she sat down, he kissed her cheek.

"You look great."

"Thanks."

"Any ideas for the wedding present?" he asked as she opened her menu.

"Not really. Something they'll enjoy for a long time, but what? They have enough furniture between them to stuff that house they're moving into." Bob had been fortunate enough to purchase the house as soon as it came on the market, and now Jan would live close to Elaine and would be able to walk over to the tearoom each morning and continue her baking as long as she enjoyed doing that.

"Seems to me you're the one who will come up short on furniture after the wedding," Nathan said.

"That's right. Most of what's in our private quarters belongs to Jan." Elaine had been a military wife for many years, and she'd come to the tearoom with only a small number of personal belongings compared to what Jan had brought. "In fact, she's leaving half her furniture for me to use. Maybe we should get them something symbolic."

"*Hmm.* Or some art." Nathan arched his eyebrows at her.

"That's a great idea too. A painting or something?"

They gave their orders to the server, and Nathan gazed at her across the table.

"I'd like to give them something they'll both love."

"So would I," she said.

"I guess that leaves out an antique Hoosier cupboard or a china cabinet."

"Jan would love either of those, but I doubt Bob would care."

"Right," Nathan said. "Let's look for something special. It doesn't have to be expensive, but something that will mean something to them."

Elaine sighed. "That sounds like a tall order."

"I'm sure we'll find just the right thing," Nathan said.

Two hours later, they stopped at a diner for coffee and a breather. They had been to three department stores, an art gallery, an import store, and an upscale antique shop, but they seemed no closer to finding the elusive wedding gift than when they had set out.

"Maybe you can find something online," Elaine said. Nathan had extensive contacts with dealers in antiques and rarities through his auction business.

"What about something like a membership at the fitness center where Sasha works now?"

Elaine considered that. Her daughter had recently moved back to Maine and was building a business as a personal trainer, in connection with a local fitness training center. "They might enjoy it, but I'm not sure Jan would have time to go regularly. And they might think we were saying they weren't fit."

Nathan chuckled. "We wouldn't want to insult them. Maybe we should stop by Mainely Bargains."

"Why not? They're open year-round now."

"Why not indeed?"

Elaine smiled. "Now, don't make fun of the flea market."

"I'm not."

"Jan and I have made some really interesting buys there."

"You certainly have. And I've picked up a few unusual pieces there myself." Nathan looked at his watch. "Come on, we might as well see what they've got today."

"Okay, but let's just go for fun. Don't even think about wedding gifts. That way, if we see something, it will be a delightful surprise."

"You're on."

Elaine scooped up her purse, and they headed for Nathan's car.

She had always loved Mainely Bargains, and Elaine and Jan frequented the large building. On the day they had first taken possession of the tearoom house in Lancaster, they had stopped at the flea market and found a unique piece of china that had taken them on an adventure. Ever since, Elaine held the business in higher esteem than the first impression given by the stark hall and shabby tables. Not only that, but they'd also been on many more adventures since then—even, of all things, solving mysteries together. And it had turned out that they were pretty good at it. Although Jan was getting married and moving out, Elaine hoped that there would still be more adventures to come for the cousins.

Elaine and Nathan strolled the aisles hand in hand for a while and paused to look at a vase, an old camera, and a group of cast-iron toys. Elaine spotted a vintage scrapbook and lingered over it while Nathan moved on to the next booth. Antique valentines. Her pulse quickened. Some of them were lovely, all hearts and flowers, with quaint verses. She remembered the lacy card Nathan had sent her last week, along with a dozen roses. He was a romantic at heart, and sometimes she got the feeling he wished she would let him express his feelings for her more flamboyantly.

As she leafed through the scrapbook, thoughts of love simmered. She was so in love with Nathan. She wanted to spend the rest of her years with him. That was easier to picture now that Jan was marrying Bob. True, her cousin would not be far away, but Elaine was ready to think about a new life for herself. One that included a husband—a particular husband.

Nathan had been so considerate, so sweet. They had talked about Ben and her grief. Nathan had told her he would give her all the time and space she needed to deal with that, but that he loved her and would be there for her. Was he ready to propose if he knew she felt the time had arrived? She ran her finger over an embossed card depicting a chubby cherub about to loose his arrow of love.

In her mind, she saw them as husband and wife. If she married, she wouldn't want to leave the tearoom house, and she would want to continue the business with Jan. Could Nathan be happy giving up his house in Waterville and living beside the lake? He'd have a longer commute to the auction house, but it was only a few extra miles. His grandchildren could come and stay on weekends if they wanted to, and he could entertain his mom and other family members in their home.

Elaine smiled at her mental picture of her new extended family. She wanted that very much.

"Find something?"

She looked up into his blue eyes, and her pulse sped. "Oh, it's these old valentines. Aren't they sweet? Brings back memories and a lot of thoughts."

"Romantic thoughts?"

"*Hmm,* you never know, do you?" She laughed.

Nathan closed the album and checked the price. "Too bad we just had Valentine's Day. But I think that would make a nice gift for you anyway."

"It's not my birthday."

"We don't need an occasion."

"Well, thank you."

He bought it and carried it in a shopping bag the vendor gave him. Elaine took his hand. She couldn't stop smiling as they continued their leisurely browsing.

Again, her mind was miles away when Nathan stopped abruptly.

"Look at that," he whispered near her ear.

"What?" She glanced at him and followed his gaze. Nathan was staring at something on a table laden with china.

"That teapot." He nodded toward the table.

Elaine scanned the dishes and spotted a teapot that looked old but somewhat ordinary, a white teapot with a brown Transferware floral design. Nathan whipped out his phone and started clicking away. She figured he was looking online for comparisons. Curious, she moved closer and picked it up.

"I think it's Spode," Nathan said in her ear. "Turn it over."

She held the lid on carefully and flipped the teapot. Sure enough, the maker's mark was on the bottom.

"It's nice, but it can't be all that rare, can it?"

"Not only rare, but unique. I think it's the one that's been missing from the Hamlin family set for a hundred and fifty years. I have to buy it!"

FROM THE
GUIDEPOSTS ARCHIVES

This story by Pat Dexter of Mesa, Arizona,
originally appeared in *Angels on Earth*.

"L et's get you back to class," I told the five-year-old I had
been tutoring. I loved volunteering as a reading coach for
the kindergartners, especially on Valentine's Day. At 77, and
a widow, I was no one's valentine anymore. Still, I could enjoy
watching the kids make and exchange their sparkling cards.

Back in the classroom, the teacher signaled for everyone to
line up. "The children really appreciate your help, Ms. Pat. They
want to give you something special," she announced. Each child
came forward, one at a time, and presented me with a card.

"You are all angels," I told them. "I will wait till I get home
and then read each and every one."

When the bell rang, I walked to my car swinging my bag of
valentines. *The kids must have had so much fun making these cards,*
I thought. I imagined them busy with their glitter and glue,
content to make a card no matter who it was for. I was glad I
could help make the day special for the kids.

At home I dropped the cards on the kitchen table and dropped myself onto the couch for a long nap. When I woke up I tidied the house and worked for a bit in the yard. It wasn't until I'd eaten dinner and cleaned up the kitchen that I took the bag of valentines from the table up to bed. I wanted to give each card the attention it deserved, with no distractions. I owed it to the kids.

I picked the first card from the bag and read the envelope: "Ms. Pat, I love you." I recognized Diego's handwriting immediately. When I opened the envelope a slew of tiny plastic hearts and flowers fell onto my lap. *Oh, my!* I thought, surprised. I reached in the bag for another card. This one was from Jennifer. "You are awesome," the cover read. I flipped it open and sequins flew out, mixing with Diego's hearts and flowers. My plain white sheets turned Technicolor. "I light up for you!" the next card read. It spit out sparkles. I burst out laughing.

What a mess! By the time I got to the bottom of the bag, I was half buried in hearts, flowers, sparkles, sequins, glitter— and memories of special moments with these kids. I felt like a princess in a bed full of roses.

I'd worry about the mess tomorrow. For now I just lay down my happy head on my pillow. I thought Valentine's Day wasn't for me anymore. So God sent a classroom full of angels to shower me with love.

A NOTE FROM THE EDITORS

We hope you enjoyed Tearoom Mysteries, published by the Books and Inspirational Media Division of Guideposts, a nonprofit organization that touches millions of lives every day through products and services that inspire, encourage, help you grow in your faith, and celebrate God's love.

Thank you for making a difference with your purchase of this book, which helps fund our many outreach programs to military personnel, prisons, hospitals, nursing homes, and educational institutions.

We also create many useful and uplifting online resources. Visit Guideposts.org to read true stories of hope and inspiration, access OurPrayer network, sign up for free newsletters, download free e-books, join our Facebook community, and follow our stimulating blogs.

To learn about other Guideposts publications, including the best-selling devotional *Daily Guideposts*, go to Guideposts.org/ Shop, call (800) 932-2145, or write to Guideposts, PO Box 5815, Harlan, Iowa 51593.

Find more inspiring fiction in these best-loved Guideposts series!

Mysteries of Martha's Vineyard

Come to the shores of this quaint and historic island and dig in to a cozy mystery. When a recent widow inherits a lighthouse just off the coast of Massachusetts, she finds exciting adventures, new friends, and renewed hope.

Tearoom Mysteries

Mix one stately Victorian home, a charming lakeside town in Maine, and two adventurous cousins with a passion for tea and hospitality. Add a large scoop of intriguing mystery and sprinkle generously with faith, family, and friends, and you have the recipe for Tearoom Mysteries.

Sugarcreek Amish Mysteries

Be intrigued by the suspense and joyful "aha!" moments in these delightful stories. Each book in the series brings together two women of vastly different backgrounds and traditions, who realize there's much more to the "simple life" than meets the eye.

Mysteries of Silver Peak

Escape to the historic mining town of Silver Peak, Colorado, and discover how one woman's love of antiques helps her solve mysteries buried deep in the town's checkered past.

Patchwork Mysteries

Discover that life's little mysteries often have a common thread in a series where every novel contains an intriguing whodunit centered around a quilt located in a beautiful New England town.

To learn more about these books, visit Guideposts.org/Shop